# THE KITCHEN GOD AND HIS WIVES

# THE KITCHEN GOD AND HIS WIVES

A MODERN CHINESE FOLK EPIC

TRANSLATED AND INTRODUCED
BY WILT L. IDEMA

CORNELL EAST ASIA SERIES
*an imprint of*

CORNELL UNIVERSITY PRESS
*Ithaca and London*

Number 223 in the Cornell East Asia Series

First published 2025 by Cornell University Press

Printed in the United States of America

Librarians: A CIP catalog record for this book is available from the Library of Congress.

ISBN 9781501779121 (hardcover)
ISBN 9781501779138 (paperback)
ISBN 9781501779145 (pdf)
ISBN 9781501779152 (epub)

# Contents

# Acknowledgments

The Henan Renmin Chubanshe (Henan People's Publishing House) graciously granted permission to publish a full English translation of *Guo Dinxiang* as published in 2007 in *Guo Dingxiang yueduben*; it also granted permission to publish English translations of some sections of *Guo Dingxiang* as published in 2009 in *Guo Dingxiang quanben*.

"Appendix I: The Textualization of *Guo Dingxiang*" is a shortened and somewhat revised version of my article "The Textualization of *Guo Dingxiang*," *Chinoperl: Journal of Chinese Oral and Performing Literature* 41, no. 1 (2022): 7–36, https://doi.org/10.1353/cop.2022.a862267. It is printed here with the permission of the University of Hawai'i Press.

The cover illustration is based on a woodblock print from Wei County in Shandong Province, depicting in its upper level the stove god and his two wives, whereas the lower section depicts various symbols of prosperity and longevity. That print is reproduced in Po Sung-nien and David Johnson, *Domesticated Deities and Auspicious Emblems: The Iconography of Everyday Life in Village China* (1992) and has here been used with the permission of the Chinese Popular Culture Project.

# THE KITCHEN GOD AND HIS WIVES

# Introduction

*Guo Dingxiang* 郭丁香 is a narrative poem of epic length that tells the harrowing tale of the origin of the stove god and his divine spouses. In late-imperial China, the stove god (also often referred to in English as the kitchen god, especially since the publication of Amy Tan's 1991 novel *The Kitchen God's Wife*) was revered in the kitchen of every house and was believed to ascend to heaven at the end of each year to report on the behavior of its inhabitants. Like many other gods in premodern times, the stove god and his spouse were supposed to have lived on earth before they had received their divine appointment upon death.[1] Over the centuries, many legends narrated the circumstances that resulted in their apotheosis, and one of those combined the tale of a splendid wedding with that of a gruesome divorce, a suicide, and a visit to hell. This particular legend circulated in many shapes, from simple folktales to epic-length songs. *Guo Dingxiang*, named after its virtuous female protagonist, is based on the performance of this legend in "stove singing" (*changzao* 唱灶), a genre of performance literature that enjoyed its heyday from the mid-nineteenth to the mid-twentieth century.

Stove singing most likely originated in Gushi 固始 District in southeastern Henan, and from there it also spread to adjacent regions in Anhui and Shandong. Throughout the century of its greatest popularity

(1850–1950), it remained an oral genre; at least, no early manuscripts or printed editions are known. One distinctive characteristic of the genre was its close association with carpenters. While local priests also might perform stove singing, the genre was best known for performances by carpenters during the evening hours after a full day of work at the home of their patrons. The performance of a single story could be adapted to the length of the engagement and might vary from a few weeks to a full month. The genre likely derived its name from the fact that the most frequently performed item in the repertoire was the tale of the origin of the stove god and his wife, who in this part of China are known as Zhang Wanliang 张万良 and Guo Dingxiang 郭丁香. Such a performance would be introduced by an elaborate ceremony in veneration of the stove, asking for the stove god's blessings for the patron and the performers. Depending on available performers, the tale might be performed as a narrative in verse (*zaoshu* 灶书; stove tales), as a very simple play (in which all roles were distributed among two or three performers), or as a more elaborate play (*zaoxi* 灶戏; stove plays). Stove tales and stove plays to a large extent shared the same texts. Tunes, musical instruments, and, in the case of plays, costumes were all of the most simple kind. In view of the drastic reorganization of the rural economy in the early decades of the People's Republic and the many intensive ideological campaigns of those years, it is small wonder that the genre was on the verge of extinction by the early 1980s.[2]

## The Stove and the Stove God

In traditional China, no house was complete without a stove. In most places, the stove would be built out of brick. At the bottom there would be an opening to feed the fire, and on top there would be at least two round openings: the largest one for using the wok, and the smaller one for using smaller pans (for instance, when heating water). In northern China, a vent would lead the hot air of the fire below the *kang* (a raised brick platform) in the main living room. The stove itself would be located in the kitchen, on the eastern side of the house. As an essential part of the house, indispensable to the family living there, the stove was also venerated as a deity, known as the god of the stove, the king of the stove, or the lord of the stove. During the last one thousand years or so, well into the twentieth century, a woodblock-printed image of the stove god and his retinue was pasted to the side of the stove to be venerated (very simply) on the first and fifteenth of every month by the male head of the household. The stove god would receive more elaborate offerings of sweet foods near the end of the year (in most places on the twenty-third of the last month), when he was believed to ascend to heaven in order to report on the behavior of the family during the preceding year. The print was then removed, to be replaced by a new print on the day in the new year when the stove god was believed to return to his post. Such prints could vary from very simple and crude to quite elaborate and fanciful.[3]

The belief that the stove god reported on the sins and virtues of the members of his family to the celestial authorities can be traced back for many centuries and may well be as old as the cult of the stove itself. It may already be implied in the following puzzling passage from the *Analects*, which collects pronouncements by Confucius (551–479 BCE) and records discussions between the Master and some of his students: "Wangsun Jia asked, 'What is the meaning of "It is better to toady to the Stove than to toady to the southwest corner of the house"?' The Master replied, 'Not so! If one has offended against Heaven, there's no one whom one can pray to.'"[4]

One of the earliest texts to explicitly state that the Stove God regularly reports to Heaven on the behavior of the inhabitants of the house is the *Baopuzi* 抱朴子, by Ge Hong 葛洪 (283–343), who states, "Also, on the last day of the month, the god of the stove ascends to Heaven and reports on man's transgressions. For major ones, a Period is taken away [from one's allotted lifespan]; a Period is three hundred days. For minor ones, a Counter is taken away; a Counter is three days."[5] As one of the many gods who report on the behavior of humans, the stove god, too, during the last millennium was honored with the two syllables *siming* 司命 (master of fate) in his title.[6]

By the Song dynasty, the veneration of the stove god was already very similar to current practices and beliefs. The well-known official and poet Fan Chengda 范成大 (1126–1207) wrote, "On the night of the twenty-fourth of the Last Month, people make offerings to the stove. They explain this by saying that on the next day the stove god pays court in Heaven to report on the affairs of the entire year, thus they pray to him in advance of this time."[7] Fan's accompanying poem reads as follows:

Since ancient times the twenty-fourth of the Last Month each year
You, stove god, will ascend to heaven to report on our behavior.
Please halt your coach of clouds and storm-wind horses for a while:
We have prepared the cups and plates to offer sacrifice.

The pig's head is well-cooked and hot, the fishes are both fresh;
The bean-paste is so sweet and loose, the powdered cakes are round.
It is us men who hold the gifts—the women keep their distance—
As we, to please the god, pour out the wine and burn the money.
You never heard the fights and quarrels of the servant girls,
And do not blame us for the dirty deeds of cats and dogs.
Have a good trip to heaven's gate now you are drunk and sated!
Please do not mention any minor matters anymore
But, pray, bring us prosperity to share on your return![8]

As in later times, it was men, not women, who sacrificed to the stove god. The god was treated to meats and sweets, and he also received some alcohol. The money that was burned was, of course, sacrificial paper money in huge denominations. The god was implored to forget anything inappropriate that may have happened over the course of the year in his domain and to come back from his celestial trip with ample blessing for the whole family. In modern practice, the god in many places is treated to many sugary and sticky foodstuffs, so his lips will be sealed when he arrives before the Jade Emperor to report (a practice still known as "toadying to the stove god" [*meizao* 媚灶]). Several religious tracts of the Ming and Qing dynasties urge their readers to treat the stove god with greater reverence in view of his importance, but their impact would appear to have been limited among the population at large. Such tracts may credit the god with more and more elaborate titles and also may identify him with divinities of great power.[9]

In the earliest references to the stove as a divinity, the stove has no personal name. Some early sources identify the god of the stove with the god of fire or with the divine first cook, but those identifications probably are only speculations by their learned authors.[10] Some works from the first millennium credit the stove god with the appearance of a beautiful woman. The first author to provide the stove god with not only a title but the surname Zhang 张 was Duan Chengshi 段成式 (d. 863). In his *Youyang zazu* 酉阳杂俎, he wrote, "The deity of the stove is named Wei 隗. Its appearance resembles that of a beautiful woman. Also, the god has the surname Zhang 张 and the name Dan 单. His cognomen is Ziguo 子郭. His wife's cognomen is Qingji 卿忌, and he has six daughters, all named Chaqia 察洽. He always rises up to heaven on the dark of the moon to report on the situation of man's transgressions."[11] Duan goes on to provide a long list of the names of the stove god's underlings. One of the earliest texts to provide the god with a mortal life before receiving his divine appointment is the late Ming novel *The Appointment of the Gods* (*Fengshen yanyi* 封神演义). This work makes an effort to provide all gods in the popular Chinese pantheon with a fitting background. The novel describes the moral degradation of King Zhou of the Shang dynasty, the moral stature of the King Wen, and the campaign of his son King Wu to topple the Shang dynasty. Most of the novel is taken up by an extended description of the victorious campaign of King Wu that results in the foundation of the Zhou dynasty. At the conclusion, the slain generals on both sides are all appointed to divine office. According to *The Appointment of the Gods*, the stove god is the apotheosis of Zhang Kui 张奎, one of King Zhou's loyal generals who dies in a battle.

Over the course of the twentieth century and into the twenty-first, many quite different folktales have been recorded from all over China, providing legends about the mortal life of the stove god up to his divine appointment.[12] The many characters who are identified in various tales about the origins of the god of the stove as his mortal incarnations include figures ranging from the mythical royal father of the bodhisattva Guanyin and a tutor of the Qianlong emperor to an expert builder of stoves and a voyeur, while some tales provide the god of the stove with a mortal life as a woman. One of the most popular tales on the mortal life of the god of the stove (and that of his wife) is a variation on the theme of the meeting of a divorced couple. In this type of tale, the male protagonist insists on divorcing his wife even though she has not given him any reason to do so. Following that divorce, the man falls into extreme poverty, while his former wife brings prosperity to her second husband. One day, her first husband, reduced to begging and overcome by shame and remorse, realizes that the food he was given was prepared by his divorced wife. This is a type of tale found all over East Asia. When adopted as the origin legend of the stove god, the remorseful husband often commits suicide by jumping into the stove, where he is burned to death. In its many variations, this legend of the origin of the stove god was not only told as a simple folktale but also adapted into many local genres of popular performative literature all over China, whether as long ballads or plays.

Usually the first husband wants to divorce his wife because she has a poor background, so her family has a much lower social status than his own. There are also versions in which the husband wants to divorce her because he discovers on the wedding night that she is ugly.[13] In the tale of Zhang Wanliang and Guo Dingxiang that was adopted in stove singing in Gushi as the origin legend of the stove god and his spouse, both husband and wife share the same upper-class status and she is described as the acme of female beauty and virtue, so the tale needs a different reason for the husband's hatred of his wife and his urgent desire to divorce her—a reason it finds in his love for another woman and that woman's underhanded machinations. In order to be able to receive his divine appointment, Zhang Wanliang has to die violently and does so, as in many other versions, by jumping into the stove. In order to enable Guo Dingxiang to become his divine spouse, she has to die quickly too (in the translated version due to an illness caused by Zhang's revengeful ghost!).[14]

One study claims that all basic motifs in origin legends of the god of the stove that belong to the wedding-and-divorce type can be traced back to elements in the earlier legends concerning the divinity and related ritual practices. For instance, the author links the episode of the husband who is reduced to begging to the custom of beggars dressing up as the king of the stove (or the lord of the stove and the lady of the stove) in the last month of the year and visiting the homes of the more affluent members of the community, driving out the accumulated evil of the old year. welcoming the new year with auspicious phrases, and expecting some gifts.[15] This custom was a relic of more ancient end-of-year exorcist rituals and by Qing dynasty times was known as "Dancing the King of the Stove" (*tiao zaowang* 跳灶王). During the final decades of the dynasty, inside the palace, "Dancing the King of the Stove" was performed with fitting grandeur on the twenty-third day of the last month of the year, as forty actors were summoned from the beginning of that month to be properly trained.[16] The humbler version is recorded from several regions in China during the last millennium, and in certain places survived into the twentieth century.

The stove tale translated in this volume repeatedly claims that the god of the stove originally was surnamed Li and only later became surnamed Zhang. This reflects the traditional Chinese belief that gods may be moved from one position to another in the pantheon, just as officials may be moved through the imperial bureaucracy. One historical individual who, according to legend, served as god of the stove was Li Shaojun 李少君, a magician who was active at the court of Emperor Wu (r. 140–87 BCE). Li claimed to be able to prepare the elixir of immortality and venerated the stove.

## Stove Tales and Their Performance

Stove singing is only one of the many local genres of Chinese traditional performative literature. According to some Chinese publications, the performance of stove singing originated from a single carpenter telling stories in prose. Later he or his pupils would have switched to verse. As stove tales were performed by groups of carpenters, they started to divide the individual speeches among two or more people, who might then accompany their performance with a few items of costume and some simple gestures. Such use of narrative ballads for the performance of plays is also encountered elsewhere in China. Eventually, if sufficiently capable performers were available, all individual speeches would be assigned to separate carpenters who adopted local tunes to sing their lines. One characteristic of these stove plays was that the individual characters were not performed by fixed role types, but that the roles were assigned to the members of the troupe at the start of the performance. During the period 1850-1950, the musical instruments developed from carpenter's tools, beaten to indicate the rhythm, to simple drums and some other instruments.

The *Gushixian quyizhi* 固始县曲艺志 (Gazetteer of the minor performance arts of Gushi District) (1989) provides a more detailed reconstruction of the development of the performance of stove singing, distinguishing three stages.[17] During the first stage, prose narration dominated over singing. Sung sections were limited to set pieces, such as transitional episodes, climaxes, and scenes of violent emotion, and these sung sections only repeated the earlier information. In this stage there would be only one or two performers, and the accompaniment was provided by carpenter's tools, such as saws, planes, and chisels. In the second stage of development, singing predominated over prose narration, and a good singing voice became a major consideration in accepting apprentices for carpenters, giving rise to proverbs like "With skill but without a fine voice / One cannot be a good carpenter." Because of the increasing importance of song, stove singing also acquired its own instrument, the "stove drum."[18] The singer could play the drum himself, or it could be played by someone else. At most there would be up to five people, all of whom would still be seated while performing. In the third stage of development, stove singing would completely rely on sung lines (apart from rare inserted short jokes). If there was only a single performer, he would have to be able to sing as a man and a woman; if there were more able singers, roles would be divided on the basis of their voice qualities. But the performers would still not play their roles or assume costumes that fit their roles, apart from the men who performed female roles, who might wrap their heads in handkerchiefs. During this stage, some more instruments might be added. Once the performers adopted stage costumes, stove singing had developed into stove plays.

In the absence of any written materials on stove singing from the period before 1949, this periodization can have been constructed only on the basis of oral traditions. When Cao Jiazhen 曹家振 and his colleagues "discovered" the genre in the late 1970s, they encountered single elderly carpenters who could sing only short sections, so it made sense for them to organize the materials they recovered as a long narrative ballad, whether they derived from stove tales or stove plays.[19] In the 1980s, others made attempts to revive the tradition of the performance of stove plays. Several episodes were performed with varying degrees of success. In the decades following the 1981 publication of "Guo Dingxiang," some more performers of the ballad version became known. Pan Jing'e 潘景娥, a local actress, apprenticed herself in 1988 to one of them, becoming in this way the first female performer of stove tales. Her repertoire is said to include a version of *Guo Dingxiang* in 4,231 lines.[20]

Yang Xianru 杨纤如 has provided a relatively detailed description of stove singing as a rudimentary play by only two or three people. The carpenters might perform on their own initiative or at the invitation of their patron. The performances would start each day in the evening after dinner and last until midnight, and the audience would bring their own benches each night: "This form of performative art [*quyi* 曲艺] has its special characteristics. It includes song and dance, but it does not include any spoken dialogue.[21] The dances are also very simple and even the melodies are not too complicated. But once the performance has started, it will last for at least half a month, and if it lasts longer it can reach all nights of a month.[22] From the first to the last, the audiences never tire of listening and people speak of the 'series of the stove.' "[23] According to Yang Xianru, two of the performers played the roles of Zhang Wanliang and Guo Dingxiang, but they may also have played some of the other roles when needed. The play was never performed on a formal stage; a carpet on the ground was sufficient. Costumes would be very simple, and specific pieces of clothing might be borrowed from the family at whose home the performance took place. The man who performed the role of Zhang Wanliang would also play the "divine drum" while he sang and danced.

This instrument is described as follows: "The divine drum is made of an iron ring covered with sheepskin. The handle is more than one foot long, and at the end of the handle there are three prongs, and from each prong hang some copper rings. The man who performs Zhang Wanliang holds a stick in his hands with which he repeatedly strikes the divine drum. Shaking the copper rings and playing the drum he dances and sings to the music. He can use the copper rings of the divine drum's handle to produce brilliant patterns."[24] The play contained no prose dialogue at all but was fully conducted in verse. Yang Xianru praises the ability of the actors to express a wide variety of emotions in a tender and delicate manner despite the simplicity of the performance.

The performance of stove singing was preceded by venerating the stove.[25] The *Gushixian quyizhi* provides the following description of the ceremony for venerating the stove and its change over time:

Before their performance, the stove tale performers must sincerely and orderly venerate the stove. And each evening before performing . . . they also must venerate the stove. In front of the stove in the kitchen of the house of the patron, not only must the performers provide incense, sacrificial paper money, and vegetarian offerings, but there is also an extensive song [*changci*] that resembles a prayer, for instance:

My father and mother gave birth to this little boy,
Now grown up, he has a mouth and eats from the four directions.
While eating with his mouth, he thinks in his heart
That with all his heart he wants to venerate the king of the stove.
Our patron has spread out a big and red mat of felt,
And we kneel down in the middle strictly according to the rules.
In my left hand I light the gold and silver sacrificial paper money,
In my right hand I light the ambergris incense.
Lifting these in both hands I perform a kowtow,
Hitting the floor with a bang I kowtow to the king of the stove.
Sincerely I bow a first time to the king of the stove
So I may not lose my voice when singing of the stove;
Sincerely I bow a second time to the king of the stove
So all may go well once outside this kitchen;
Sincerely I bow a third time to the king of the stove
So the family of our patron may prosper and rise!

When stove tales were performed in the later period, the ceremony had been much simplified even though the rule of venerating the stove still existed. Often the performers made only a light bow to the king of the stove. Or they went in a procession in the house of the patron from the hall in front to the room in the back, all the while singing while marching. In general, these were all lines of praise and flattery. For instance:

Our revered patron has invited us to sing of the stove
But without a voice, with a hoarse throat we are at a loss.
We receive ample food and drink at your fine manor,
So if we would not sing, our face would lack all luster.
So let it be! We will sing a while,
We will sing of the fine state of your noble mansion!
It is not that we are out to please you by our praise,
But the buildings of your mansion are well designed.
The storied buildings look down on the lower roofs,
The southern rooms strictly face the northern brick building.
The gate building has been constructed as three drops of water,[26]
While five-man cannons support both sides of the gate.[27]
The doghouse and the pigpens are made of glazed tiles,
And those lacquered pillars and those white-washed walls!
When our patron in the future will become an official,
A pavilion for receiving officials is built on the southern threshing ground![28]

## The Discovery of Stove Singing and the Three Editions of *Guo Dingxiang*

Stove singing and *Guo Dingxiang* were first introduced to a national public in China in the fall of 1981 by two publications. The first of these was a short article by Yang Xianru, titled "Jieshao changzao" 介绍唱灶 (An introduction to stove singing),[29] which begins with a discussion of the name of the genre and continues with a detailed summary of the tale of Zhang Wanliang and Guo Dingxiang and their unhappy marriage.[30] Zhang Wanliang does not like Guo Dingxiang despite her beauty, virtue, and hard work, and he is persuaded by another woman to divorce her. Following this divorce, Dingxiang marries again and makes her new husband a rich man, while Zhang Wanliang is soon reduced to poverty. When the beggar Zhang Wanliang one day realizes that the woman who has been feeding him is his former wife, he is overcome by remorse and commits suicide by jumping into the stove. He then becomes the god of the stove and Guo Dingxiang his divine spouse upon her death. Yang Xianru's article also discusses the performance of the tale as a very simple play (quoted above), provides a few snippets of text, and concludes with a discussion of the music.

The second publication, which appeared in the national journal *Minjian wenxue* 民间文学 (Folk literature), provided a version of the stove tale, titled "Guo Dingxiang,"[31] that had been "collected and edited" by Cao Jiazhen 曹家振 (b. 1945), Peng Huahou 彭华后, and Li Haihua 李海华. Whereas Yang Xianru had provided only short snippets of a stove play version of *Guo Dingxiang*, Cao and his coauthors claimed they were providing a full version of the story as a stove tale, in 1,350 lines of seven-syllable verse.[32] These two publications coincided with the moment in Chinese folklore studies when academics became aware of the existence of several living oral traditions of long narrative songs among the Han Chinese folk.

The metropolitan editors of *Minjian wenxue* enthusiastically hailed the publication of "Guo Dingxiang" as yet another discovery along these lines:

> Who says that the areas of the Han ethnic group don't have long narrative folk poems? In recent years we continuously have had new discoveries from regions such as Hubei and Jiangsu, and "Guo Dingxiang," a long folk poem from southern Henan that we publish in this issue of our journal, is yet another heartening example.
>
> "Guo Dingxiang" is in origin a representative song text belonging to the folk genre of "stove tales," which are popular throughout the region of southeastern Henan and northwestern Anhui. The tunes and melodies are on the verge of extinction, but the songs' words have been preserved in this poetic form because of its beautiful and moving story.[33]

Part of this enthusiasm most likely was inspired by the fact that this "stove tale" did not tell a "superstitious" story, like the creation of the world in *The Legend of Darkness* (Hei'an zhuan 黑暗传) from Hubei;[34] nor did it focus almost exclusively on adulterous love, as in long "Wu songs" (*Wuge* 吴歌), the narrative ballads in the Suzhou dialect from the Lake Tai area in Jiangsu.[35] As textualized by Cao Jiazhen and his colleagues, "Guo Dingxiang" contains hardly any superstitious elements, and while it features a divorce, it otherwise demonstrates a welcome morality: "Because 'Guo Dingxiang' sings the praises of such human virtues as hard work, goodness, and honesty and chastises evil habits such as laziness, deception, and ingratitude, and does so in simple and unadorned folk language, it is greatly liked by the masses and today still has educational meaning, so it is well worth reading."[36]

Whereas the article by Yang Xianru seems to have attracted little attention, "Guo Dingxiang" created quite a stir because some scholars also hailed the text as a Chinese epic.[37] The text garnered prizes on the national and provincial levels and was repeatedly reprinted, not only locally but also in prestigious national collections.[38] In the *Gushixian quyizhi* 固始县曲艺志 (1989), "stove tales" and "Guo Dingxiang" occupy prominent positions,[39] and the same applies for "stove plays" and "Guo Dingxiang" in the *Gushixian xiquzhi* 固始县戏曲志 (Gazetteer on traditional theater in Gushi District [1989?]).[40]

For the second stage in the textualization of the tale of Zhang Wanliang and Guo Dingxiang, we have to wait until the early years of the twenty-first century, when, in 2003, in the context of the campaigns to rescue China's intangible cultural heritage, local authorities in Gushi (and those in Xinyang 信阳, of which it now forms a part) were urged by national cadres to intensify their work of preserving stove tales and stove plays and identify "transmitters" (*chuanchengren* 传承人). This government-led project not only resulted in the discovery of new performers and new texts but also identified avid audience members who had memorized many lines, enabling the compilation of far longer texts. The application for the recognition of stove singing as a provincial-level item of intangible cultural heritage included an (unpublished) "materials edition" (*ziliaoben* 资料本) of "Guo Dingxiang" that ran to 4,300 lines.[41] This served as the basis of a published "reading edition" (*yueduben* 阅读本), printed in 2007, of over 4,800 lines.[42] Renewed activities for the collection of materials in 2006–7 resulted in a draft of more than 6,000 lines that was revised and expanded and then published in 2009 as a "complete edition" (*quanben* 全本).[43] This latter edition was reprinted again in 2017.[44]

As the materials edition and the draft of the complete edition have not appeared in print so far, this means that the common reader in China now has access to three different editions of *Guo Dingxiang* that not only vary considerably in length but also show major discrepancies in content and approach, even though the basic plot is the same. This translation is based on the 2007 edition of the text, the reading edition. Precisely the fact that it contains several inconsistencies and episodes that awkwardly fit into the narrative suggests that this text stays relatively close to the transcripts of performances, the unpublished materials edition. A selection of the additional materials from the more heavily edited 2009 edition is included as an appendix.

The original is basically composed in seven-syllable verse. Occasionally there may be a few longer lines of ten syllables. The full text maintains a single rhyme (-*ang*) throughout. The translation follows the Chinese editions' division into sections and paragraphs.

The Chinese scholar Bai Gengsheng hailed *Guo Dingxiang* as an "epic on folk life." If creation epics deal with a distant past and heroic epics with the upper classes, *Guo Dinngxiang* stands out for its devotion to the details of daily life in everyday society, often as perceived by its female members. As it is a tale of marriage and divorce, many chapters deal with the wedding, ranging from the negotiations between the two families through the preparation of trousseau to the wedding day itself, and the first visit of the unhappy bride to her parental home. As we are dealing with an arranged marriage, we should not be surprised that the groom does not automatically fall in love with the bride at first sight. He does, however, fall in love with the wife of a cousin, who with the help of a lying soothsayer leads him to believe that his wife is infertile and urges him to divorce her so he can marry her younger sister. In order to have a socially valid reason to divorce his wife, Zhang Wanliang tries various means (including violence) to make Guo Dingxiang lose her temper, all to no avail. When she has been divorced, Guo Dingxiang marries again, and when she and her new husband celebrate the birth of a baby by feeding beggars, her suddenly impoverished first husband is one of them; he recognizes her by the taste of the noodles she has prepared. Upon his suicide, Zhang Wanliang visits the underworld and witnesses the cruel punishment there of sinners in an episode that provides a summary description of conventional beliefs concerning the afterlife. It is only because of his and Guo Dingxiang's celestial background that the couple's case is reassigned to heaven, where her enduring love for her first husband and his newly discovered love for his original wife make them choose a destiny as a divine couple on earth rather than a passionless existence in higher spheres.

As an "epic on folk life," *Guo Dingxiang* not only is a product of rural society in southeastern Henan but also reflects the hopes and fears of its original creators and audiences: hopes for a happy marriage and a rich and healthy life; fears of disunion, poverty, and disease. If *Guo Dingxiang* has a message, it is that the best a man can hope for is a devoted wife, and that a devoted wife has to hope for a husband who is not a lazy spendthrift and an easy victim of crafty seduction. The story of that message is told in simple language and with great gusto, reaching high points in describing the construction of the wedding bed and the preparation of superior noodles. What more can one wish for?

# Guo Dingxiang

## 1. *Venerating the Stove*

Joy to our host, may his family prosper,
May he make money and buy more fields.
Elder and younger colleagues, more than ten of us,
Have come to your manor to do our work.
You've treated us well with food and drink, tobacco and tea,
So we thank our host and the lady in charge of the till.
This evening today we will let our axes rest for a while
And sing the Book of the Stove to express our thanks.
By coming today to sing of the stove at your manor,
We've caused such confusion that everybody is busy.
The grown-ups are busily setting out the tables,
The little kids are busily carrying in the benches.
The men have left the house to borrow firecrackers;
The women have opened the chests to select clothes.
This one Book of the Stove causes thousands of tears:
For seven lives these two could not become a couple.[1]
If one would want to sing the book from its beginnings,
These seven lives of doomed lovers make it too long!

Nipping off the head, removing the tail, we start from the
    middle,
Singing the part of Wanliang divorcing Dingxiang.
And if we cannot sing that to the end this very night,
We'll continue tomorrow night and the night thereafter.
When singing of the stove the rules are that one first
    venerates the stove:
One's throat will be clear only after bowing to the stove.
Once when they sang of the stove but didn't bow to the stove,
Their legs folded below them as a result while performing;
Once when they sang of the stove but didn't bow to the stove,
They sang to the beat but they had forgotten the tune;
Once when they sang of the stove but didn't bow to the stove,
You rose and I fell, unable to continue;
Once when they sang of the stove but didn't bow to the stove,
They opened their mouths to sing but had lost their voices!

In the past those who sang of the stove numbered twelve;
Today our singing troupe is made up of six twosomes.
If you have enough for all roles, you can sing of the stove,
If you cannot fill the roles, you cannot put on a performance.
Who will play the grown-ups, who will play the children?
Who will play the father, who will play the mother?
Who will play the female roles?
Who will play the male roles?
Who will play Young Man Shi?
Who will play Wang Manxiang?
Who will play the father's elder sister?
Who will play the mother's younger sister?
Who will play the little boy An, as naughty as a monkey?
Who will play the young servant girl with big feet and big
    hands?
Who will play the matchmaker with her oily mouth and sweet
    talk?
Who will play the soothsayer who wags his head and sways his
    brains?
Who will play the huffing and hawing old nabob?
Who will play the stooped and hunchbacked Fourth Lady
    Ou?
Who will play Zhang Jinyu?

And who will play Guo Dingxiang?
Now that the roles have all been properly assigned,
We will go all together to the eastern kitchen.
The kitchen is actually the palace of the lord of the stove:
In the stove lord's palace we bow to the king of the stove.
While we are on our way, we have a good look
To inspect the fine manor of our host:
The eastern building has been erected facing the western
    building;
The southern building exactly faces the northern wing's
    rooms.
The gate building has been erected as three drops of water[2]
While five-man cannons support the gate on both sides.[3]
Tiles have been laid out to make a smooth floor
And chalk has been applied to make for white walls.
The dog shed and chicken pen are constructed in brick,
And even the outhouse has brightly painted beams.
It would appear our host has been an official:
A Pavilion for Receiving Officials is built on the southern
    threshing ground.
While we are walking we also are looking around,
And all of a sudden have arrived at the eastern kitchen.
By the sides of its gate one reads two lines of a couplet;
Please allow me to ask what has been written out there?
If you had not asked me, I would not have told you,
But as you have asked me, now please let me explain:
"The eastern kitchen, palace of the stove lord of the four
    directions,
With its rice and flour, its oil and salt, its onions, garlic and
    ginger."
"The five tastes are in harmony" is inscribed over the gate:
This parallel couplet is perfect for the three directions.
In the past the king of the stove was surnamed Li;
At present the king of the stove is surnamed Zhang.
Whether he is surnamed Zhang or surnamed Li,
Despite these changes of surname, he's still king.
Having read the couplet, we enter the kitchen
While the host is setting off the firecrackers.
In front of the stove we get gold and silver paper[4]
And burn our incense in the purple-gold burner.

The men all kneel down, the women kneel down;
Men and women kneel down all together.
Having performed a kowtow, we make a bow,
Venerating the king of the stove and his lady.
The king of the stove is busy, his lady is busy:
The Jade Emperor sent you down from heaven.
Descending from heaven the stove king and his lady
Were appointed to reside in the eastern kitchen.
In every household you are revered with incense;
Every family honors your image on the stove base.
The stove base is changed each year at New Year;
The stove print is always put on at New Year's Eve.
Why do the people of this world all revere you?
You are in charge of the main ancestral sacrifices
And each year you return to the celestial palace
On the night of the twenty-third of the Last Month.
Every family sends you off with fine incense,
Sends you off on your return to the celestial palace,
Praying that you will tell only good things in heaven,
Praying that you'll preserve blessings down on earth.
Today we pay our respects to the stove
Because we are going to sing the Book of the Stove.
After we have made a kowtow we perform a bow,
And back on our feet we will go to the green room.
The male protagonist says that he is in no hurry
But first will go into the high hall for a while.
The female protagonist stretches out her hand, stopping him,
And says, "Jeune premier, please listen to me.
Paying respect to the stove we did so as a troupe,
But it is your responsibility to greet the guests.
A sow may be big, but she never plows the fields;
A calf may be small, but it still can pull a harrow.
When the female role has put on her veil,[5] it covers her eyes,
And she is then unable to welcome the guests,
So you should go ahead and greet the guests,
While I go into the powder room to put on powder."
The female protagonist dresses as the girl Dingxiang,
The male protagonist changes into Zhang Wanliang.
Wanliang and Dingxiang are married as husband and wife,
But matched as husband and wife they don't form a couple.

One bumpy, oh so bumpy road for three full years:
Love and resentment cause thousands of tears.
Those thousands of tears make for a long story,
Written up as this Book of the Stove we will sing.

## 2.  *Opening Piece*

Green beans turn out green beans, brown beans brown;
The big rice and the small wheat are proper grains.
A loving pair of husband and wife grow old together,
But a doomed marriage will not result in a couple.
Why could this passionate girl for seven generations,
Life upon life, never form a lasting bond of love?
It was a debt of a sin from a former existence
For which she had to pay through seven lives.
That Wanliang and Dingxiang became no couple
Had its roots in the halls of heaven high up above.
There in heaven you have the Jade Emperor Zhang,
With, at the Jade Emperor's side, the Queen-Mother.[6]
Her Majesty the Queen-Mother invited the immortals
From all eight directions to her Flat-Peach Party,
And when the immortals of the eight directions had arrived,
The banquet was laid out for that Flat-Peach Gathering.[7]
When the Flat-Peach Banquet was served at Jasper Pond,
Golden Page and Jade Maiden were overcome with joy,
Because ordinarily the two of them didn't see each other.
Meeting each other today, their passions were aroused!
If you cast me a glance, a glance, I will give you a wink;
If you come up with the tune, I'll compose a refrain.
When Her Majesty the Queen-Mother saw their behavior,
A raging fury involuntarily surged up in her heart.[8]
The Queen-Mother pronounced an edict by which
The two of them were banished from heaven's halls!
When Golden Page descended to the common dust,
He changed into a stalk of reed by the side of a river.
Jade Maiden turned into a river wren who descended,
As she descended, on the very top of that one reed.
Her only thought was to rest her feet for a while,
But who knew that she brought about a disaster!
The stalk of reed bent down, unable to support her,

Sinking down and raising up it had lost all strength.
Bending down and stretching again for seven times
Had driven Golden Page completely to distraction:
"Now you have made me suffer for these seven times,
I will have you suffer for seven lives as my wife!"
And because he had pronounced these cruel words,
The poor girl wept her heart out for all seven lives:
In her first rebirth as the poor-fated Meng Jiangnü
Who married the poor-fated Wan Xiliang;[9]
In her second rebirth as the suffering Zhu Yingtai
Who ran into that stupid fool brother Liang;[10]
In her third rebirth as the suffering Qin Xuemei
Who lived a widow's life weeping for Shang;[11]
In her fourth rebirth as the suffering Li Aijie
Who prayed to the Buddha in her lonely cell;[12]
In her fifth rebirth as the suffering Lan Yulian,
Drawing water, filled with longing by the well;[13]
In her sixth rebirth as the suffering Zhang Guizhi
Who took fragrant tea to her short-lived husband.[14]
Who was the suffering girl in the seventh rebirth?
Zhang Wanliang's divorced wife Guo Dingxiang!
Because Wanliang divorced his wife Dingxiang,
He threw himself into the stove, so losing his life.
His death in the stove left the Book of the Stove,
The Book of the Stove in praise of Guo Dingxiang.

When we colleagues sing the Book of the Stove,
We must sing the Book of the Stove from the start.
How did Golden Page become young man Zhang?
And how did Jade Maiden become Guo Dingxiang?
Disaster and luck in our lives are settled by Heaven,
The divine lord up in heaven is Jade Emperor Zhang.
It was all because Sang Family Mountain in Henan's
Guangzhou Prefecture was such an excellent place!
If in front of the mountain the Zhangs were the richest,
Then the Guos were the strongest behind the mountain.
The Zhang family produced Grand Commandant Zhang,
While the Guo family produced Executive Censor Guo.
The two of them served in office for several decades
But didn't forget their fine estates at Sang Mountain.

One of them quit his job to go back to his native village;
The other "cited his age" to return to his hometown.[15]
Riding their official sedan chairs they met each other,
And hand in hand they stepped into a thatched hall.
They sat down in the open pavilion in front of the hall;
Speaking of this and that they expressed their feelings.
The Zhang family had no son and had also no daughter,
The Guo family had no daughter and had also no son.
Now that they returned to their home village they hoped
To extend the ancestral lines by accumulation of virtue.
In the hot summer months they donated tea and water,
And in the cold winter months they handed out clothes.
When a gentleman on the road lacked traveling funds,
They gave him the silver he needed to return home.
The two families competed in practicing good deeds
By building bridges, repairing roads, donating medicines.
Above, they prayed to Heaven, and below, to Earth,
Praying and praying Her Majesty to send them a son.
If the two families would both be blessed with a boy,
They would send them together to the southern academy;
If the two families would both be blessed with a girl,
To the eastern pavilion to practice embroidering ducks.
But if one family had a boy and the other had a girl,
It was a heaven-made match of Dragon and Phoenix!

When Mr. Zhang came back home, he erected a temple;
When Mr. Guo returned home, he constructed a shrine.
The Zhang family each day submitted yellow memorials;[16]
The Guo family each night burned high-rising incense.
When submitting yellow memorials and burning incense,
The incense smoke wafted up and ascended to heaven.
Drifting into the celestial palace the smoke of the incense
Disturbed and startled divine lord Jade Emperor Zhang.
Seated in his Beyond-Welkin Hall, the Jade Emperor
With jumping eyes and burning ears didn't feel at ease.
Holding a book in his hands he made a computation,
Trying to compute where the problem was happening.
He was trying to compute where there was a drought,
He was trying to compute where there was a flood;
He was trying to compute where there was a surplus,

And trying to compute where granaries were empty.
He was trying to compute where he should bring aid,
He was trying to compute where he should show pity.
Computing this on his fingers he reached a conclusion:
He saw that this concerned Guo Town, Zhang Village.
The Guo family wanted to continue the ancestral line,
The Zhang family was praying for the birth of a son:
There were plenty of boys and girls in all-under-heaven—
No need for both families to remain without offspring!
While His Majesty the Jade Emperor did his computations,
Her Majesty the Queen-Mother returned from Jasper Pond.
When the Jade Emperor had told the whole story to her,
Her Majesty the Queen-Mother soon reached a decision.
Golden Page and Jade Maiden suffered their punishment:
Their karmic bond had been played out for six existences.
There still was this one lifetime of doomed union
That had to be served out by these two characters.
The Zhang family was fated to be blessed with a boy;
The Guos were not so fortunate: a daughter was born.
Golden Page was reincarnated in the Zhang family;
He was reincarnated in the Zhang family as a son.
He was given the personal name of Zhang Jinyu
And the elegant social name of Zhang Wanliang.
Jade Maiden was reincarnated in the Guo family;
She was reincarnated in the Guo family as a girl.
Her father and mother called her Big Sister Guo
And they gave her the name of Guo Dingxiang.
How was the karmic enmity of these two ended?
It is all to be found in the Book of the Stove.

## 3.  *Big Sister Guo*

The Sang River winds and curves, going on and on;
The Sang Hills rise high and higher, range upon range.
The stream around the Sang Hills: a dragon sweeping its tail;
The hills so close to the Sang River: a phoenix facing the sun.[17]
In front of the hill and behind the river: mulberry trees in
    groves;
Amid those groves there is a place called Guo Family Village.
The Guo family there has a virgin daughter

Who from birth has been called Dingxiang.
At the age of one and two she was held in her mother's arms;
At the age of three and four she never left her mother's side.
At the age of five and six she could distinguish good from
    evil;
At the age of seven and eight she embroidered mandarin
    ducks.[18]
When Dingxiang had reached the age of more than ten years,
A teacher was hired to teach Dingxiang to read and write,
And before she had studied the books for three full years,
She understood the Three Mainstays and the Five
    Constants.[19]
When Dingxiang had reached the age of sixteen years,
Big Sister's beautiful features were famed all around.
People of this world praise flowers and moon as pretty,
But those could not compare to Dingxiang's fine shape.
Her black tresses bound up by silk rivaled dark clouds;
Without any use of cypress oil they were lustrous by nature.
Her apricot eyes were sparkling like late-autumn streams;
Her fine eyebrows were curving like long willow leaves.
A powdered face, peach-like cheeks, and red lips so bright;
Silver teeth like kernels of rice, and a fragrant jade-white skin.
In a black dress and a green skirt, on red embroidered shoes:
When walking outside she resembled a wind-swayed willow!
Whenever Dingxiang would go out to pick mulberry leaves,
The butterflies so informed would busily spread the news.
The peony hearing the news would busily apply her powder;
The rose hearing the news would busily put on her makeup.
The crab apple hearing the news would put on her lip gloss;
The lotus flower hearing the news would change her dress.
But when Dingxiang eventually passed in front of them,
The comparison told them their efforts had all been in vain.
The peony was so ashamed that she bowed down her head—
A covered face and closed eyes, her heart all bewildered.
The rose was so ashamed that her face changed color—
What one moment was white, the next moment was brown.
The crab apple was so ashamed that she could not bear it,
She turned away so she could shed her tears unobserved.
The lotus flower was so ashamed she had nowhere to hide
And rolling down the slope she jumped right into the pond!

Dingxiang was not only beautiful but also quite clever
In spinning thread, weaving cloth, or doing embroidery.
She was competent in both heavy work and lighter tasks
And equally expert in heating the wok or firing the stove.
Whenever Dingxiang would be cooking her red congee,
The fragrance of the rice would spread ninety-nine miles.
Whenever Dingxiang would embroider blooming trees,
Honeybees would hurry over, flying in noisy swarms.
Whenever Dingxiang would water the vegetables,
Gourds would pair off and melons line up in rows,
And whenever Dingxiang was weeding the cotton,
The summer heat was tempered by frost at night.
Thousands and myriads of tongues praised Dingxiang,
As the countryside in all directions extolled Dingxiang.

## 4.  *The First Absence from the Academy*

On the sunlit Sang Mountain, the earth all turns yellow;
In front of the mountain there's Zhang Family Village.
When in the year before last the rich man Zhang died,
He left behind his one son, known as Big Boy Zhang.
The school name he had been given was Zhang Jinyu;
The social name he was given was Zhang Wanliang.
Hoping that her son might quickly head the family,
His mother sent him at the age of seven to school.
She hoped that her son would devote himself to study
And stuff his belly with the scholarship of fine texts.
Who could know that Wanliang had no taste for study
And that his thoughts were not attracted to these books?
He didn't study the Masters and the Hundred Schools;
His mind was occupied by the wild stories of romance.
In ancient times there was an Emperor Yang of the Sui
Who in the flower garden in the back raped a girl.
The name of that girl was Lanying
And she was a blood relative of that Emperor Yang.[20]
Close relatives as elder brother and younger sister:
They shared the same father, had different mothers!
This love affair of an elder brother and younger sister:
That was the text that obsessed the heart of Wanliang!
While at school Wanliang was obsessed by passion;

Not studying the Classics he went mad with desire.
In his heart he longed only for this one single person:
His cousin's wife, his cousin-in-law Wang Manxiang![21]
When he had visited the Shi family to see his aunt,
His soul had become attached to that body of hers,
Because the pair of man-catching eyes of that woman
Would drive any man she but looked at to distraction!
She had not only embraced him but even dragged him,
And completely seduced he had entered her room.
And when he had groped her breasts with his hands,
The meat of her two steamed buns was so fragrant!
He had wanted to have some fun with her
But had been afraid to cause a disaster:
If his cousin were to catch them in the act,
The two families would break off all contact!
And if his father's sister were to know about it,
The old woman would lose all face for two lives.
How hard it had been to let go of that opportunity—
With hanging head, dispirited, he had come home.

Yesterday he had met someone who told him
That his cousin had departed on a business trip.
This was a heaven-sent rare opportunity
For him to go and meet with Wang Manxiang!
When he and she, related through marriage, would meet,
Their passion would soar: fierce fire in dried kindle!
If someone was there, he'd pretend he came for a chat;
If no one was there, they'd engage in battle for sure![22]
The more he thought of her, the more he longed for her: his
     heart was on fire!
The more he longed for her, the more he thought of her: the
     fire raged higher.
Once he had made up his mind, he took to his heels—
He didn't practice his characters anymore or read the books!
Without informing his teacher he left the academy,
Got on his horse, and set out on that ancient road.
Traveling all by himself he felt cold and lonely, so
Varying on an old poem, he sang to amuse himself:
"In the season of Clear and Bright, the rain is falling,[23]
The traveler out on the road is about to collapse.

When he asks where to look for an inn serving wine,
The herd boy points far away to Apricot Village.[24]
In Apricot Village you can find beautiful girls;
In Peach Blossom Village they've fat wenches.
In Orchid Village the girls you find are romantic;
In Pear Blossom Village the women are easy!
Some girls may be fat and others may be slim;
As for their skin, there's dark, light, and sallow.
There are some people who love their girls slim,
And there are others who love their girls fat;
There are some people who love their girls light,
And there are others who love their girls sallow.
Fat or slim, light or dark, which one is the best?
The opinions expressed by the crowd all differ,
But I, Wanliang, I say that that girl is the best
Whose pretty charms are concentrated in her eyes.
If but the eyes of a beauty can speak, then that girl
Resembles my cousin-in-law Wang Manxiang."
As he was talking to himself he went quite fast
And had already arrived at Shi Family Village.

In Shi Family Village this Wang Manxiang
Was the wife of her husband, Shi Dawang.
The pair did not have that many children:
She had given birth to one boy and one girl.
Once over thirty, one's carnal desires are strong:
Her heart was filled by cousin Zhang Wanliang.
"That Wanliang is actually a handsome student,
Far more attractive than that Dawang of mine.
I'll not be the first for romance with a fine gent
And that cousin seems to be the romantic sort.
That day when he and I met for the first time,
The mutual passion was honey-steeped sugar.
It was only because that Dawang was at home
That this fine pair of ducks was scared apart.
Ever since we parted from each other that day
I have been longing for Wanliang day and night.
Now I am sitting here in my embroidery room;
I'm too listless to do any embroidery work at all.
This cousin has wormed his way into my heart:

Longing for him in my heart I call his name.
This cousin has wormed his way into my eyes,
And all I see all over the place is Wanliang!"

Wanliang had left the academy, riding on horseback,
Obsessed by the thought of seeing Wang Manxiang.
Impatiently riding his horse, he went very fast and
Arrived in the wink of an eye at Shi Family Village.
Jumping across the drawbridge he entered the house
And ran straightaway to the room of his cousin-in-law.
But in front of the room, he didn't dare raise his voice:
As a novice in adultery, he still lacked the experience.
His legs were not freezing, but still they were shaking,
The words rose to his mouth, but he couldn't say them.
Turning thrice to the left, he turned thrice to his right:
His urgent heart was on fire, his whole body itching!
He wanted to open the gate and rush into that room
But then was afraid his cousin might have returned.
But if he would get on his horse and go back again,
His trip would have been all in vain—what a shame!
Suddenly he heard the sound of a bamboo curtain
And saw Wang Manxiang peeping out of the window.
She gave him a wink and beckoned him with her hand:
Too bad that she was unable to push down that wall!
As soon as he saw her, Wanliang's heart was all joy:
[He resembled] a tomcat in heat that has gone mad!
In one jump he rushed through the gate, going inside:
Embracing his cousin, he swung her unto the bed.
He not only nibbled her lips but also bit them;
He stroked her upper body, groped the lower part
To her lascivious sounds and lascivious sighs,
As—"Aiya—aiya"—Manxiang slowly grew hoarse.
Wanliang couldn't speak as he heavily breathed;
He was drenched in sweat from his top to his toes.
It was too bad that his cousin-in-law was no water
So he could dive into the water, hide in the water!
It was too bad that his cousin-in-law was no loam
So the loam could stick to his body for all eternity!
This rakish lout only lusted for one moment of joy,
Unaware that this was bound to lead to disaster!

## 5.  *Marriage Proposals*

When Dingxiang had reached the age of eighteen,
Matchmakers proposing marriage became a crowd.
The main road before the front gate was impassable;
On the small path to the back door all grass was gone.
The proposal from the eastern village failed to succeed,
The proposal from the western village did not work out.
The Zhang family therefore hired two matchmakers
Who came to Guo Family Village as a pair, a couple.
One of them was Third Sister Wang from East Range,
The other was Fourth Woman Zhu from West Range.
Now both Third Sister Wang and Fourth Woman Zhu
Were famed for their eloquence and persuasive powers.
Having from birth the mouth of mountain sparrows
They relied on their matchmaking to make a living:
They could persuade a life fish to wildly blink its eyes;
They could persuade a dead child to clap its hands.
They could persuade lame woman Liu from East Village
To marry that crooked Mr. Li from West Village;
They could persuade Four Times Bald from South Village
To marry Shining Plate Monster from North Village.
They could persuade the incense burner to marry the
     candlestand;
They could persuade the lintel to marry the gatehouse.
That day when they passed by the milling room,
The mule was persuaded to marry the millstone;
The day they passed by the chicken coop,
The rooster was persuaded to marry a newly hatched chick;
The day they passed by the dunghill,
They persuaded a carrying pole to marry a shit bucket!

They arrived at the Guo Family in the First Month
And urgently urged the match till the wheat yellowed.
When Double Five had passed, they came once more[25]
And urged the match till the Sang River was frozen.
They talked their mouths dry and still were refused,
So pretended to commit suicide at the house of the Guos:
Third Sister hung herself from a beam in the hall and
Fourth Woman jumped into a water vat in the kitchen.

When her father and mother saw things going wrong,
They were flustered at heart and lost their right mind:
They hastily agreed to the marriage proposal, and so
Dingxiang became engaged to Zhang Wanliang.

Peach flowers are red, apricot flowers are yellow;
When pears start to bloom, they are white all over.
A spring breeze was moving the purple bamboos:
Alone in her embroidery room sat Guo Dingxiang.
While she was busy embroidering mandarin ducks,
Her girl servant came in and told her to go down.
The ducks were put aside, the shoe basket abandoned,[26]
And following the servant she went downstairs.
Speeding forward they arrived quite quickly,
Had already arrived in the main hall of the house.
Before she spoke a word, she first bowed down,
Bowed to her mother, the woman who bore her.
First she asked, "Dear Mother, how are you doing?
Then she asked, "Dear Mother, are you feeling well?
I was upstairs, embroidering mandarin ducks,
So what is the reason you had me called for?"
Her mother addressed her: "My dear Dingxiang,
Your mother has something to discuss with you.
My child, you are quite a grown-up at present,
I'm afraid you can't stay much longer at home.
Which girl does not go away to be married?
Which young lady does not leave her mother?
You already have reached the age of eighteen,
So it is the right time to discuss your marriage.
As long as a daughter's marriage is not settled,
Her parents cannot feel at ease in their hearts.
In front of the mountain lives the Zhang family,
And that Zhang family happens to have a son.
The personal name he is called by is Zhang Jinyu
And the social name he goes by is Zhang Wanliang.
This year he reached the age of eighteen years
And so like you was born in the year of Sheep.
Just get out an abacus and make up the accounts,
Compute whether or not he makes a fine match!
He is a student, studying at the southern academy,

He is knowledgeable and smart, and writes well.
Your father and mother have already agreed,
That's why we called you here to talk it over."
When Dingxiang heard her mother's words,
She was involuntarily overcome by confusion:
Considering the matter from all possible sides
This marriage proposal was not fitting at all!
"Even though the Zhangs have great wealth,
I have no idea of the young master's character!
If he by any chance happens to be a violent type,
How do you want me to deal with such a guy?
If every few days I have to be carried home twice,
How could I spend there, then, many days on end?
Let's forget your daughter's miserable suffering,
It would also cause my parents much grievance.
I, your daughter, am young and inexperienced,
But why, Mother, didn't you consider this well?
I, your daughter, have barely reached that age,
But why must you drive me from my natal home?
If I could stay here at home for a few more years,
Mommy, it would be for providing you company.
How much rice would I be able to eat here at home?
How many old clothes could I then wear through?"
This long speech that Dingxiang delivered
Like a steel needle pierced her mother's heart.
"Even if you hadn't told me so, I would know!
Your mother and you, we feel exactly the same!
Your mother doesn't force you to marry early,
Your mother doesn't force you to leave home!
My child, you are your mother's darling daughter,
You are tied to my stomach, hang from my bowels!
How could I hate you for eating your mother's rice?
How could I fear that you wear out your clothes?
'When a daughter is born, she is facing outward;
When she grows up, she will leave her mother.'
And even though Mommy agreed to the match,
It actually was your daddy who made the decision.
'A marriage of Zhang and Guo was made in heaven:
Eighteen years ago I already signed the agreement:
"If the two families would both be blessed with a boy,

They would send them together to the southern school;
If the two families would both be blessed with a girl,
To the eastern pavilion to practice embroidering ducks.
But if one family had a boy and the other had a girl,
It was a heaven-made match of Dragon and Phoenix!"
Eighteen years of light and shadow have passed—
I never raised the issue but I remember the words.
The Grand Commandant may have passed away,
But Executive Censor Guo still is very much alive.
So if the Zhangs come today to propose marriage,
The promise is still firmly imprinted in my heart!'
Your daddy is the head of this whole household;
Outside the house people call him the local squire.
Now in case we do not agree to this marriage,
I have to fear that your father will lose all face."
When Dingxiang heard these words of her mother,
She was dumbstruck for a while, and then said,
"As heads of the household you have agreed,
So how could I as your daughter dare complain?
You, Father and Mother, have raised your child,
So whatever you want me to do, I surely will do.
Still there is one thing that keeps me worried,
So forgetting all shame, Mommy, I have to ask:
What is the character of that Zhang Wanliang?
Does he mean nightfall or does he mean light?"
As Dingxiang kept on asking this question,
Her old mother was at a loss how to answer:
"I only know what the matchmakers told us;
His qualities are without peer in this world.
The Zhang family has a long tradition of study,
They have mules and horses, and many fields.
We only wish you will make a good match,
Only then will we feel relieved on this issue."
When she had heard her mother's confession,
Dingxiang at her side answered as follows:
"I as your child are the flesh of your heart:
The matter of my marriage is yours to decide.
'Marry a cock, then follow the cock, cluck cluck cluck;
Marry a dog, then follow the dog, bowwow, bowwow.'
How my life will turn out will all depend

On my fate as it is determined by Heaven.
If my fate will be fat, I won't have to worry
About hairpins of gold and clothes made of jade;
If my fate will be poor, my back will be broken
By the many loads, I'll be tormented by hunger!"
The more she spoke, the more she felt disturbed:
Rain hit the black mountain, shrouded in mist.
Secretly she turned to Blue Heaven and prayed,
Prayed that High Heaven might grant its blessing:
"Grant that I, Dingxiang, will enjoy a good fate,
Grant that I, this silly girl, will marry a loving man;
Grant that I will be rich and noble, lucky all my life,
That the love of husband and wife will last forever!"

## 6.   *Discussing the Trousseau*

The matchmakers came to Guo Family Village
To settle on the date of the wedding ceremony.
"The fifteenth of the Eighth Month is a good day
For Wanliang and Dingxiang to bow in the hall."[27]
When Dingxiang heard the date had been settled,
She looked for her mother in her upstairs room.
"Mother, ever since you agreed to this marriage,
I, Dingxiang, I haven't dared make any comments.
But now the wedding date is quickly approaching,
I only feel my heart is in turmoil and in confusion.
Let's forget for the moment all other matters;
I have rushed here to ask about my trousseau!
Mother, as I, Dingxiang, am the flesh of your heart
The trousseau you provide must be well arranged!"
When her mother heard this, she heartily laughed,
"My girl, you talk as one who doesn't understand!
Your mother has considered this from an early date,
How she'd provide Big Sister with a fine trousseau.
If I'd be unable to provide you with such a trousseau,
Your mother at heart would not have felt at ease.
Now, Big Sister, first let me know which items
You want your wedding trousseau to include."
When Dingxiang heard this, she was overjoyed,
And counting on her fingers described the items:

"First of all I need my mother's big dragon chest,
Secondly I need my mother's two dragon boxes.
Thirdly I need an eight-sided table of fragrant wood,
Fourthly I need a golden bowl for starching clothes.
Fifthly I need five sets of clothes in all five colors,
Sixthly I need head jewelry both in silver and gold.
Seventhly I need *ruyi* scepters and golden hooks,
Eighthly I need a long skirt with a hundred plaits.
Ninthly I need a caltrop-flower round bronze mirror
For when I comb my hair and apply my makeup,
And tenthly I need a pair of mandarin-duck cushions
To grow old together in love alongside Master Zhang."
Hearing this her mother pursed her lips and smiled.
"My dear smart little daughter, my dear Dingxiang!
Big Sister, my child, whenever you open your mouth,
Your mother can match each and every item of you!"
To the first, I'll add a gold-thread, red-silk curtain;
To the second, I'll add an eight-step ivory bedstead.[28]
To the third, I will add three stone of polished rice,
To the fourth, I'll add four stacks of glutinous rice.
To the fifth, I'll add golden bricks to support the legs of the
     bedstead;
To the sixth, I'll add silver bricks to prop up the boxes.
To the seventh, I'll add golden hooks to be hung from both
     sides;
To the eighth, I'll add silver rods for drying your clothes in
     the sun.
To the ninth, I will add one big dragon chest,
And to the tenth, I will add two dragon boxes.
That big dragon chest and the two dragon boxes,
Placed here and there, will make two mountain walls.
The boxes will carry three hundred ounces of silver
As your private capital when running the household.
These articles are not the full sum of your trousseau;
There are also the relatives who'll add to your boxes."
The more Dingxiang heard, the more pleased she was.
"My dear mother, you really care for your Dingxiang!
If you, my parents, provide me with a rich trousseau,
All members of the Guo family will gain much face!
When drummers and pipers play as I enter his home,

This all-new trousseau will fill the wedding chamber,
And when the guests come and inspect the trousseau,
They all will praise the Guos as very magnanimous!
You, my parents, gain face; I, your daughter, gain face—
If a knife cuts through tofu, it's bright on both sides!"[29]
Her mother took Dingxiang by the hand, and she said,
"There is still one more thing that I have to explain.
On your behalf I have busied myself for three years
In embroidering a gown that is something precious.
From the eastern village I invited your big aunt;
From the western village I invited my younger sister.
I have spent several hundreds of ounces of silver
And also used up some big vats of the finest oil.[30]
Your aunt and my sister set to work all together,
Embroidering a precious gown for hot and cold.
On the front lapel they embroidered ten clusters of flowers;
On the inside lapel they embroidered ten pairs of flowers.
On the flowers of the front lapel they embroidered butterflies;
Below the flowers of the inside lapel they did mandarin ducks.
On the two sides they embroidered a dragon and a phoenix:
The flying dragon and dancing phoenix spell happy blessings.
Once a phoenix couple soars up, they spread their wings
    together;
When a dragon rises into the sky, winds and clouds stretch
    widely.
If you want to know what the use may be of this precious
    gown,
It is meant for a blessed man to enjoy its luster:
When he wears it in summer, he'll feel no heat;
When he wears it in winter, he'll feel no cold."
On hearing this Dingxiang was overjoyed:
"I will take this precious gown with me,
Take this precious gown with me to the Zhang family
And there give it to my man, Zhang Wanliang!"

## 7.   *Instructing a Daughter*

Hearing her mother describe her trousseau
Truly left Dingxiang completely speechless.
"When you add this and when you add that,

You'll give your daughter quite some face.
When I on that day will set out on the road,
The trousseau will go on for miles on end!"
The trousseau very much pleased Dingxiang,
But she had another question to ask Mommy:
"When I arrive as bride at the Zhang family,
I will still have above me my mother-in-law.
Then there's also to be my husband, Zhang Jinyu,
Her son, the young master, Zhang Wanliang!
That Wanliang is the only heir of the Zhangs;
I, Dingxiang, was the Guos' king of the girls.
But I have no idea how things will turn out
When Wanliang and I are husband and wife.
Here at home what I do is always perfect,
And when I make a mistake, you forgive me.
But if I make a mistake at my in-laws' place,
People might gossip about Guo Dingxiang!
Me losing face may be only a minor matter,
But it also means loss of face for my parents.
You have borne me and you have raised me,
So you cannot just push me out of the house!
How to play the young wife at my in-laws'—
Mother, I have not the slightest idea at all!
But Ma, as you have been through it yourself,
I ask you to let me receive your instructions."
Her mother pulled Dingxiang closer to her.
"My child, what you say really pains my heart!
The wedding date comes closer with every day,
The wedding ceremony is fast approaching!
My child, you'll soon go to the Zhang family,
So how could I as your mother not be worried?
It is a good thing you asked me that question;
Hadn't you done so, I still would have told you.
Being a daughter at home is perfect indeed;
Once you get to your in-laws', it's not the same.
Early at dawn, Big Sister, you'll still be a Guo,
But inside their gate you'll be surnamed Zhang.
Listen to your mother as she tells you in detail
How a virgin maiden has to act as young wife.
On leaving to marry, a girl doesn't touch the earth:

Your brother carries you downstairs on his back.
Take your chopsticks and throw them behind you,
Leave your rice bowl here in Guo Family Village,
Because otherwise once you've entered their gate,
You will reduce all the Guos to poverty, and me!

Conducting a wedding is always a happy event,
But rich people and poor folks do it differently:
At the weddings of poor folks the guests are few,
At the weddings of rich people they are a crowd.
Now when you arrive as a bride at the Zhangs',
You have to fully understand the latest fashion:
When relatives and neighbors 'disturb the room'[31]
You have to show yourself truly magnanimous.
Only on the third day grown-ups and kids separate—
Old and young are all allowed to disturb the bride.[32]
Rude language and dirty talk—let them chatter;
As a married wife you are no virgin anymore!
Let them all have a look and let them all spy,
Let them all say their thing and let them all talk.
On no account can you show yourself obstinate
And refuse to listen to their chatter and talk.
If you cover your face with both your hands,
If you turn yourself around and face the wall,
If you grasp the bed-curtains, not letting go,
If you shout at them and if you are going to yell,
You offend your elder and younger brothers-in-law,
You offend relatives and friends, and neighbors too:
'That Guo family girl does not know how to behave,
That girl of the Guo family lacks all common sense!'
The aunts and sisters-in-law who disturb the room,
I would think, do so in order to see your trousseau.
They'll have a look at the boxes, a look at the chest,
They'll have a look at the bedding, a look at the bed.
They want to see the clothes the new bride brought,
And want to see whether she is as pretty as rumored.
These women won't want a smoke or a cup of tea,
But will scatter some fruits and scatter some sweets.
Give them a little present when they take their leave,
A handkerchief as a keepsake, to wipe their mouth.

When that evening you'll have the wedding dinner,
My child, you must have a solid seat at the table.
You can take from all the bowls, each kind of dish,
But you should not try to taste one single noodle!
Because if you would try to take noodle strings,
They would be all over the place, going on and on.
On the one hand you would fail to fill your bowl,
On the other they would cover all those dishes!
On seeing this unsightly spectacle, the people
Would not say a word but talk behind your back:
'The bride the Zhang family acquired is a moron!
The bride the Zhang family acquired is a nutcase!
The way she takes her meal is an awful disgrace:
If you have to watch it, it is beyond description!'
After three days of hiding in the wedding room,
The moment has come for you to go to the kitchen.
Rinse the plates and dishes, the bowls and chopsticks,
Scrub the big woks and small pans spotlessly clean!
Ask your mother-in-law what you should prepare,
You cannot make any decisions now on your own!
You will have to use the big pan to cook the rice,
You will have to use the small pan to heat water.
Rinse onions, garlic, and vegetables till they're clean;
When the knife cuts the tofu, it's bright on both sides.
Add soy sauce when you're roasting pork or chicken;
When baking a fish, it must be brown on both sides.
When your mother-in-law prefers her food sour,
You just add some additional vinegar to her food,
And if your mother-in-law prefers her food spicy,
You just add some additional pepper and ginger!
When putting in salt, you must use just enough,
So the food will not be too salty and not too bland.
When you've cooked the rice and the side dishes,
You first of all serve the food to your mother-in-law.
Also bring water to wash the face, rinse the mouth,
And ask her to wash her face and rinse her mouth.
With your right hand you serve her a bowl of rice,
With your left hand you serve her a bowl of soup.
Place these in front of her, your mother-in-law,
And then address her reverentially as 'Mother!'

If your mother-in-law still finds fault with you,
You cannot give her tit for tat and oppose her.
With a soft voice, slowly speaking, you concede—
To reason with her talking back is just not done.
To practice filial piety in front of elder persons
Surpasses burning fine incense in a temple hall:
Wait until you have served your mother-in-law
And then fill a bowl to offer it to your husband.
Display love and affection toward your husband;
Make sure that you do not provoke him at all!
Place the finest morsels at the bowl's bottom
And cover them over with rice or with soup.
Now, this is called 'rich in love on the inside,'
But make sure that others don't laugh at you!
Wait till the others have all finished their meal,
And only then, my child, can you eat yourself.
But while you are eating, you must pay attention:
And refill the bowls of those who are finished.
Allow them to eat as much food as they want;
If they spill much and eat little, don't complain.

Observe threefold obedience and fourfold virtue;[33]
Diligently manage the household, it is your task!
At evening keep busy into the night's first watch,
And don't go to bed as soon as darkness sets in.
When the rooster crows twice, you must get up,
Properly put on your clothes, and leave your room.
When your family has guests who come and visit,
You will set out the benches and wipe off the dust.
And when you have made your guest comfortable,
You go to the kitchen to help your mother-in-law.
When your man goes out to meet with his friends,
Quickly open the chest and quickly open the boxes.
Provide the young man with some money to spend
And find him some clothes that will fit him well.
While the young man buttons the buttons up front,
You brush the gown on his back so there's no crease.
If his clothes have been neatly arranged on all sides,
They will all have an equal length on all four sides.
When out on the street there's a slovenly fellow

He for sure back at home must have a lazy wife;
When out on the street there's a handsome dresser,
He for sure back at home must have a diligent wife!
When the young master is praised when outside,
You, my child, will also gain face!
When the young master has had too much drink,
Show a smile on your face as you help him inside.
Take his hat and then place it inside the hatbox;
Take his clothes and hang them out on the rack.
Make sure that his cushion is propped up higher,
That he has the room to spread his arms and legs.
If his clothes became soiled, you must wash them;
If the blanket is dirtied, you will have to clean it.
Prepare your husband a jug of the strongest tea,
And also make him some hot green-bean soup,
And when he wakes up from his drunken slumber,
The tea and the soup can't be too hot or too cold.
Hand your husband a bowl, so the fragrance
Will dispel his hangover and slake his thirst.
No one's joy is as important as your man's joy:
When your husband is happy, you'll be at ease.

When people invite you over, my big daughter,
You have to react with all due modesty for sure.
But when you ought to go, you also have to go—
Don't act peevishly, without any understanding.
When out on the road, walk alongside elderly people,
Don't walk together with those unmarried bare sticks![34]
Don't talk with men who wear their hat askance;
Don't speak to men who don't button their buttons!
If others walk in the middle, you walk on the side;
If others walk on the side, you walk on the bank.
Once there, when sitting down to eat, act modestly;
Make sure that the old lady is given the best place.
While your sisters-in-law will sit down at the side,
You, my daughter, will sit down at the lower end.
You can eat, of course, from all the fine dishes,
But also take a taste of those you do not like.
When you take vegetables, take your time to do so;
Your chopsticks shouldn't look like they are fighting a battle.

Pointing and snatching they resemble lances at play,
What's taken from one bowl is inserted into another.
The bowls and the chopsticks bump into each other
With such a din that those who see it find it a mess.
My child, if you lack all rules when with others,
You cause people to talk about you and to gossip.
My child, if you everywhere show your breeding,
Your mother back at home likewise will gain face.

If there is any kind of needlework you don't know,
You should ask your mother-in-law for advice.
Making shoes, stitching socks, embroidering flowers—
It's only perfect if you join your own handiwork.
If, my child, by any chance you make a mistake,
Acknowledge your mistake and don't be obstinate.
If your husband beats you, don't strike him back;
If his mother scolds you, don't respond to the tune.
If his mother scolds you, just pretend not to hear it,
But if you scold her, they will gather at her side![35]
To be a young wife, you must learn to bear a lot;
Those unable to do so prove themselves harsh.

My daughter, this is based on my experience,
And now I have told all I have learned to you.
You know the Three Mainstays, Five Constants,
So all around people praise you as virtuous.
If you act according to your mother's words,
I will in a few days welcome you back home.
But if you will not act according to my words,
We, mother and daughter, will end all contact:
I will burn a written statement at a crossroads
That I consider my little Dingxiang as dead."

When Dingxiang had heard her mother's lesson,
She was pleased at heart and clapped her hands.
"No wonder my aunts and all the old ladies
Praise you, my mother, as virtuous and wise.
Dear Mother, please set your mind at rest,
Have no worries about your little Dingxiang.

Here at my mother's place I have been spoiled,
But at my in-laws' home I'll be a proper wife.
Many thanks, Dear Mother, for your instructions;
I will follow your example and not go astray.
When little chicks come out, they are all yellow,
But nine of ten maidens turn out like their mas."

## 8.  *Leaving Home to Marry*

The sun appears and brilliantly shines
When the wedding sedan chair enters the village.
In front of the procession comes a proud horse,
And on the horse a young man is properly seated.
He presents the marriage gifts and makes a bow,
As he waits for the bride while the band is playing.
Today is the day that Dingxiang will be married
By making her bows in the fine hall of her in-laws.
Combed and washed and all dressed up early on,
She has been waiting for the sedan chair to arrive.
Serving girls and maids accompany the bride
As she straightaway walks up to the sedan chair,
But how she as the bride should mount the chair
Is a matter that causes the girl quite a headache!
"If I would want to mount the chair from the left,
I'll impoverish my in-laws and enrich my mom;
If I would want to mount the chair from the right,
I'll enrich my in-laws and impoverish my mom.
So let me mount the sedan chair from the middle
So the two families may both equally prosper!"

While two strings of firecrackers were exploding,
The wedding procession departed from the village.
Carts and horses carrying the trousseau filled the road,
Covering the road for a distance of three miles on end.[36]
There were eight hired hands to carry the sedan chair,
There were eight hired hands to carry the wedding boxes,
There were eight hired hands to blow the trumpets,
There were eight hired hands to join in the music.
Relatives and neighbors from far and near saw her off;

Dingxiang's departure from home was quite spectacular.
The one-hundred-sons firecrackers exploded to heaven
As she left the village to the music of pipes and drums!

Firecrackers all along the road, fireworks along the road:
The sedan chair carriers belted out their songs all the way.
The girl of eighteen was seated inside that sedan chair
For the very first time since the day of her birth.
While Dingxiang was sitting inside the sedan chair,
She kept on thinking about her father and mother.
Thinking about past and future she grew confused,
But then she had arrived at Zhang Family Village!

At the Zhang manor a wedding takes place today!
In front of the manor a crowd has already assembled.
The gate building has been festooned up to the top
And big red lanterns have been hung on both sides.
In front of the gate a red carpet is spread on the ground;
The wedding shed is erected in the courtyard's center.
The people milling around there all show a happy face;
The whole courtyard is filled with a happy spring breeze.
An eight-sided table has been placed in the middle:
The wedding steelyard is inserted into a flowery bushel.
The bushel is completely filled with silver-white rice,
And two strings of copper coins hang from the beam.
In front of the bushel stands a caltrop bronze mirror
That facing the sun and moon receives heaven's light.
In a purple-gold burner the incense glows brightly,
While pairs of wax candles are brilliantly shining!
Young boys bringing joy paste up wedding couplets,
The character "joy" in bright red, "becoming a couple."
The wedding band performs "Magpies on a Branch,"
And the fireworks form "mandarin ducks at play."
Those observing the bride are crowding together,
And the well-wishing guests are lining up in rows.
While flustered men are smoking the wedding tobacco,
Agitated children are stealing the wedding candies.
Girls and young wives are coming hand in hand
And press closely together observing the new bride.
They all say that the new bride has a fine figure:

Not too tall, not too short, and also not fat at all!
While standing she resembles a solitary flower,
While walking a willow that is swaying in the wind.
Her full head of black hair looks like ink or lacquer,
Without any use of cypress oil so fragrant by nature.
Her pair of apricot eyes contain autumn streams,
Her curved eyebrows are as long as willow leaves.
Her nose, as tiny as a pimple, is quite becoming;
Her little mouth like a cherry is one dot of fragrance!
She wears a bright red jacket embroidered with flowers;
Her skirt with its hundred plaits trails behind her.
The three feet of white silk reach down to her feet—
On her feet a pair of embroidered shoes of red satin.
Embroidered shoes of red satin with high white soles;
To the embroidered flowers little bells are attached,
So when she takes one step, these bells jingle and jangle;
When she takes two steps, these bells jangle and jingle.
And when the bride walks in steps that form a circle,
They clink and they clank, they clank and they clink!
The groom stands to the west, the new bride to the east:
Husband and wife make their bows in the great hall.
With their first bow they bow to Heaven and Earth;
With their second bow they bow to the ancestors.
The pair bows to each other, so completing the rite,
And the new pair is escorted to their wedding room.

## 9.  *The Wedding Room*

Serving girls rushed forward as busy as could be,
And came first into the room to make up the beds.
They laid out two beds with coverlets of red silk
And laid out a couple of mandarin-duck cushions.
The cushions ought to have been placed together
But they in their hurry placed them at the two ends.
Even worse, one of the serving girls spoke stupidly,
Shouting, "Let the new bride enter the sick room!"
The others all said that this girl had misspoken,
And this serving maid hurriedly changed her tune:
"The ivory couch, as you see, has been prepared,
Please, new bride, please enter the wedding room!"

According to ritual, Dingxiang sat down on the bed,
Her head covered by a veil, waiting for the groom.
When she peered through her veil to have a look,
The ivory bed had been fitted out most expertly.
The bed-curtains of red gauze, the streamers green;
The golden hooks hung aslant, the tassels were long.
The coverlets and mattresses were shimmering satin;
The embroidered cushions gave off a fine scent.
On their bed had been placed seven dates;
Five peanuts were put next to the cushions.
The peanuts and dates all have their meaning
As an omen: "Quickly give birth to a noble son."[37]
"May seven sons come home as dragon and phoenix,
May five sons pass the exams at the top of the list."
Red lanterns and wax candles shone brilliantly,
Illuminating the new room, arranged to perfection.
Dingxiang stepped on the red carpet on the ground.
Her steps were an uneven, never an even, number:
If her steps were uneven, she would first have a son,
If they were even, she would first have a daughter!

Four colorful lanterns hung in the four corners
That lighted the wedding room with bright light.
The first lantern had been fashioned quite artfully,
Showing An'an delivering rice to the temple;[38]
The second lantern had been fashioned quite well:
With a slice of her liver Haitang saves her mother.[39]
The third lantern had been fashioned quite artfully:
Guo Ju buries his son and receives Heaven's boon;[40]
The fourth lantern had been fashioned quite well:
Wang Xiang lies down on the middle of the ice.[41]

The two newlyweds entered the wedding room,
And everyone was eager to "disturb the room,"
But the master of ceremonies first gave a speech;
The master of ceremonies had his words to say:
"May this one burner of incense rise to heaven,
So a fine marriage may descend to this home.
'Following the examples' you enter the room;
'Isn't this a joy': we congratulate the groom.

'Like friends from afar': such is your meeting;
'Thrice scrutinize yourself': I'll say a few words.[42]
As master of ceremonies I may have little learning
And my classical scholarship may lack all pattern,
But as master of ceremonies I must give a speech,
So as master of ceremonies I'll admonish the bride.
Yesterday, new bride, you were still at your home,
But today you've been married into this fine house.
Yesterday, still at home, you were a pampered virgin
And no one dared say anything about your behavior.
Now today you've crossed the gate to become a wife;
You must show yourself magnanimous to all people.
If they speak flippant words or serious phrases,
You cannot let those enrage you—just let it pass!
Only on the third day old and young are separated—
Without the disturbance a wedding lacks all glamour.
If I as master of ceremonies don't tell you so clearly,
Each and every one will say that I don't know my job.

I call on the maids, I order the serving girls
To hand me the happy plate so I can sprinkle the bed.[43]
The first hand I sprinkle on the mandarin-duck cushions;
The second hand I sprinkle on the ivory bed.
The third hand: may father- and mother-in-law enjoy good
	health;
The fourth hand: may husband and wife enjoy pleasure
	and joy.
The fifth hand: may the sisters-in-law all be modest and nice;
The sixth hand: may all relatives equally praise you!
The seventh hand: may your seven sons all be reunited;
The eighth hand: may your blessing last like a flowing stream.
The ninth hand: may your nine sons assist you;
The tenth hand: may you prosper in all ten perfections!"

When he opened the red bed-curtains with both his hands,
He displayed the red silk that covered both the beds.
"When I carefully inspect those coverlets,
The embroidery shows us several pictures.
The first picture is tree peonies and herbaceous peonies;
The second picture is cape jasmines and crab apples.

The third picture is a carp jumping across the Dragon Gate;[44]
The fourth painting shows Weaving Maiden meeting
    Oxherd.[45]
The fifth picture shows a cat catching a mouse;
The sixth picture shows lotuses filling a pond."
Having observed the hundred designs on the coverlets,
He then observed the one pair of mandarin-duck cushions.
"The mandarin-duck cushions have been put together,
Waiting for husband and wife to sleep as mandarin ducks.
If husband and wife sleep as mandarin ducks together,
They will hold a little baby boy in their arms next year."
When he had blessed the new couple with lucky words,
Relatives and friends set to disturb the wedding room.

## 10. *The Eight-Step Bedstead*

In the wedding room Dingxiang was seated on the bed,
An eight-step big bed that was very broad and wide.
This eight-step bed was said to be eight steps wide
Because it combined two beds into a single bedstead.
At the top it was furnished with a celestial-dragon canopy;
Below it was furnished with a flat square bottom.
The canopy was decorated with dragons and phoenixes;
Incised in the flat square bottom were mandarin ducks.
Four posters were provided in the four corners,
Decorated on both sides with the immortals of Harmony.
Let's not talk about the quality of the workmanship;
I'll only say that the materials were from famous shops.
In constructing this bed they had used a sal tree
That grew on the Dragon and Tiger Mountains.[46]
On the fifth day of the Third Month the seed was dropped,
And on the fifth day of the Fifth Month a sprout appeared.
When the great sun emerged from the earth, it did so too,
When the moisture of dew came back to life, it did so too.
After ten years it had only reached a height of three feet,
And only after a hundred years attained ninety-nine rod.
Before the natives in the mountains would sell such a tree,
His Lordship had to pay as much as the wind blows.[47]
Three hundred two big branches must be cut off;
Four hundred pairs of small branches must be cut off.

On dry land the tree had to be carried by hand and foot,
But on a river the trunk could be loaded onto a boat.
When it had been transported to the house of the Guos,
They hired the best craftsmen from the country around.
There they used it to build this eight-step bedstead;
The carpenters and lacquer workers shared in the glory.
They could ask for any salary they might want;
Their meals came on time, and the wine was fragrant.
It didn't matter how much their treatment might cost,
But His Lordship told them before they got started,
"This bed so tightly must fit that you don't see a seam!
When one strokes it, it must be gleaming on all sides.
It must be lacquered in such a way to show all colors,
It must be painted in a manner that strikes the eye."

A sal tree, so straight and spotless! There are rules
When you want to apply an axe or to use a saw.
First the old master will use a string to draw a line,
And then two apprentices will busily work the saw.
If you use only a single saw, you'll get two planks;
But if you use double saws, you'll get three planks.
And if you use triple saws, you'll get five planks:
Two of those will be yin, and three of them yang.
Hammering and planing they constructed the bed;
They applied the lacquer and produced paintings.
On the eastern side they painted the big red sun;
On the western side they painted a white moon.
When you have a red sun and a white moon,
That means you have one yin and one yang.
If the sun is not red, just apply some lip-red,
And if the moon is not white, put on powder.
And they applied lacquer, and they did paintings,
Painting the Eight Immortals on the bed's sides:
The Eight Immortals as they were crossing the sea,
Each of the immortals with his own magic weapon.[48]
The first of these immortals was Zhongli of the Han:
Bare feet, unbound hair, and a belly that's exposed.[49]
His eight-treasure magic fan carried four characters:
"Best wishes and congratulations" was written there.
The second of these immortals was Lü Dongbin,

Sporting a waving beard, dressed in a yellow habit.[50]
The four characters written on his clappers spelled
"Gold and jade" first, and then "Fill your home."
The third of these immortals was Zhang Guolao;
Riding backward on his mule, he looked backward.[51]
The four characters on his "fisherman's drum"
Read, "May a lucky star shine down on you all."[52]
The fourth of these immortals was Cao Guojiu,
A black hat on his head and dressed in a court gown.[53]
The four characters on the court tablet in his hands
Read, "Free and easily" roaming through the world.
The fifth of these immortals was Iron Crutch Li;
He looked like a beggar with his free-flowing hair.[54]
The gourd that he carried showed four characters:
"Nine generations living together" reeking of wine.
The sixth of these immortals was Lan Caihe,
Clear eyebrows, bright eyes, merrily laughing.[55]
The four characters on his jade flute performed
"The whole family united in joy" as a refrain.
The seventh of these immortals was Han Xiangzi,
Who practiced self-cultivation in the eastern hills.[56]
The four characters engraved on his fine sword
Resplendently said, "Riches and status combined."
The eighth of these immortals was Maiden He;
A pure and gracious maiden, she is a big girl.[57]
Her flower basket supported the four characters
"A myriad of blessings for generations to come."

Having observed the new bride's eight-step bed,
They further observed the new bride's trousseau.
The embroidery on the white curtains was artful,
The scenes of its hundred patterns were stunning.
The first was Guanyin seated on her lotus throne,[58]
The second was the Old Master in his refining room.[59]
The third was the Queen-Mother's Flat-Peach Banquet,
The fourth was Lü Dongbin flirting with a courtesan.[60]
The fifth was Golden Page paired with Jade Maiden,
The sixth was Weaving Maiden united with Oxherd.
The seventh was Second Sister Song sitting at the gate,
The eighth was Hu Yanzhang departing from the inn.[61]

The ninth was West Lake's Broken Bridge reunion,[62]
The tenth was Tang Yin picking Autumn Fragrance.[63]

This was a fine trousseau, a wonderful trousseau
What with its tall chest and with its low boxes!
Four golden bricks supported the dragon chest;
Eight silver bricks propped up the dragon boxes.
The chest and the boxes had green bronze locks;
For the corners were used iron-leather fittings.
The clothes rack, the washing stand, the makeup table
Were painted with flowers and decorated with beasts.
The clothes rack displayed carved orchids and flowers;
On the washing stand had been painted mandarin ducks.
There also was a pair of red-lacquered washing basins,
Each of which had been painted in a different manner:
A baby was lying between lotuses, sat in a cluster of lotuses,
And Yulan hauled water from the stream that flowed on.[64]
The makeup table was inlaid with golden phoenixes;
Dragons playing with a pearl were carved on the sides.
Right in the middle had been inserted a caltrop mirror
That was left there for the new bride to do her makeup.

In praising the trousseau of this new bride
We have not yet mentioned its four pearls:
The flood-preventing pearl could prevent floods;
The storm-preventing pearl prevented tornadoes;
The fire-preventing pearl could prevent fires;
The night-shining pearl emitted light at night.

## 11. *Burning the Precious Gown*

On the ivory bed Dingxiang was seated upright,
She had stilled her heart, waiting for the groom.
Dingxiang was not a madly lascivious woman,
And understood that he had to see to the guests.
When well into the second watch she heard steps,
She guessed that he entered the wedding room.
Indeed, when she had a peek through her veil,
It turned out to be the groom, Zhang Wanliang.
He had had so much he was drunk like a skunk

And muddle-headedly he barged into the room.
The bride he had married was Guo Dingxiang
But the wench on his mind was Wang Manxiang!
Drunk as a skunk he entered the wedding room
And belted out to Dingxiang, "Dear Manxiang!"
When Dingxiang heard this, she had to smile:
"Drunk as he is, my groom is mixing up names!"

But once young Zhang sat down, he unexpectedly
Still kept on addressing her as Wang Manxiang,
And judging by his manner, it wasn't the drink,
Because the words that he spoke were quite clear!
Dingxiang only then secretly started to suspect
That it was not Dingxiang who was on his mind.
When speaking out, she didn't resent anyone else;
She resented her mommy, her own dear mother!
"Why did you so lightly agree to this marriage?
Four ounces of cotton and no spinning was done!
What was the character of this young man Zhang?
Could it be that young Zhang was a debauchee?
If young Zhang has a secret lover,
That would spell disaster for me, Guo Dingxiang!"

Let me not tell about the confusion of Dingxiang—
Zhang Wanliang on his side also started to speak:
"Today I have married you, this girl of the Guos,
But as I look you over, you've not much of a figure.
People all told me that this Dingxiang was a beauty,
But as I see your face, you're nothing special at all."
Raising his leg he wanted to mount the bedstead:
"An unripe melon tastes bad whatever you may try!
I will not mount the wedding couch this night—
But can a bride be left to 'guard an empty room'?"
In this dilemma, he could not make up his mind;
Caught in a quandary, he couldn't reach a decision.
Then he clenched his teeth, saying, "It's too bad!"
And turned around and disappeared into his study.
There in his private study he quickly sat down,
Feigning reading a book by the light of a lamp.

When Dingxiang lifted her veil to look around,
She didn't see her husband anywhere in the room.
Lightly moving her lotus steps, she went outside,
And in one go had discovered his private study.
There she saw young man Zhang snoring loudly
With, under his elbow, the book that he studied.
Using this opportunity she observed the groom:
That young man Zhang cut a handsome figure!
His figure was not too tall and not too short;
His face was not too round and not too square.
His body was not too fat and not too slim;
His skin was not too dark and not too sallow.
That young man Zhang had a handsome figure;
That could be counted Dingxiang's blessing!
She wanted to step forward and wake him up,
But then she felt that that wouldn't be proper.
As a man's wife she had to act with sense—
Her mother's instruction still rang in her ears:
"'If your husband has had too much drink outside,
Don't nag and whine when he returns home.
Bring him instead a bowl of white sugar water,
And prepare him a steaming bowl of green tea.'
Now my husband has fallen asleep,
I cannot allow him to catch a cold!"
From the bright chamber she entered a side room,
And inside that side room she opened the boxes.
Three layers on the inside, three on the outside:
She took out the precious gown from her trousseau.
She would cover him with that eight-jewel gown,
So he would not suffer heat and not suffer cold!

When the drum tower sounded the fourth watch,[65]
Zhang Wanliang woke up in his private study:
A moment ago he still had felt cold all over,
But now his whole body was covered in sweat.
Could it be that the wine was showing its strength?
Could it be that the weather had suddenly changed?
When he lowered his head to observe his body,
His body was covered in some strange garment.

Two weird beasts with their wide-opened eyes
Stretched out their tongues—the length of a span!
With open maws and moving claws set to devour him—
Though only an illusion they looked quite real.
At that sight Wanliang was so filled with fear
That he tore off that gown and ran to the bridal room,
Cursing out Dingxiang as a damned little slut
Out to kill her husband on the day of the wedding!
When Dingxiang opened her mouth in order to explain,
Wanliang took the gown and ran from the room.
Straightaway he went to the back flower garden,
Where he made a fire to burn that precious gown.
As soon as that precious gown was on fire,
An explosive thunder resounded for a while.
Suddenly two dragons soared up and returned
With swaying heads and waving tails to heaven.
Dingxiang blamed herself for arriving too late,
And vented her spite: "My man, Zhang Wanliang,
I would not care if you had burned anything else,
But you shouldn't have burned this precious gown.
This precious gown was made by my mother,
Who hired two women to help her with this job.
Horse loads of lamp wicks were needed for this,
And quite some vats of fragrant oil were used.
Those many hands embroidered this garment;
The embroidery took three years to complete:
In front of it they embroidered a big red sun;
On the back they embroidered a white moon.
On its sleeves they embroidered two pythons
To chase away the cold and ward off the heat.
When I saw that you, my lord, had fallen asleep,
I took out this precious garment to cover you.
First of all I feared that you might catch a cold;
Secondly I feared you might have a bad dream.
From the bottom of my heart I wanted the best
As husband and wife have to assist each other.
Who could know you would burn this garment—
The best intentions turned into a donkey's guts!"
When Wanliang heard this, he stamped his feet:
"How could the situation have been like this?

When I was covered by your precious garment,
My whole body felt like I had been set on fire!
My only thought was that you wanted to kill me,
So in my anger I burned your precious garment.
Forget about that garment now that it is burned.
If it was a mistake, I will suffer for my deed."
When she saw that her husband spoke this way,
Dingxiang had no option but to soften her anger.
As her man had acknowledged his mistake,
There was little that Dingxiang still could say—
She acted this way for a peaceful wedding night
And for the eternal love of husband and wife.

Dingxiang was washing her hands in the pond
And wanted for fun to bamboozle her husband.
"My dear husband, please look below my hands:
There are twelve jugs here all filled with silver.
This silver is not the silver of the Guo family;
It must be the savings of the Zhangs buried here.
Silver of the Zhangs should be used by Zhangs,
So take it out and then use it on improvements.
Hire able craftsmen and capable carpenters
And let's build a five-horse revolving pavilion!"[66]
Once Wanliang heard this, he disagreed,
And shaking his head he berated Dingxiang:
"Girl, what you say makes no sense at all!
That silver is mine and I'll have a use for it.
I will buy me a racing track for the horses,
And I also will build me a gambling house.
The racing track is in order to gain prestige;
The gambling house is for making money."
Hearing this, Dingxiang did not like it,
And with subtle words she spoke to him:
"If you build a five-horse revolving pavilion,
The neighbors all around will praise you for it.
On the four corners we'll hang colored balls,
And from the balls chimes will hang down.
When the east wind blows, they will jingle;
When the west wind blows, they will jangle.
All the people will see it and all will praise,

Will praise us the Zhangs for being so grand!"
When Wanliang heard this, he was enraged
And addressed her in language most foul:
"You this fine Dingxiang, you this little slut,
In all things you must have the better of me!
Since ancient times 'man leads, wife follows.'
How can a hen announce the dawning sky?"
Having said this, Wanliang swept his sleeves
And abandoned Dingxiang there in the garden.
Dingxiang involuntarily heaved a heavy sigh:
"This Wanliang is in truth an irascible fellow.
Since we crossed lances on our wedding night,
I have never since enjoyed a pleasurable day."
Pondering her situation she grew more annoyed,
And in a while she came to feel quite lonely.
When she spoke, she vilified the matchmakers,
Vilifying the matchmakers as without morals.
"Why not tell the truth proposing the match?
Your invented blind talk has victimized me!"
A thousand, ten thousand words of grief and resentment—
Dingxiang's heart might be strong; her fate wasn't so.

## 12. *Returning Home*

When Dingxiang had been married for three days,
She returned on the third day to Guo Family Village.
These three days at the Zhangs' she had found so cold;
Now back at her mother's place, she felt the warmth.
Her old father was seated on the right side,
Her old mother was seated on the left side;
Her elder brother was standing opposite her,
Her sister-in-law stood at her brother's side.
The whole family showered her with kisses
And they asked her about this and about that.
The sister-in-law took Dingxiang by the hand
And observed her carefully from top to toe.
"Dear Dingxiang, we haven't seen you for three days,
So how come, Dear Sister, your appearance has changed?
Dear Sister, while at home you were bright and chubby,

So what is the reason your face has now turned sallow?
One line of a cloud of sorrow hovers over your face,
As if you're hiding a story you would like to narrate—
Your eyes resemble a pair of red peaches, so inside
There for sure lurks a story that must be revealed.
On the third day you should return as a couple,
So why don't we see your husband here with you?
Could it be that your mother-in-law treats you badly?
Could it be that your Wanliang has an evil nature?
Could it be that this marriage is not to your liking?
Please tell your sister-in-law the details of the case!
If there is someone, Dear Sister, who bullies you,
Please tell your sister-in-law and tell her at length!
Your elder brother is a man who knows no fear;
Your sister-in-law is a woman who can go mad.
Believe me, in all other things I am unqualified,
But when it comes to a fight I'm really an expert.
The two of us will go over and beat up the Zhangs,
And create a scene of the turtle disturbing the pond!"
Facing these questions Dingxiang felt quite sad—
She hastily hid the tears in her eyes in her stomach,
Pushed her sorrow from her face to display a smile,
And with her face in a smile, she answered thusly.
"Dear Sister-in-Law, please don't act in this way!
It wouldn't be right for you to bother the Zhangs!
My mother-in-law actually treats me quite well,
And as to Wanliang and me, I cannot complain!
It is only that I, your sister, having barely left home,
Find it hard to be away from Guo Family Village.
I kept thinking of my father, thinking of my mother,
Thinking of my sister-in-law and my elder brother.
If you would go over and bother the Zhang family,
I'm afraid it may cause disaster without any reason.
They would say that my family had declared war,
That the Guos, though in the wrong, bullied the Zhangs.
Feud will follow on feud, crime follow on crime,
So we could not stay a couple of husband and wife.
Dear Sister-in-Law, go to the kitchen and cook the rice,
And let me here in front chat awhile with my mom."

When her brother and sister-in-law both had left,
Her mother pulled Dingxiang somewhat closer
And said, "Dingxiang, your mother's dear child,
Your coming home today is not the normal way.
As soon as I did not see my son-in-law's face,
My heart was already overcome by great worry.
There can be no doubt that something has happened;
Now please tell your dear mother all the details!"
When she was questioned this way by her mother,
Dingxiang felt as if a river roared in her heart.
Softly, so softly, she said, "Mommy, Dear Mother";
As words rose to her mouth she changed her tune.
"Since Wanliang and I bowed to Heaven and Earth,
Our affection as husband and wife has been lasting.
If he did not come now when I return home on this day,
It is because he is studying at the southern school.
For Wanliang his studies are extremely important;
Only through study can he have a great future."
The old lady shook her head and said, "No way!
Dingxiang, don't even try to deceive your mother!
I was looking forward to your third-day return,
Hoping to see the couple together here at home.
If student Zhang does not know how to behave,
His study of the Classics will be utterly in vain.
What is at the bottom of the present situation?
You cannot suppress it—don't hide it from me!"
When Dingxiang saw that her mother got angry,
Her tears gushed forth before she had said a word.
"I have been away from home for three days,
Three days that seemed to last three years!
From the early morning I longed for sunset,
At midnight I urgently longed for sunrise.
Day and night I was longing for my natal home,
And the thought of you would break my heart.
The proverb says, 'None knows a daughter as well as the
     mother,'
And indeed you looked straight into my heart.
My mother-in-law treats me quite friendly,
Good-natured and kind, she has no comments.
The only problem is that on the wedding night

Young Zhang was drunk, didn't enter the room.
He was studying all alone in his private study
And had fallen asleep, crouched at his desk.
When I, Dingxiang, at midnight observed this,
I was afraid the young man might catch a cold!
I, your daughter, remembered my mother's words:
'Husband and wife, united in love, assist each other.'
So I fetched the eight-jewel gown from its room
And lightly, so lightly, covered him with the gown.
Who could know that he could not support it:
His whole body felt hot as if he suffered a fever.
He also said that huge pythons had scared him,
Wanting to devour his body from top to toe!
He also said that these pythons had large eyes
And stretched out their tongues as long as a span.
With each and every word he claimed that I
Wanted to murder my own husband Wanliang!
In his rage he ran off to the flower garden
And there he burned this precious garment.
Of course I wanted to argue with him, but alas,
This was our very first night in the bridal room!
After Wanliang had burned that precious gown,
He could of course not face you, Dear Mother!
In embroidering that eight-jewel garment
You had spent three years of light and dark!
Remembering the instructions of my mother,
I suppressed my rage and said not a word.
So be it if that precious garment was burned—
Just act as if the gown had never been given.
My husband at that time still acted friendly,
And he addressed me with many friendly words.
He permitted me to roam the garden with him,
To go and watch all the sights of the garden.
While washing my hands in the lotus pond,
I wanted to tease him by telling a little joke.
I said that below the water I saw some silver,
That we should promptly decide on its use!
He said he wanted to buy mules and horses;
I said that we should build a pavilion in brick.
Now, buying mules and horses still made sense,

But he said he wanted to build a gambling den!
Exchanging some words, we were at odds,
So he got up, left for the southern academy.
So my husband left and went to his school,
And on this third day did not come with me.
I don't mind that he didn't come on this third day—
This 'eight-jewel boy' is too quickly aroused.
But as young man Zhang is a student of books,
He should know how to behave as a gentleman.
Bickering between husband and wife is normal,
But who'd expect he would not cede half a pace?
If you hadn't asked me, I wouldn't have told you,
As telling you would only increase your sorrow.
It happens that a young wife may flatter both sides:
'Apply powder left and right—both cheeks are bright!'
But a young wife cannot be obstinate to both sides,
Erecting a wall between her natal and new families.
A young wife needs to have a large stomach;
She cannot have small chicken guts in each case.
I firmly remember your instructions, Dear Mother,
A drop dripping down—I'll follow your example.
When on a later day his rage will have subsided,
My husband and I will come and pay you a visit."
Her old mother repeatedly said, "Yes, yes, yes,
Your words, my daughter, indeed make sense.
Bickering between husband and wife is normal,
And the two families should not try to interfere.
Even successful interference is not taken well,
And unsuccessful interference breeds disaster.
Heartfelt concern remains heartfelt concern,
As I hope the two of you will have a good life.
My daughter, you must go quickly back home—
May you never forget the married wife's Way."

## 13. *Managing the Estate*

When Dingxiang returned to Zhang Family Village,
She wholeheartedly served her mother-in-law.
But after only half a month she came to realize that
The Zhang family was strong in name, not in fact.

She had thought the Zhang family owned millions—
How could she know they were utterly impoverished?
In their stables you didn't find any mules or horses;
The tiled buildings they lived in were broken-down.
The rents of ten *mu* of poor fields remained unpaid;
The rents stayed in his aunt's Shi Family Village.
The whole family was reduced to only two people:
There were only her mother-in-law and Wanliang.
Zhang Wanliang had always been a dissolute loafer,
Unacquainted with plantings or sowing the fields.
He was listed as a student at the southern academy,
But in fact spent his time inanely loitering about.
Dingxiang pondered the matter and was quite upset:
She might have a strong nature, but not a strong fate!
But when she spoke she did not resent other people;
She resented only her parents as too muddleheaded!
"Too lightly you agreed to this wedding proposal—
Condemning me, Dingxiang, to this miserable life.
But all my resentment and all my regret are useless;
I had better come up with a solution on my own.
As long as I, Dingxiang, have this pair of hands,
I don't have to worry that I'll have no good life;
As long as I, Dingxiang, have this pair of hands,
This old house will be replaced by new buildings."

Having made up her mind, bolstered her courage,
She turned around and hastily entered the room.
Raising her voice she called for Zhang Wanliang,
And she told him, "My husband, now listen to me!
People say that of the eighty and eight occupations
The best is by far the sowing of fields on the farm.
If you and I exert ourselves in reclaiming wasteland,
For sure we are bound to later enjoy a good life.
From the earth we can grow yellow gold sprouts,
From the mud we can harvest the grain of white rice.
Mulberry trees will turn in a wink to satin and silk;
The chicken and ducks can be sold for fine silver!"
On hearing these words Wanliang heaved a sigh,
And bereft of spirit and energy, he answered thusly:
"Because I married you, all my grandeur is gone,

I am deeply in debt to King Yama, ruler of death![67]
At present I do not have any cash to my name,
So how do we buy a big hoe or acquire a plow?"
Dingxiang had already considered this matter,
And her face all in smiles she told her Wanliang,
"My dear husband, there's no need for sad sighs!
I have come up with a plan to restore the estate.
These pieces of jewelry are only useless things;
By wearing them I cannot fill a hungry stomach.
So we should pawn them for a spade and a hoe,
And open the spring of riches to let them flow."
When Wanliang heard this, he was quite elated:
He made a bow to pay his respect to Dingxiang.

When the agricultural implements had been bought,
Husband and wife set out to reclaim the wasteland.
Using the hoe they removed the clods of stiff earth;
Using the plow they drew furrows in the new land.
They slaved under the stars and under the hot sun,
They slaved under the hot sun and under the moon.
They labored till their waists and legs were hurting
And the sweat poured down along their backbones.
The more Dingxiang worked, the stronger she grew;
The more Wanliang worked, the weaker he became.
On his hands, blood blisters linked with blood blisters,
And his shins and thighs were all covered by wounds.
When blood from broken blisters mingled with sweat,
It seemed as if a golden needle was piercing his heart.
Wanliang felt such pain that he howled and cried;
Dingxiang felt such pain that tears filled her eyes.
She supported her husband to a grove of willows,
And in their thick shade the couple rested awhile.
Extracting the thorns and piercing the blisters
She did not stop from admonishing her husband:
"It is sufficient for me if you keep me company.
Don't touch the hoe as I reclaim the wasteland!"

Wanliang took his rest each day in the willow grove,
While Dingxiang each day reclaimed the wasteland.
One inch of sunlight was one inch of land:

Each inch of land required so much time!
When in front she cleared a piece of new land,
Rank weeds grew up in a wink behind her back.
Despite all their bitter effort, they saw no progress,
So Wanliang vented his resentment at Dingxiang:
"Let's forget about it all, let's forget about it!
Like carrying water in a basket, it's wasted effort!"
In her heart Dingxiang also was filled with sorrow,
And after some hard thinking, she replied thusly:
"Dear Husband, there is no need yet to complain.
I have come up with another way of doing this.
It is now exactly one month since we were married,
So tomorrow I will go home and visit my parents."
Wanliang answered her in these words: "I won't go;
I'm off to the southern academy to resume my studies.
As of now I leave managing the household all to you.
Do not hope for help anymore from me, Wanliang!"
Having said these words, Zhang Wanliang strode off,
Enraging Dingxiang so much that she was all tears.

Returning home, Dingxiang made great haste
And in a wink had arrived at Guo Family Village.
Having greeted her parents she made her bows
And then asked her parents how they were doing.
Her parents were seated in the high hall
And listened attentively to their daughter.
"My in-laws live at a swamp before the hill,
Hill slopes and riverbanks are all wasteland.
Your daughter has already made up her mind
To reclaim that wasteland and plant the field."
On hearing this, her parents were pleased
And both of them praised their daughter:
"Smart and hardworking, you're a good girl;
This means your parents don't have a worry.
Here at home we have mules and horses;
We also have gold and silver to help you.
We have here a cow as well as a calf—
You choose the one you want to lead away.
We also have here two oxcarts at this place—
You choose the one you want to take along."

When Dingxiang heard this, she was happy
And busily made her choice, took her pick.
She took whatever she thought she needed
And she yoked an ox to one of the oxcarts.
The cart was loaded with golden grain seed,
And behind the cart were tied pigs and goats.
The boxes were filled with silkworm eggs;
On its back the ox carried mulberry sprouts.
She took her leave from her parents to return
And went back to her farm like a firestorm!

When the oxcart stopped at the Zhang house,
This caused her mother-in-law utmost joy,
And as soon as he saw it, an elated Wanliang
Seated himself in one jump on the back of the ox.
Pleased and self-satisfied he forgot himself
And he addressed Dingxiang in this manner:
"If this calf would be a high-spirited horse,
You would see me ride it in a grand manner!"
"If you want this calf to turn into a horse,
It all depends only on you, Zhang Wanliang!
You'll have to devote yourself to your studies
So one day you can pass the exams as the best.
Then you can ride a high-spirited big horse,
Dressed in red, decorated, above all others.
It's needed that you and I work hard together,
Each day even stronger than the day before!"

Dingxiang was by nature a hardworking girl,
And this time she was even busier than before.
Below the southern slope she plowed the old fields;
Below the northern slope she opened the wasteland.
At the eastern rapids she planted the mulberry trees;
On the western swamp meadow the ox was to graze.
At home she fed the pigs, raised chickens and ducks;
Her happy mother-in-law helped her in her chores.
Mother-in-law and daughter-in-law slaved together,
Hoeing the cotton at dawn, transplanting seedlings
    at night.

But that Wanliang was one freeloading loafer;
He hid himself wherever he could hang around.
At dawn he feared the dew, at noon the heat;
At night he feared being wounded by snakes.
He loudly blamed Dingxiang for showing off:
She should not reclaim the overgrown range!
But as soon as one told him to do some work,
He would claim that he had to study his books.
The wrong kind of friends came by often;
He engaged outside in all kinds of mischief.
This enraged his old mother to such a degree
That she grasped a club to give him a beating:
"A profligate will not change his nature despite a hundred
    warnings;
A lazy mule will not turn the millstone despite a thousand
    lashes!"
Wanliang was so angered by this beating
That he pushed his old mother to the ground.
"You don't have to beat me or to thrash me.
Beat me once more and you're not my mother!
I will leave this house and I'll live on my own,
And I'll never return to Zhang Family Village."
Dingxiang stepped forward and intervened,
Saying, "Dear Mother-in-Law, please listen!
Wanliang has always been your only child;
He has been pampered and spoiled all his life.
According to me, we should forget about this
And allow him to devote himself to his studies.
I will take care of the farmwork here at home,
And for inside the house, we'll depend on you."
Wanliang said repeatedly, "Yes, that's right!
What Dingxiang is saying makes perfect sense.
I will pursue my studies at the southern school,
And you two at home can plow all your fields.
From now on each of us will go his own road
And none of us will still think of the others.
The first of us to mention one of the others
Will grow a big ulcer on his mouth;
The first of us to think of one of the others,

His liver and innards will rot away."
Having said this Wanliang went out the door,
While his poor old mother collapsed from rage.

Spring: sowing; fall: harvest—time passed quickly;
In the wink of an eye three years had flown by.
Old Heaven does not betray hardworking people:
These three years had changed the Zhang manor.
Year after year Sang Mountain's harvests were rich:
The golden grain they harvested filled the granaries.
They had not enough room for all harvested grain,
So they sold it to the big grain brokers in the city.
They had not enough room to put the silk cocoons,
So they sold them to the spinning shops in the city.
Chickens and ducks, pigs and goats became herds
That they drove to the city and sold for good silver.
Now that they had the silver, now that they had the cash,
They rebuilt the manor—a magpie redoing its nest!
Destroying the wattle work, they replaced it with brick;
Pulling down the old house, they replaced its buildings.
High-spirited horses now filled the stables,
And inside its shed stood a wonderful cart.
The fame of the Zhangs surged from this day on:
For ten miles around, people praised Dingxiang!

## 14. *The Second Absence from the Academy*

While Wanliang studied at the southern academy,
His heart was occupied only by Wang Manxiang.
His heart was filled with his love for his cousin-in-law,
So he had no desire to recite the classical texts.
Behind his desk the teacher explained the books,
The long tale of the ancient deeds of ancient men.
First there were the Three Lords and Five Rulers;[68]
Then there were Yao and Shun, and Yu and Tang.[69]
King Wen searched for a saint, found Jiang Ziya;
King Wu raised an army and fought evil King Zhou.[70]
Five hegemons, seven states: spring and autumn;
The First Emperor of Qin gobbled up the six states.[71]
Xiang Yu burned down Epang Palace, but Liu Bang

Eventually trapped the Hegemon-King at Wu River.[72]
Wang Mang usurped the throne, drove Liu Xiu away;
Cao Cao, controlling the emperor, lived at Xuchang.[73]
The Three Kingdoms emerged: Wei, Shu, and Wu;
Jiang Gan stole the letter, eager to bring men down.[74]
At Long Bank Slope, Zhao Yun showed his courage;
Qin Qiong fought in the ring: whip matching lance![75]
Seven trips to the South: Emperor Yang of the Sui;
The Zhenguan reign's peace established the Tang.[76]
The coup d'état at Chenqiao of Zhao Kuangyin;
Then Judge Bao sentenced criminals in Kaifeng.[77]
Yue Fei served his dynasty with utmost loyalty;
The brave guard of the Three Passes: Sixth Son Yang.[78]
The teacher discussed the former Tang and later Han,
But Wanliang listened without the slightest interest.
The lecture room was to his mind a boudoir;
His desk was to his mind a two-person bed.
The book was to him a mandarin-duck cushion:
Wanliang dreamt only of Wang Manxiang!

Dingxiang in her boudoir was struck by a thought;
As she thought of Wanliang, she was very annoyed.
Her husband had been at his school for three years,
And in these three years he had never come home.
"Even if I gather that you've forgotten Dingxiang,
Your old mother is still here living at your house!"
When she had written a letter to Zhang Wanliang,
She called over a serving girl, the little Meixiang.
"Today I called you over here for no other purpose
But to send you to deliver this letter to the academy.
When you deliver this letter at the southern school,
Hand it over to my husband, that Zhang Wanliang.
When you deliver this letter to his lordship Zhang
Have him come immediately back to his hometown."
Meixiang answered that she had fully understood,
And with her little steps hurried along the path.
Meixiang's only concern was to move forward,
And doing so she arrived at a fork in the road.
At that fork in the road she was in a quandary,
Unsure which road would lead to the school.

As she sat down there to rest just a little while,
There arrived a student—his name, Li Erlang.
When Erlang saw Meixiang, he didn't know
Why she was sitting there by the side of the road.
He wanted to step forward and speak to her,
But it isn't proper for a boy and a girl to talk.
But he also couldn't pass her by just like that—
One has to come to the aid of people in need.
So he stepped forward and greeted her, saying,
"Girl, allow me, this student, to ask you a question:
Did you lose your way going back to your mother?
Or miss the turn on the way to your mother-in-law?
Or did the two of you have some misunderstanding
And did you run off unbeknown to your husband?"
When Meixiang had heard the student's questions,
[She said,] "Dear brother student, now please listen.
I didn't lose the way on the way back to my mother,
Didn't miss the turn on my way to my mother-in-law.
It's also not the case of a couple's misunderstanding;
I'm not here out on the road unbeknown to my man.
I am a serving girl employed by the Zhang family,
Taking a letter to the southern academy in a hurry.
A letter addressed to my mistress's husband, Sir Zhang;
My mistress's husband is called Zhang Wanliang.
At this crossroads I do not know where to go,
Do not know which road leads to the academy."
Erlang promptly replied, "That's a coincidence!
I also happen to study at that southern school.
Wanliang and I even happen to be roommates,
Sharing room and desk, as well as our bench.
Wanliang and I happen to be sworn brothers,
I am, so to speak, your brother-in-law, Li Erlang.
If you are willing to believe what I've told you,
Just come along with me as I go to the school."

Wanliang had dozed off and again had a dream.
In his dream his family was struck by disaster:
The house had caught fire and was burned down,
And his mother was burned to death in the fire!
Wanliang woke up with a start and sat straight up,

When he saw Meixiang who appeared before him.
When he asked Meixiang why she had come there,
She handed him the letter that came from home.
That letter from home was written by Dingxiang,
So Wanliang opened the letter to read it through:
"Dingxiang kowtows to you and kowtows again;
Bowing, she greets her husband, Zhang Wanliang.
While you were studying at the southern school,
The family, please know, was struck by disaster.
After you left to pursue your studies at the academy,
The god of fire has visited Zhang Family Village,
Burning down thatched rooms and tiled rooms—
Thatched and tiled rooms were all burned down.
The heat turned the gold into green-bean porridge;
The heat turned the silver into glutinous rice soup.
When the big fire was over, the plague god arrived—
The plague god was sitting astride the ridge pole.
Your old mother in the high hall caught the disease,
While the serving girls and maids all grew ulcers.
This leaves only your wife, who is still rather well,
But during the day and also at night I suffer fevers.
If it just was this fever, it still wouldn't be so bad,
But my whole body is covered by pus-filled boils.
I now have Meixiang deliver this letter to you,
This letter to be handed to my honored husband.
When you, Sir Zhang, have received this letter,
Please hurry back to your home village, please!"

Once Wanliang had read this letter to the end,
It seemed as if his heart were a burning inferno.
He promptly went to the back room of the school
And hastily informed the teacher of the situation.
In the front hall he also made a bow to the Sage,
He took his leave from the Sage as he returned.[79]
He next made his bows to his fellow students,
And he also took his leave from his roommate.
When Wanliang stepped into the courtyard,
He lifted his head, observing the screen wall.[80]
On that screen wall a unicorn had been painted,
And above that unicorn a couple of phoenixes.

Above the phoenixes three rows of characters:
"Top of the List, Second Place, Flower Snatcher—
In this academy there are eighteen students in all,
But who of them will be honored by such a title?"[81]
As men we all have the ambition to rise in status,
Because who would otherwise study the texts?
When he had left the school, he went forward;
The stable was not far, by the side of the road.
He stretched his hand and untied a horse, then
Took his position on the horse-mounting stone.
Setting his foot ever so firmly in the stirrups,
He sat in the saddle in one swoop like a falcon.
Wanliang spurred on the horse to run quickly,
In one ride returning to Zhang Family Village.

When Wanliang halted his horse to have a look,
He saw one large manor, a truly fine dwelling!
Having made three rounds around the estate,
He was both surprised and pleased in his heart.
"While I was away at the school for three years,
This poor family struck it rich—quite a change!"
The gate, three rod high, admitted a running horse,
And stone lions guarded the gate on both sides.
Above the gate a golden plaque had been hung,
Showing as big as a bushel the character "Zhang."
The eastern building was facing the western hall;
The private study stood opposite the guest room.
The inner courtyard was paved with black tiles,
And the large reception hall occupied the north.
When he peeked into that hall for a moment,
He saw his old home hanging on the back wall.[82]
It was on both sides accompanied by a couplet,
Forcefully written by the hand of a famous man.
"Spring fills the painted halls, increasing the colors;
Petals drift through pavilions, spreading their scent."
Below these, the benches of seven feet and a half
Were made either of fine pear wood or of buxus.
Peacock feathers, inserted slantingly into ancient vases,
Were swaying to and fro, more than three feet in length.
On four plates the longevity peaches were big as bowls;

Buddha's hands and wood gourds were yellow like wax.
Some eight-immortal tables had there been set out,[83]
And four folding chairs were arrayed on the sides.
The tabletops had been polished, spotlessly glowing;
The tea set had been scrubbed till it gave off a glow.
The tea jug from Guangxi came with a silver bottom;
The teacups from Jiangxi had been inlaid with gold.
When he then also had a peep at the two side walls,
He saw the painted screens placed against the walls:
Qin Xuemei while breaking the loom to teach her son;[84]
Meng Jiangnü bringing down the Wall by her weeping;
The triple visit to the thatched cottage to invite Zhuge;
The oath in the peach orchard of Liu, Guan, and Zhang.[85]
One glance was not enough to see the reception room's beauty,
So he walked on to the rooms facing the back courtyard.
The partition panels had been painted parrot green,
But both sides were dusted with gold powder.
On the red gate screen, a phoenix couple was painted,
And chimes were fastened to ancient bronze hooks.
When he lightly lifted the gate curtain to look inside,
The fragrance of osmanthus flowers drifted outside.
And when he took a second look at the dark interior,
That dark interior was stronger than brightest day:
The makeup table was shining and brilliant;
The caltrop mirror gave off a very bright light.
"That stunning beauty sitting in front of that table
Cannot but be my own wife, Guo Dingxiang!"
Wanliang wanted to keep on looking still longer,
But that would not be proper for a husband to do,
So he let the curtain fall and retreated some steps;
He retreated to the courtyard, right out in the sun.
There in the courtyard Wanliang made some noise,
Trying out in that manner his young wife Dingxiang:
If Dingxiang was a woman who knew her manners,
She would come outside to welcome Zhang Wanliang;
However, if Dingxiang did not know her manners,
She would stay in her room, acting high and mighty.

Dingxiang was sitting by herself in that side room,
Thinking and thinking of her man, Zhang Wanliang.

"He pursues fame and glory by his study at school
And for three full years has never once come home.
It is clear that he lacks all affection and love for me,
But I am filled with love and affection for him!
Each day I long for him till late after midnight!
Each night I long for him till the break of dawn!
Each day I stare at the road to the southern school,
And each year I wait till the wheat turns yellow!
In the three years I waited for him without result,
I managed to restore the manor to its former glory.
In front of the gate I planted a thousand willows,
For my husband to enjoy there their cool shade;
By the back gate I planted a myriad of pine trees—
Pine and crane—a long life—create a fine sight."[86]
Right when Dingxiang was thinking of her man,
She suddenly heard someone coughing in the yard.
Who could be coughing outside in the courtyard?
This had our Dingxiang guessing for quite a while.
"It doesn't sound like that little boy An, as naughty as a
    monkey;
It doesn't sound like little Meixiang, shuffling on her
    baby feet.
It doesn't sound like the cat that has caught a rat;
It doesn't sound like the rooster jumping onto the altar table.
It doesn't sound like my old mother-in-law,
And it doesn't sound like Second Aunt next door."
Big Sister Guo did not know what was going on,
So she peered outside from behind the curtain.
As soon as she had had a peek at the courtyard,
She saw that a student had made his appearance.
Looking a first time, he resembled Zhang Jinyu;
Looking once more, he looked like her husband!
That her husband had finally returned
Filled the heart of Big Sister with joy.
Her husband resembled a medicine's sugar:
This concoction fitted her symptoms perfectly.
This was a well-cooked drug that she swallowed,
And that terrible sickness was completely cured!
"There's no need for talk, no need for discussion;
This must be my husband who has returned home."

Without any makeup and without any jewelry,
She was dressed only in her everyday old clothes.
She pushed back the Zhao-lord hairpins in her bun[87]
And brushed the woolen thread chaff off her sides.
Around her waist she tightly bound a gauze skirt belt;
Bending her waist she pulled up the sides of her shoes.
Raising her feet she then stepped forward;
She went to the front to have a good look.
Not wanting to stumble, she of course did stumble;
Not wishing to be nervous, she of course was nervous.
Raising her feet she wanted to greet her husband,
But then she felt she might so be acting too rashly.
"If the man in the courtyard is my husband,
No one can criticize me for welcoming him,
But in case this man is not my husband,
It would be improper to make such a mistake."
After quite some thinking, [she said,] "This is it,
There can be no harm in me asking a question."
Now when Dingxiang had made up her mind,
She lifted the curtain and went out of her room.
Raising her voice she called out to the student,
Addressing him thusly: "Student, please listen!
Have you perhaps on your way to school lost the way?
Have you on a vacation missed the turn to your village?
Could it be that the two of you had a misunderstanding
So you've fled to this village, unbeknown to your wife?
If you don't make yourself scarce right now,
I, Big Sister Guo, will not treat you so nicely.
I will call little boy An from the eastern place,
Call for little Meixiang from the western side.
If they carry a wooden club, it's a wooden club;
If they carry a rolling pin, it is a rolling pin.
They'll beat you thirty-two times with the club
And twice sixteen times with the rolling pin!
They will beat you for this lack of decency,
Barging into a decent house in broad daylight!"
As Dingxiang said this, she was ready to shout,
So Wanliang from his side hastened to answer.
"Damn you, little slut, for all lack of decency!
Damn you, little slut, for being so arrogant!

I am your own husband named Zhang Jinyu.
How can you subject your man to a beating?"

Dingxiang hurriedly ran up to her husband,
Shouting, "Husband, you must forgive me!
For three years on end I haven't seen your face,
So I was afraid that I might make a mistake.
But as it is you, my husband, who returned,
You should quickly follow me into the room.
Please sit down, now please quickly sit down,
Sit down, rest awhile, and then we can talk."
So saying, she carried over a lacquered chair
That she lightly placed at the head of the table.
She dusted it thrice with a chicken-down duster
So it would not soil her husband's garments.
On his side Wanliang started the conversation
By addressing her as "My wife Guo Dingxiang"
[And said], "At the academy I received your letter,
So I hurried to come home as fast as I could.
What is the disease my dear mother attracted?
Did you ask a physician to write a prescription?"
On her side Dingxiang answered him thusly:
Addressing him as "My husband," [she said,]
"My honored mother-in-law is healthy and hale;
Physically she is actually doing quite well.
The maids and the servants are without disease,
And I, your wife, am not plagued by a fever.
As you are studying at the southern academy,
I would not dare disturb you without a reason.
The five-horse storied building is completed,
So I invited you home to please have a look.
Please, my husband, let me hear your opinion:
Where might it be too high, or where too low?"
When Wanliang heard this, he pursed his lips,
And said with a smile, "You are extraordinary!
You, Dingxiang, have special abilities indeed—
For what purpose do you still need Wanliang?"
Dingxiang on her side quickly put on a smile.
"Dear Husband, what you say makes no sense!
Even with greater abilities I'd still be a woman,

And women and men are after all not the same!
The rent that's our due at Shi Family Village
We have not received for three years on end!
When I sent our boy An to collect the rent,
Those people tied him to a post for the ox;
When I sent Meixiang to collect that rent,
Those people tied her to the rope of the mill.
After your wife had been humiliated twice,
I myself went for the rent to Shi Family Village.
When I came to the Shi family for the rent,
I infuriated your cousin-in-law Wang Manxiang.
Your cousin-in-law resembled a female tiger,
Inserted above the main gate and second gate.
I just got some food but she didn't receive me,
And filled with rage I was at a loss what to do.
Only when I was at my wit's end completely,
Did I urge you by letter to come back home."
Once Wanliang had heard this whole story,
He was so angered that his face turned sallow.
"I'll go there tomorrow and collect that rent
And then I'll confront that lunatic woman!"
Dingxiang on her side hastily urged him,
"Don't let such a small matter anger you!
Now quickly come with me to the high hall,
To greet my mother-in-law, your mother!"

As Dingxiang led the way as they went there,
She was closely followed by Zhang Wanliang.
Husband and wife entered the high hall together
And made their bows in front of his old mother.
His old mother wiped the tears from her eyes
And cursed him out as an unfilial little boy.
"You went to that southern school to study,
But why did you never return for three years?
Dingxiang has been an extraordinary woman,
Restoring the Zhang family to its former glory,
Quite unlike that ne'er-do-well that you are,
With your face that predicts the family's ruin.
You may have an imposing figure of seven feet,
But you cannot match a single pampered girl!

Say that you have devoted yourself to study,
But your belly is devoid of any fine writing;
Say that you didn't devote yourself to study—
The skin on your face is as thick as a wall!
Dingxiang all year worked herself into a sweat,
But she never saw you come and offer help;
Dingxiang all year worked herself to death,
But you stayed away and enjoyed the breeze.
Dingxiang all year was concerned about you,
But you stayed away and sang opera tunes.
Your mother was all year concerned about you,
But you didn't care that her hair grew white.
Do I know in which life I committed the sins
That left me with you, such a useless milksop?"

## 15. *The Dispute*

The more his mother spoke, the angrier she became;
How she would have liked to slap him in the face!
Wanliang on his side could not stand it anymore;
He breathed heavily and his face changed color.
Angrily he said, "Mother, you are too cruel!
With each word you speak you only wound me.
When using chopsticks to eat lotus roots, you only pick
    the eye;
When rubbing the itch, you only rub the old sore.
With each and every word you praise Dingxiang,
But in my eyes Dingxiang is not all that special.
In spending the money she spends it stingingly;
In managing the family she is not magnanimous."
Once his mother heard this, she exploded in rage,
And pointing at his face, she vilified Wanliang:
"Wolf's heart and dog's lungs: a liar's language!
Telling lies, then running off, you are only a crook.
Away from home you loafed around for three years;
Now you have the face to come back and comment!"
Wanliang did not wait for his mother to finish,
But he laughed out loud as he beat his breast.
"When you break a plate, you discuss the plate,
When you buy a water jug, you discuss the jug.

I, your son, have my own plan to raise the family,
So, Mother, there is no need to display such rage."
When he said that he had a plan to raise the family,
Dingxiang was so happy that her eyebrows flew up.
"Dear Husband, if you have a plan, please tell it,
So I can saddle and bridle the horse once again."
Wanliang all of a sudden became enthusiastic;
The words gushed from his mouth like a river.
"What I am telling you is no idle boasting:
The time and hour has come: luck without limit!
As the first step I will start from this very family;
As a second step I will address the whole world.
Let's buy three thousand *qing* of good fields,[88]
Let's buy two hundred pairs of mules and horses.
Let's hire the farmhands to work the fields;
Let's hire the cooks to work in the kitchens.
Dear Mother, you will then be Her Ladyship,
Enjoying pure blessing for the rest of your life;
Dingxiang, you will become the Master's wife,
And the rich proprietor will be me, Mr. Zhang!
I imagine how the eight hundred fine tenants
Each year will bring tribute and pay the rent;
I imagine how the eight hundred fine boatmen
On rivers and roads all will be called Zhang.
I imagine I'll have eight hundred pawnshops,
So all treasure of the world will be kept by me;
I imagine I'll have eight hundred money shops,
So all cash of the world will be managed by me.
I imagine how black gauze will replace my felt hat,
And how purple pythons will replace my felt vest.
And if I am allowed to rule all-under-heaven,
I'll select the prettiest woman to be my queen!"
Wanliang had still wanted to go on speaking,
But he had on her side so annoyed his mother
That, supported by her cane, she rose to her feet
And slapped Wanliang twice, smack in the face.
"You're a rotten scoundrel telling rotten lies;
Your whole belly is loaded with bad intentions.
Today I am forced to discipline you, my son,
You, evil sinner bereft of any sense of shame!"

Raising her arm she wanted to strike him again,
But Dingxiang on her side hastily stopped her.
"My husband spoke without thinking beforehand
And so caused his own mother to be annoyed.
But who in this world doesn't long for riches?
Who doesn't powder her face if she has powder?
But striving for wealth depends on one's hands—
One cannot conceive any poisonous schemes.
The one who harms others will harm himself;
The use of brute force will not lead to results.
As long as Old Heaven doesn't cut off my hands,
You'll have rice to eat, and the pigs their chaff."

Dingxiang still wanted to go on with her speech,
But an invitation was delivered there in the hall:
Tomorrow his aunt would celebrate her birthday,
And she invited her nephew Zhang Wanliang.
On seeing this, Wanliang was quite pleased,
And he used the opportunity to brag once more:
"Dingxiang may well be a fine housekeeper,
But the outside affairs she cannot manage at all.
When rent must be collected at Shi Family Village,
She still sets her hope on me, Zhang Wanliang!
So tomorrow I will go to Shi Family Village
For the celebration of the birthday of my aunt.
First of all I will offer her my congratulations,
And secondly I'll collect the outstanding rents.
But there is something I would like to mention
Even though it may not be appropriate to say:
When I go outside, I am young master Zhang,
But the clothes that I wear do not fit the name.
What is lacking, alas, is a fine vest of gauze—
When I go outside no one is impressed by me.
Now, if I had a gauze vest, I could show myself;
Without such a vest, I cannot present myself."
When hearing this, Dingxiang very well grasped
That he deliberately was putting her on the spot:
"A single gauze vest is only a minor matter;
He wants to test how competent I really am.
If I will only suggest that I cannot make it,

My needlework will not do, I lack breeding.
But if I say once that I can make such a vest,
I will be busily occupied all through the night.
Wanliang does not show me any affection,
But I, Dingxiang, cannot follow his example.
Not steaming the buns, he just vents his spite—
I cannot believe he'll remain cold as ice.
I had better give in to him on this matter,
Not compete with him over who's the best."
When she reached this conclusion, she said,
Unhurriedly and with a smile on her face,
"I, Dingxiang, have a pair of capable hands,
Expert at embroidering Dragon and Phoenix.
Now please choose the model for your vest,
Then let me take your size for good measure.
Tonight I will embroider you a gauze vest,
In time for you to join the anniversary party."
When the sun was setting, the day getting late,
Dingxiang strode off to her embroidery room.

## 16. *Embroidering the Gauze Vest*

As the twilight descended and the evening breeze grew cooler,
Dingxiang walked away and entered her room.
With a gold hairpin she stirred the silver lamp to shine
    brighter,
Wanting to embroider a garment for her husband.
She opened the boxes and she opened the chest,
Fitting silks and satins together in a perfect way.
At the same time she got her shoe basket out
And took the ruler and the scissors in her hands.
The big cuts and small cuts she thrice checked,
The long and short pieces she measured thrice.
Bright red threads were matched with second-red threads;
Parrot green was matched with old ginger yellow.
The tiny flower stiches resembled wheat sprouts:
Passing the thread through the needle she embroidered
    the garment.
Her fingertips were sharply pointed, the silver needle
    was short;

The silk threads went on endlessly, the colored threads
    were long.
With a smart mind and nimble hands she worked as fast as
    she could,
While the flying needle and racing thread were as busy as
    could be.
While Dingxiang was occupied with embroidering the gauze
    vest,
She didn't notice the hare had already risen in the East.[89]
First she embroidered sparrows that did not grow up;
Secondly she embroidered swallows loving their two beams.
Thirdly she embroidered a magpie as cute as a white flower;
Fourthly she embroidered an old crow that was black as ink.
Fifthly she embroidered the mynah that can tell a tale;
Sixthly she embroidered the oriole that can sing a song.
Seventhly she embroidered one falcon
That can snatch the little pulls on the ground;
Eighthly she embroidered a wutong tree,
And on that wutong tree descended a phoenix couple.
Ninthly she embroidered carp jumping from the lotus pond,
And tenthly she embroidered frogs carrying lances.
When she had embroidered all fishes and insects, flowers and
    birds,
She went on to embroider all ancient figures:
First she embroidered one man, one horse, and one lance;[90]
Secondly she embroidered Second Son carrying mountains
    chasing away the suns.[91]
Thirdly she embroidered the triple oath in the peach
    orchard;[92]
Fourthly she embroidered Sima Guang breaking the jar.[93]
Fifthly she embroidered the five tiger generals of Western
    Shu;[94]
Sixthly she embroidered Sixth Son Yang at the Three Passes.
Seventhly she embroidered the miserable death of Seventh
    Son Yang;[95]
Eighthly she embroidered the Eight Immortals crossing
    the sea.
Ninthly she embroidered the nine daughters of the
    Queen-Mother,

And tenthly she embroidered Jade Emperor Zhang up in
    heaven.
When she had embroidered these ten patterns of ancient
    figures,
She embroidered flowers and birds on the gown's borders.
During the first watch she finished embroidering the front
    lapel:
Peonies were flowering on his breast.
During the second watch she finished embroidering the four
    corners of the gown:
Colored clouds were drifting by.
During the third watch she finished embroidering the sides
    of the gauze vest
With magpies on a branch of a blooming prunus tree.
During the fourth watch she finished embroidering double-
    headed lotus flowers:
Their pink flowers and green leaves spreading their fragrance!
During the fifth watch she completely embroidered her own
    wish:
Two mandarin ducks flying as a couple, wing to wing!
When this five-colored gauze vest had been embroidered,
Her whole body felt sore and she couldn't open her eyes.
But when she gathered her strength to inspect the new
    garment,
This new garment had been embroidered just brilliantly!
She fastened off the threads and straightened the corners;
She brushed it and folded it, and scented it ever so lightly.
When her husband wore this, his whole body would smell:
Sweeter than honey or sugar to the mind of Dingxiang!
"When out on the street there's a slovenly fellow
He for sure back at home must have a lazy wife;
If your husband from top to toe is dressed in new,
You too, Dingxiang, will equally gain in face."

## 17. *Offering Birthday Congratulations*

A gauze vest, a silk scarf: dressed to perfection,
Wanliang mounts a horse and leaves the village.
When he went out earlier, he looked like a beggar

In his worn gown, torn vest, and straw shoes.
But going out now, he's the right young master,
With new shoes, a new hat, and smelling nice.
When going out earlier, he was shorter than others,
But when going out now, he is taller than others.
When going out earlier, he took the back alleys,
But when going out now, it is the main road.
When going out earlier, no one took notice,
But when going out now, he creates a hubbub.
The more he thinks about it, the more he is pleased:
Spring breeze filled his face: overflowing joy!
Riding his horse he gave it the whip to run faster
And in a wink had arrived at Shi Family Village.
The little horse groom came running out promptly
And with both hands took over the horse's reins.
A whole group of people came out to receive him;
Greeting him politely they welcomed Wanliang.
The one walking in front was his male cousin,
Who was followed by his wife, Wang Manxiang.
Cousin and wife both came out to welcome him
And together they led Wanliang into the hall.

Having bowed to his aunt, they joined the table,
Where all guests ceded first place to Wanliang.
A thousand ounces could not buy such respect:[96]
Wanliang was so satisfied he almost swooned.
With jade-white arms his cousin-in-law raised the jade pitcher
And personally she poured Wanliang his wine.
It is not the wine that intoxicates people—people do so
     themselves:
Wanliang could not stop himself from ogling Manxiang.
Manxiang served him with even more diligence;
With her arms she brushed against his shoulders.
First she poured her younger cousin another cup,
And then she lilted in a most titillating manner,
"Cousin, you've been blessed with great wealth;
Drink two more cups to increase your blessings.
Today your aunt celebrates her sixtieth birthday,
So drink a few cups more to increase good luck."
Outwardly Manxiang was pressing wine on him,

But in her heart she harbored a crooked scheme:
Today Wanliang had come at the right moment
To set her trap and trap that sex-obsessed fool.
Because he had married that girl Dingxiang
Who managed the estate with a divine insight,
The old house had been replaced by new buildings
And herds of horses and mules filled the farm.
The cousin-in-law early on had grown jealous:
The vinegar jug was replaced by a vinegar vat![97]
Her obsession was to push out that Dingxiang
And have him marry her sister as a substitute.

Manxiang deliberately set out the wine trap;[98]
Wanliang, all unawares, rushed into the trap.
An unexpected arrow is more poisonous than a visible lance:
An innocent man cannot guard himself against devious types.
Manxiang on her side had come up with a scheme
To instigate Wanliang to divorce Dingxiang.
Once Wanliang divorced Dingxiang,
She would then have her sister become his wife.
Her younger sister was called Wang Miaoxiang:
A white skin, soft flesh, and a pretty figure!
Her outstretched arms outdid lotus roots;
Her slender fingers resembled onion shoots.
She was as seductive as the ancient vixen Daji
And as gorgeous as Consort Yang of the Tang.[99]
If Miaoxiang could become Wanliang's wife,
She would be in charge of the Zhang millions.
If her little sister was in charge of these millions,
Manxiang too would somewhat share in that glory.[100]
Having worked out this vicious, poisonous plot,
She pulled her cousin by the hand, and she said,
"My dear cousin, you are in high spirits today!
In my side room I've set out another private meal,
So, Dear Cousin, please come with me to that room
As there is something I want to discuss with you.
Among my relatives there's a certain Master He,
Who is an expert in physiognomizing people.[101]
Dear Cousin, you are destined for a great future,
So let him read your face—it can do no harm."

It was partly because he had had too much drink
That Wanliang believed Manxiang so readily.
Following her, he arrived in that side room,
Where again he was given the seat of honor.
On one side he was accompanied by Sir He;
On the other side Wang Manxiang sat down.
Toasted by them, Wanliang had three more cups:
He had drunk so much his head was spinning.
Manxiang thereupon proposed to Master He,
"You are an expert in the art of physiognomy.
Why don't you use the occasion of this party
To read the face of my cousin by marriage?"
Wanliang replied, "Let's forget about it.
Why interrupt this happy drinking together?
A good prediction makes one impatient,
A poor prediction only creates anxiety."
The soothsayer said, "That won't be the case.
One rarely finds a face as promising as yours.
I find that you are young and strong in years:
A golden rock hitting the ground that resounds!
When your fortune arrives and blessing blazes,
You'll later be rich and noble beyond measure.
When I am going to read your face this time,
I will tell you the truth, nothing but the truth!
If my prediction is poor, then don't be upset;
If my prediction is good, do not praise me!"
At first sight Wanliang fell into his snare,
So the master continued to employ his skills.
He widely opened his eyes like large lamps,
And, playing the part, observed him closely.
"Mr. Zhang, you have from birth a fine face,
A blessed face that brings glory to the Zhangs.
The virtue of the three hills matches the height of the five
    marchmounts;[102]
Your eyebrows take the eight-bushels part; your eyes are
    luminous.[103]
Left and right are cinnabar phoenixes; the black and white are
    clear.[104]
Your forehead corners produce a glow, a clear sign of good
    fortune.

Your bearing is imposing, out of the ordinary:
Eventually you will be appointed chancellor."
Wanliang repeatedly said that it was too much;
Manxiang repeatedly praised his skills as divine.
As soon as the master saw his time had come,
He returned in his words to his former theme.
"A gentleman's mouth voices no flattery;
Physiognomy has never yet told us a lie.
Observing your fate, it spells great wealth,
But there's one thing I had better not tell."
Wanliang repeatedly said, "Don't be shy!"
Manxiang repeatedly said, "Tell the facts!"
"Mr. Zhang's fate promises great wealth,
But alas, it doesn't bode well for offspring.
Could it be that your spouse has some problem?
Could the eight characters perhaps be in conflict?"[105]
Who could have known that the master's words
Exactly matched the worries in Wanliang's mind?
He had been married to Dingxiang for three years,
But she had not yet borne him a son and an heir.
Once Manxiang saw the fish was caught in the net,
She tightly pulled the net's string to urge him on:
"You should ask Sir He to read the eight characters!
First pull out the weeds, and then plant the sprouts!"
Wanliang explained the eight characters to him;
The master computed yin and yang on his fingers.
He mumbled *zi, chou, yin,* and *mao* for a while,[106]
Then suddenly his face turned as yellow as wax.
"How can the hexagrams turn out in this way?
Brother Zhang is not destined to suffer such fate!
But the workings of Heaven cannot be disclosed:
If I disclose these secrets, I am bound to perish.
But for a friend I am willing to murder myself;
Risking my life I will tell the truth of the matter.
Brother Zhang and your sister are meant to marry;
A marriage of drops of dew cannot last for long.
Your fate belongs to Fire, Guo's fate to Water:
When Water quenches Fire, your life will end.[107]
The person who in the past arranged this match
Miscomputed the flowing years to your detriment."[108]

With lowered head, Wanliang did not say a word,
But Manxiang used this opportunity to comment,
"Ai ai ai! That is really too bad!
What do you say now? What do you mean?
That Guo Dingxiang is so smart and intelligent!
That Guo Dingxiang is so pretty and charming!
Who'd think that their fates were incompatible,
That her fate lacked a son and defeated her man?
When I too long ago once scrutinized Dingxiang,
Her features, I found, did not spell good fortune:
Behind her left ear she had a red cinnabar mark
And behind her right ear she had a hitching post."[109]
The master hastened to add his own comments;
The two of them seemed to be singing in harmony!
"The art of physiognomy allows us to see this clearly,
The divine numbers spell it out without a mistake.
A red cinnabar mark or mole precludes children;
A hitching post spells the death of the husband.
And when children and husband have been killed,
It later will even extend its harm to the parents.
If you don't divorce this woman fated to live alone,
Within three years, the Zhang family is killed off!"
The more Wanliang heard, the more he was upset;
His brain feverish from wine, he could not decide.
Turning his eyes, he again ogled his pretty cousin,
Whose words were extraordinarily unrestrained.
"My dear cousin-in-law, my dear cousin-in-law,
How could the situation have come to such a pass?
Cousin-in-Law, if you are willing to take my advice,
Consider this carefully and think about the future.
When keeping pigs, the aim is to dine on the pork;
When keeping goats, the aim is to enjoy goat soup.
In marrying, the aim is to sire sons and daughters—
What is the aim but to sire and raise children?
If at thirty you still have no son, that is fine;
If at forty you have no son, you'll suffer hunger.
And if in old age you lack sons and grandsons,
Who will inherit the great wealth of the Zhangs?
In front of the gate you'll be 'Childless Zhang';
Behind the house you'll be 'Impotent Zhang.'

Now I may be only one year older than you,
But we have already gotten three little sons.
When your cousin comes home from outside,
The children run out to welcome him at the gate.
While the oldest one takes him by the hand,
The second one flings his arms around his neck.
And when we go to sleep in the evening,
The baby appears from under the coverlet.
He crawls this way calling, 'Daddy!'
He crawls that way calling, 'Mommy!'
Dear cousin Wanliang, just think by yourself,
How much glory that brings to the two of us!
If you but divorce that woman Dingxiang,
I, your cousin, will select a pretty girl for you.
That pretty girl is even better than your cousin:
It is my baby sister named Wang Miaoxiang!
If you mention Miaoxiang, who doesn't know?
People praise her as a flowering crab apple tree!
A fine person, a fine fate, and blessings galore:
She would be the perfect woman to be your wife."

When Wanliang heard this speech of hers,
The feelings in his heart resembled a raging river.
Dingxiang, he considered, had no major failings;
Thinking of divorce he couldn't open his mouth.
Dingxiang, he considered, had perhaps a poor fate,
But in managing the household she had a method.
Dingxiang, he considered, was smart and bright,
But then, she had not been blessed with any son,
And if the Zhang family would not have an heir,
It was wasted effort—carrying water in a basket!
He thought this way and that way with no conclusion;
He thought that way and this way, unable to decide.
When Manxiang observed Wanliang's indecision,
She added ice to snow, and to snow added frost.
"Cousin-in-Law, you're a fellow of seven feet tall;
When a man has to act, he cannot be mired in doubts.
He must act like a sharp knife in cutting tangled hemp;
He must act like a huge flood in toppling a mud wall!
The proverb says that without venom one is no man!

Divorcing your wife is like changing a set of clothes.
Those much-loved old clothes do not keep you warm;
Once you have changed them, the new ones are better!
If you don't remove the blighted grain from the granary,
You will have no place left to store the good rice."
Before Manxiang's voice had lowered in intensity,
That master already continued the argument, saying,
"Brother Zhang, your face promises wealth and status,
So do not let a star of disaster cover your features.
Since ancient times beauties marry men of talent—
How can a pheasant hen ever marry a phoenix?"[110]
When Wanliang heard this, his heart was on fire;
With swooning head and brains he spun around.
When he opened his mouth, he said to Manxiang,
"I would like to have a look at that Miaoxiang!"
When Manxiang heard this, she chuckled,
"Heaven is fated to couple these mandarin ducks.
If you would like to meet my sister Miaoxiang,
It just so happens that she is here at our house."

## 18. *Meeting Miaoxiang*

Miaoxiang was waiting in a room in the back
When she heard her elder sister calling for her.
Her elder sister Manxiang had explained to her,
"That Zhang cousin-in-law is called Wanliang."
She had told her Wanliang had a good nature,
That his family was rich—grain-filled granaries;
That Wanliang had a wife, named Dingxiang,
But after three years of marriage had no child.
If she could trick him into divorcing his wife,
She would let Miaoxiang become her substitute.
If Miaoxiang married into the Zhang family,
This marriage would not be some trifling matter!
First of all this Wanliang had a good character;
He was an unrestrained romantic, and handsome!
Secondly the Zhang family was very wealthy,
And she would be in charge of their millions!
Thinking of this, she was overcome with joy
And hastily went forward to meet Wanliang.

Swaying her silken skirt she entered the room;
Bashfully blushing she half composed her face.
To one side she saw the soothsayer Sir He;
On the other side her cousin-in-law Wanliang!

When Wanliang opened his drunken eyes to watch,
His six spirits lost control and his soul went awry:[111]
This was a person like a flower, resembling jade;
An immortal maiden had appeared next to him!
Her full head of black hair seemed dyed in ink,
And washed with soap still had a lingering scent.
The snow-white face-oval outdid a ball of flour;
Her skin like a chicken egg outshone its second layer.[112]
Her eyebrows were curved like green willow leaves;
Her apricot eyes were glistening like rising streams.
She had a cherry-like little mouth with its two red lips,
A nose as small as a pimple, its nose bridge straight.
Her upper body was dressed in a purple silk vest,
While her peony skirt was just as long as her body.
To the left and right she wore satin-made shin wraps;
Her embroidered silk shoes had uppers with flowers.
When Wanliang saw her, his soul left its shelter,
But to describe her features, he lacked the words:
Say she resembled the peony's red of the Third Month,
But so did she the blooming crab apple of the Sixth Month.
Say that she resembled the gorgeous lotus flowers of the
    Seventh Month,
But so did she the fragrant osmanthus blossoms of the Eight
    Month.
Say that she resembled the chrysanthemum's yellow of the
    Ninth Month,
But so did she the pink prunus all dressed in white![113]

With jade-white hands she held the jug; her voice was lovely.
Myriad kinds of romantic feeling were lodged in her eyes.
When Miaoxiang had poured out three cups of wine,
She presented three cups of a soul-seducing elixir.
She said, "May you be blessed" and turned away,
But her eyes left their feelings, her gown its scent.
When Manxiang saw the fish had taken the bait,

She hauled in the net, pulled it up by its mainstays.
"Cousin, if you indeed want to divorce Dingxiang,
Then I, your cousin-in-law, will tell you the way.
You now get on your horse and hurry back home;
Make sure once there to slip silently into the house.
When Dingxiang comes out to welcome you home,
You throw her down in the middle of the courtyard.
Ask her who she is seeking when leaving the house;
Ask her why she is acting in such an impudent way.
When Dingxiang does not come out to welcome you,
Push her down on the bed and give her a beating.
Curse her out as a rotten woman lacking all manners;
Curse her out as a rotten woman putting on airs!
If Dingxiang kicks up a row or starts a fight,
You then throw your writ of divorce in her face!"

Dingxiang was, alas, a poor-fated woman;
Wanliang was indeed an unfaithful man.
Now that he had fallen into this evil scheme,
Disaster descended on the Zhang family.

## 19. *The First Beating and the First Divorce*

Wanliang mounted his horse and rode home,
And in his mind he had made the decision:
If he at home did not divorce that Dingxiang,
How could he marry his cousin Miaoxiang?
But if he wanted at home to divorce Dingxiang,
He would have to come up with a pretext.
If he couldn't come up with a failing in her,
He had no argument to divorce Dingxiang!
Pondering this matter he moved very fast
And had arrived at Zhang Family Village.
He wanted to curse Dingxiang outside the gate,
Curse her out as a slut who was too impudent,
But when he looked to the left and to the right,
He didn't find Guo Dingxiang outside the gate.
On entering the gate he wanted to curse her out,
To curse her out as a slut who put on airs.
But when she welcomed him at the second gate,

There was no failing in her he could mention.
First she asked him, "Husband, you must be hungry?"
Secondly she asked, "You must be extremely tired?
If you are thirsty, I will make you some tea;
If you are hungry, I'll go down to the kitchen."
Wanliang could only answer, "Forget about that!
Your long-winded questions are driving me mad!
You had better keep quiet and don't do a thing;
Come with me to my study and let's have a chat."
"My husband, as you are clearly feeling depressed,
It's only proper that I as your wife keep you company.
I don't know what problem is occupying your mind,
But please tell me and allow me to share your sorrow."
"If you ask me what problem, there's indeed an issue
That weighs down on my mind so I don't feel at ease.
You always say that your Guo family is wealthy,
While I claim that this Zhang family has more.
Do the Zhangs have more or are the Guos richer?
Today let's compare the two to see what's the case!"
When Dingxiang heard this, she replied thusly:
"What you say, my husband, is without any grounds!
What the Guo side owns is owned by the two of us.
If the Zhang side has more, the two of us have more.
The Zhang side and the Guo side make one family,
So it does not make any sense to compare the two."
"You say they are the same, but are they the same?
The Guos are the Guos and the Zhangs are the Zhangs.
Today, right here and now, we will compare them,
Compare them to see who has less and who more.
With each line you will tell the wealth of the Guos,
And I will say to their loss that the Zhangs have more.
What is the harm in comparing their possessions to see
Whether the Guos are richer or the Zhangs have more?"

"The gate building of the Zhangs is built of golden tiles."
"But the gate building of the Guos is inlaid with pearls."
"The silver and cash of the Zhangs are more than a million."
"The pearls and jewels of the Guos are measured in bushels."
"Before the gate of the Zhangs grow a thousand willows."
"Before the gate of the Guos are myriads of mulberry trees."

"Mules and horses are tied to those thousand willow trees."
"Pigs and goats graze under those ten thousand mulberry
    trees."
"Before the gate of the Zhangs lies a horse-mounting stone."
"Before the gate of the Guos stands a stone ceremonial arch."
"At the house of the Zhangs eastern buildings link up with
    western buildings."
"At the house of the Guos the study room is connected to the
    guest room."
"At the house of the Zhangs the whole floor is covered by red
    tiles."
"At the house of the Guos the back wall is covered with jade
    stones."
"At the house of the Zhangs they also have a pile of gourds."
"At the house of the Guos they even have a wild rice granary."
"At the house of the Zhangs they have twelve wells for
    drinking water."
"At the house of the Guos they have twelve ponds for raising
    fish."
"At the house of the Zhangs they have a gold stone roller."
"At the house of the Guos they have a silver threshing
    ground."
"At the house of the Zhangs they have gold treasure bowls."
"At the house of the Guos they have silver water vats."
"At the house of the Zhangs they have little gold pillars."
"At the house of the Guos they have silver crossing beams."
"At the house of the Zhangs they have thirty-two male
    servants."
"At the house of the Guos they have sixteen pairs of servant
    girls."
"At the house of the Zhangs the male servants outdo young
    masters."
"At the house of the Guos the serving girls outdo the young
    ladies."

The more they compared, the more upset Wanliang grew,
And he raised his voice, cursing her out as a rotten woman.
"In each line you say that the Guos have more wealth,
So go back to your mother's home to pass your days!
If you don't buzz off and go back to your mother's place,

You'll drive me, Zhang Wanliang, so mad I will die!"
He raised his hands against her, starting to beat her up;
He smacked her right in the face a number of times.
When Wanliang had beaten her, he proudly strode off,
Leaving Dingxiang there bitterly weeping and crying.
"It was you who wanted to compare the family wealth,
But after we had done the comparison, you went mad.
Even if you think that I shouldn't have dared compare,
Why should you want to force me to return to the Guos?
You, Wanliang, have a character that is hard to polish;
You don't show any tolerance in big or small problems.
Whatever good words I may say, it is all wasted effort,
And marital conversations all end in trivial bickering.
But today it was even worse than on earlier occasions;
You wounded me with repeatedly spoken evil words.
I, Dingxiang, have been married now for three years,
And to the end I have never committed any mistake!
Three years with the Zhangs were three years of labor,
Three years of bitter water I have tasted three years.
Three years as newlyweds were three years of widowhood:
These three years of tears flowed down as three rivers!
During the daytime I, Dingxiang, still could manage,
But then at night I, Dingxiang, never saw my groom.
So I curl myself up, curl myself up, hoping to sleep,
But while I lie asleep in my bed the tears keep coming.
Once I have closed my eyes, my husband arrives,
But when I open my pupils I see an empty room.
This marriage of the two of us is only a dream;
We've had a wedding but never became a couple.
Even if I, Dingxiang, would be a blazing burner,
I'll be unable to melt that iron heart of Wanliang!"

## 20. *The Second Beating and the Second Divorce*

Wang Miaoxiang of the Wang Family Village
Was praised by all as a blooming little crab apple.
When she had met with Zhang Jinyu two days ago,
She had made an appointment with him for today.
But when the sun had risen high and reached noon,
She still did not see Wanliang show up anywhere,

So she waited for him, her heart roaring with fire,
Guessing: could something have happened, perhaps?
Could it be that he in his heart was too spineless,
Not ruthless enough to divorce that Dingxiang?
Could it be that he has deceived me, Miaoxiang,
By promising me I would share in the glory?
But by the looks of him, he's a romantic type,
So I think that he must be a man of passion.
When we swore our oath by mountain and sea
He did not seem to perform a play on the stage.
It couldn't be this way, it couldn't be that way:
Miaoxiang was so distraught, she was at a loss!

Right when Miaoxiang was utterly distraught,
She suddenly heard the loud hooves of a horse.
When she saw the horse, it looked like his horse;
When she saw the man, he looked like Wanliang!
Making a leftward circle thrice, without dismounting;
Making a rightward circle thrice, still on horseback:
Can it be that these eyes of mine have gone blurry?
She opened the upstairs window to scrutinize him.
When she looked a first time, it was Zhang Jinyu;
When she looked again, it was Zhang Wanliang!
He had not buttoned his gown, showed his breast:
Wasn't he a smart dresser? Wasn't he marvelous?
He glances to the east and he stares to the west:
He must be expecting that I will welcome him in.
Miaoxiang hurried downstairs and went outside,
Where she stepped forward to take the bridle.
She helped her cousin-in-law to dismount
And welcomed him into her embroidery room.

Wanliang brushed against Miaoxiang's shoulder
And in his hand he offered her candied fruits.
On meeting, this cousin and this female cousin
Were wrapped in smiles without saying a word.
The two of them entered her embroidery room,
Where Miaoxiang hurried to offer him some tea.
When Miaoxiang placed the fine tea in his hands,
Wanliang grasped her hands and wouldn't let go.

He pulled Miaoxiang over to sit down in his lap,
Filling his bosom with her warmth and fragrance.
With open mouth he kissed her hibiscus cheeks,
Stretching his tongue, he licked the crab apple.
Miaoxiang in his lap just giggled and said,
"Dear Cousin, you cannot act in this manner!
I, Miaoxiang, am still a chrysanthemum girl;[114]
I am one fresh flower that still has to bloom!
If you, my cousin, truly love your crab apple,
You will have to marry me, Wang Miaoxiang.
If you have no intention to marry Miaoxiang,
This furtive groping and stroking is improper.
Today I am waiting for what you will tell me:
What is the decision that you have reached?"
When Wanliang heard this, he didn't answer,
And huffing and hawing he said not a word.
Miaoxiang involuntarily became impatient,
And, pushing a man down a slippery slope,
Pressed Wanliang by shouting, "I knew it!
I was bamboozled by you on that earlier day!
How can a crab apple compare to a peony?
How can Miaoxiang compare to Dingxiang?
I, Miaoxiang, am a girl of a small family,
In needlework and food skills unschooled.
Dingxiang is the daughter of a great house,
Schooled in needlework and cooking skills.
She can make clothes and small accessories,
And she also knows how to dye textiles.
I only have to look at what you're wearing:
That gauze vest is embroidered perfectly!
As long as the Zhangs will have Dingxiang,
They will prosper in people and in wealth;
As long as the Zhangs will have Dingxiang,
Sons and grandsons will fill their hall!
Please tell me how old your son is now.
Please tell me how old your daughter is—
Next time you come to Wang Family Village,
Please bring them along so I may have a look.
Even though people say I'm not generous,
I will take them along to the market street.

For the boy I will buy a nice silver neck lock;
For the girl I will get a bright set of clothes."
When Wanliang heard her speak in this way,
He was so enraged he seemed to blow his top.
"When beating a man, don't beat where it hurts—
Cousin-in-Law, you only hit me on my ulcer!
You know that Dingxiang is fated to be barren;
You know that Dingxiang cannot have children.
You ridicule me, Wanliang, for having no heir;
That's why you say sons and grandsons abound.
If you tomorrow will have made that neck lock,
You can lock that necklace all around my neck,
And when you then lead me across the market,
I'll call you 'Mother' with each word I speak."[115]
Miaoxiang promptly replied, "I am so sorry;
Please forgive me for speaking improperly.
I know about the situation of cousin Guo, but I
Touched the topic only once you had raised it.
There at home she may play the young lady,
But there is a rumor that's making the rounds.
Each year in summer she suffers from fevers;
Each year in winter she grows venereal ulcers.
Growing venereal ulcers and suffering fevers,
Of course she cannot conceive and give birth![116]
Moreover, Dingxiang is a baleful broom-star[117]
Who spreads calamity wherever she may go.
In her bosom she carries that iron broom of hers
That sweeps away parents-in-law and offspring.
She has only to lift her head, heaving a sigh,
And the crows will die high up on the branches.
She has only to have a look at a vegetable garden,
And nine of the ten beds of plants turn brown.
She has only to wash her hands in a stream,
And frogs and small fishes turn up their bellies.
She has only to rinse her feet in some river,
And the turtles will die on the river's banks.
She has only to haul some water from a well,
And she kills the dragon king down the well.
Today she is casting her spell on Zhang Jinyu:

No wonder the numbers will not expand.
As long as the Zhangs keep this Dingxiang,
I am afraid that you never will have a son.
Others won't care—it is not their business,
But brother Zhang, just give it some thought.
At eighteen or nineteen you have no worry,
But once past thirty, starvation looms near.
If in your old age you don't have children,
Your life will be dreary, filled with sadness.
Distant relatives will steal your possessions;
Close relatives will divide house and farm.
Dear Cousin, who will prepare your medicine
Once you are old and develop some disease?
And when eventually one day you will die,
You'll be even less than a monk in his temple.
When a monk has died, people make inquiries
And his disciples place his body in an urn.
But when a single widower passes away,
It is three pieces of rope and a single mat.
If he has dug a hole, no one will bury him:
His corpse is left on an overgrown hillside.
Male dogs come running to drag a leg away;
Bitches come running to steal his innards.
Whoever will see this will make this remark;
Whoever will see this, will have this to say:
'This was originally young master Zhang,
This was long ago that Zhang Wanliang,
But because he had no children at his knees
He ended up in this manner upon his death.'"

The more Wanliang heard, the worse he felt,
And he cried, "Miaoxiang, please don't go on!
I, Wanliang, already had my fortune told:
Dingxiang does not have a fate that is good,
And I have therefore made the cruel decision
To divorce my stinking rotten wife Dingxiang.
Ever since I first saw you, dear Miaoxiang,
I have loved you so much that I went crazy.
I want to marry you as quickly as possible.

Too bad that I cannot marry you tonight."
Hearing this, Miaoxiang laughed to herself.
"There is one thing that I still have to say.
If the Zhangs don't divorce that Dingxiang,
I, Miaoxiang, refuse to become your concubine.
So if the Zhangs want to marry Miaoxiang,
You must make haste to divorce Dingxiang.
Once the Zhangs will have married Miaoxiang,
I'll be able to bear children and breastfeed them.
As long as the provisions at the Zhangs' are fine,
I promise I will produce you a son and heir.
Once I've crossed the lintel, entered the gate,
I will bear you plenty of sons to fill the hall.
Each year a child may be an empty claim,
But two in three years is a fair estimate."
Wanliang on his side produced a forced smile.
"Dear Cousin-in-Law, you don't understand.
When I returned to my home last night,
I encountered Dingxiang and created a scene.
I cursed her out loudly, but she did not care;
I gave her a beating, but she said not a word.
The truth of the matter: she made no mistake;
As a result I don't know what I have to decide."
On hearing this, Miaoxiang was not pleased;
Turning her butt to him, she kept facing the wall.
He called to her repeatedly, but she didn't care;
Her pouting lips formed a mule-fastening pole.
"I had thought that you were a big-bellied guy;
Who could know you were a man without guts?
A rich man takes pride in his mules and horses;
A small man takes pride in his fields and farm.
Dingxiang has not born or raised a single child,
And yet you praise her as if she were a flower.
I have no clue at all to which class you belong—
You are a man who praises his wife to others!
A man who praises his wife has no aspirations;
He doesn't fear others may pierce his backbone."
Wanliang on his side smiled ingratiatingly,
Handing her fruits and handing her candies.
"Dear Cousin, please stop making fun of me,

And don't carry a grudge against your cousin.
When I mention Dingxiang, my heart explodes.
How could I praise that stinking rotten wife?
Dear Cousin, when I came here today for you,
It was for the purpose of discussing this affair.
Eager? I'm even more eager than you can be!
Flustered? I am more flustered than you can be.
Now, as there is absolutely no other way out,
I will settle accounts in an unyielding manner.
In a moment I will go to the market street
And get me a small knife of seven inches long.
I will put that knife in the inside of my boot
And then have that slut take off my clothes.
When that seven-inch knife falls on the floor,
I will grab the knife and hold it in my hand.
'Inciting your secret lover to kill your man!
You want to murder your husband Wanliang!'
That very moment I will divorce Dingxiang
So that rotten woman cannot protest at all!
My dear cousin, you are such a smart woman,
So don't be flustered and don't be impatient.
If I will not divorce that woman Dingxiang,
Then I cannot be called Zhang Wanliang!"
Hearing this, Miaoxiang was secretly pleased,
But she tied the noose for him even tighter.
"I will believe you only if you swear an oath.
A woman should not be deceived by a man!"
Wanliang was cornered, so he could only
Pull up his blue gown, kneel down on the floor.
"If I, Wanliang, have spoken any false words,
May three big torches burn down the Zhang farm!
And when these three torches set the house on fire,
Let Wanliang crawl out through the dog hole."
"Dear Brother, if you swear an oath, I'll do it too;
I, too, will wager my life in making this oath.
Dear Cousin, if I am not true in my words to you,
I will appear before King Yama stark naked!"
Wanliang thereupon said, "Rise to your feet!
You are my blooming little crab apple tree."
Miaoxiang got up and she laughed heartily:

"Cousin, I expect you to make up your mind!"
She came forward and took him by the hand.
"Come and have a look at my inner bedroom."

When she a first time pulled him into her room,
They resembled little kids "hauling wave on wave."[118]
When she a second time pulled him into her room,
He resembled Zhang Gong jumping across the wall.[119]
When she pulled him a third time into her room,
They resembled Weaving Maiden and Oxherd;
When she pulled him a fourth time into her room,
They resembled a pair of little mandarin ducks.
"Dear Cousin, please sit down, please sit down,
Please sit down on your cousin's ivory couch.
Dear Cousin, as you sit down on the ivory couch,
I, Miaoxiang, will go down to the kitchen room."
She cooked him an egg, cooked some noodles,
The chicken strings floating on top of the bowl.
With both hands she presented this to her cousin;
She presented this to her cousin: "Have a taste!
Don't blame me for putting in too many spices;
Eat some more raw ginger to open the stomach."
When Wanliang took this bowl from her hands,
It seemed he had received a brew of immortals.
When he had eaten one half, he left the other;
He left that other half to try out Miaoxiang.
He wanted to see how she reacted to him;
He wanted to see: did he cause her disgust?
But when Miaoxiang had taken the noodles,
She gulped down half that bowl in one go.
Wanliang was pleased and also in love:
Feelings of joy and love surged in his heart.
Embracing her tightly, he pulled her over:
On the ivory couch these two people
    engaged in the sport of mandarin ducks!

When Wanliang on his horse rode back home,
He ran into that old King Wen on the bridge.[120]
King Wen was a man who had lost his sight
And made a living by computing the trigrams.
He could compute disaster and misfortune;

He could compute clouds as well as sunshine.
He could compute clear skies as well as rain;
He could compute cloudy skies without sun.
He could tell the number of tigers behind a hill;
He could tell the number of wolves inside a cave.
When geese were trekking across the skies,
He could tell whether they flew singly or as a couple;
When mosquitoes passed in front of his face,
He could even tell whether they were starving or fat.
King Wen had spread his mat on the bridge,
And Zhang Wanliang rode up to him there.
"Master, please consult the hexagrams for me
And compute the fortune of me and my wife."
He reported the eight characters of their birth:
Husband and wife both belonged to Sheep.
King Wen took out his golden prediction coins
That he shook three times, flashed three times.[121]
You only heard their loud clanging resound
As these golden coins tumbled down onto his mat.
The master stroked each of these golden coins;
He stroked them to feel either head or tail.
"Your wife belongs to Sheep and so do you;
Your Sheep shares in the glory of her Sheep.
You are a Sheep of Triple Nine of winter time,[122]
When there is no grass and there is no grain—
When in fall the rice has been carried home,
Crows and sparrows have eaten each kernel.
She is a Sheep of the dog days of summer,
When there is grass and when there is grain.
When in fall the rice has been carried home,
Crows and sparrows steal not one kernel.
As it is you who asked me to spell your fate,
I tell you the truth and nothing but the truth.
If you as her man had not shared in her glory,
You would have ended up in the beggars' guild!"
Hearing this, our Wanliang was so annoyed
That he slapped King Wen right in the face.
"You rotten blind fool and your rotten fate!
How dare you insult me, using your trigrams?
I am the widely famous Zhang Jinyu, so how
Can I be said to share in the glory of my wife?

As quick as you can, compute my fate once again.
Otherwise I'll have you meet with King Yama!"
King Wen repeatedly said, "I will do it again."
Again he set out his *jia*, *zi*, and *yi*, and also *chou*.[123]
"I made a mistake in computing your future;
Forgive me for irresponsibly talking nonsense.
You are a Sheep of the dog days of summer:
Your fate has plenty of grass and of grain.
Your wife is a Sheep of the depth of winter,
So her fate is lacking in grass and in grain.
Your fate: riches and status; her fate is poor.
It's the wife who shares in her husband's glory."
Only now did Wanliang's rage turn to joy,
And he paid him as fee five ounces of silver.
"You should have talked like this from the start;
Then you would not have been slapped by me.
I find you blind are quick to change your tune.
Think twice next time when computing a fate!"
Having said this, Wanliang left on his horse,
While this old King Wen collapsed in laughter.
"Fools love to hear the most flattering words!
Too bad his mind is strong but his fate is not.
Evil men and evil deeds will earn a bad future—
Hitting me, a blind fellow, was without reason.
Good and evil, I fear, will be repaid in the end:
One day retribution will descend on your head.
You didn't take good advice but gave me a lecture:
Mean-minded men lose their houses and lives."

In her upstairs room Dingxiang embroidered mandarin ducks
When she suddenly heard from afar the tinkling bell of a
    horse.
When she looked at the horse, it was the Zhang family's
    horse;
When she looked at the rider, it was Zhang Wanliang.
She was of a mind not to go out and greet Wanliang,
But that was not the proper way of married women.
In which family is there no bickering between husband and
    wife?
And in which family do pots and pans not rattle and shake?

She only wished that her husband would change his mind
And would return to keep her, Dingxiang, company more
     often.
So she opened the door of her room and went downstairs;
Walking softly with many small steps, she walked very fast.
When Dingxiang arrived in the heaven-well courtyard,[124]
The black crows above her head were loudly cawing.
Those little crows of only half a pound
Can predict both happiness and a funeral.
Predicting happiness they circle in swarms;
Predicting a funeral they will loudly caw.
"At my mother's place the crows once cawed in this way,
And then the pigs started to die and the goats fell dead.
I've no idea what kind of event may be foreshadowed
Now that I today once again encounter these cawing crows!"

Welcoming him, Dingxiang stood before the horse;
On the horse, Wanliang proudly held his head high:
Making a leftward circle thrice, without dismounting;
Making a rightward circle thrice, still on horseback.
Dingxiang stepped forward to take over the horse
When Wanliang hit her on the head with his whip.
When beating a person, one fears he may hit first;
When murdering a man, one fears to be surprised.
With his first lash, he disordered her black hair;
With his second lash, he ruined her facial makeup.
Being thus hit, Dingxiang saw stars before her eyes,
But she didn't dare weep, didn't dare to complain.
When she had wiped away her tears, she stood up,
As before with a smile, addressing him as "Husband."
This increased the rage of Wanliang even further,
And he cursed her out in evil words, evil language.
"Guo Dingxiang, you mean slut, you rotten woman!
The skin on your face must be thicker than a wall!
I beat you and curse you but you don't understand!
With your shameless face you are one rotten bitch!
Who told you to welcome me in front of the gate?
Welcome your own father, welcome your mother!
How would you be welcoming me, Zhang Jinyu?
How would you be welcoming me, Zhang Wanliang?

For business at the front gate we have our boy An;
For business at the back door we have serving girls.
But you do not employ the boy An or a serving girl,
But you have to come outside and scout the street!
Without any restraint or control you act too freely,
Because back at home you lacked proper breeding.
But when a young wife does not behave properly,
Her foul reputation will soon spread all around.
In the fields for grazing cows you set your snares.
From among the hired hands you take the lustiest.
I reckon that those bare sticks around the village
All must have had plenty of intercourse with you!
Because if such things had not happened,
How could you have acquired the looks of a whore?
Who is the one you're waiting for outside the gate?
Who may be the romantic lover you are waiting for?"
The more Wanliang cursed her, the more disgusting he
    became,
But Dingxiang had to suppress her anger as tears coursed
    down.
"I had better suppress my anger, had better keep my mouth
    shut—
What is the harm in a husband reviling his wife?"

Dingxiang returned in tears to her upstairs room,
While Wanliang went all by himself to his study.
He pulled that seven-inch knife from his boot—
A steel knife, even unpolished, gives off a glow.
"Why don't I kill her, why not cut off her head?
The best would be to kill that damned rotten slut!"
But in the wink of an eye he thought, "Slowly!
Such a procedure would not be convenient at all.
If I tonight would kill that woman Dingxiang,
I would be locked up in jail tomorrow morning.
Since ancient times a murder has been repaid by a life;
That would mean I would lose my life all in vain.
I have to find a fault in her so I can divorce her—
There are rules for husbands divorcing their wives."[125]
Even though Wanliang had come to hate Dingxiang,

To condemn her to death would be an injustice.
If it had not been for that cousin-in-law Wang,
He would have no reason to divorce Dingxiang.
It was only in order to acquire Wang Miaoxiang
That he steeled his heart to divorce Dingxiang.

## 21. *The Third Beating and the Third Divorce*

Wanliang's feelings were like a surging river
And all night long he never closed his eyes.
Dingxiang's tears secretly soaked her cushion
And all night long, sorrow pained her heart.
When the rooster crowed and dawn returned,
Dingxiang got up and went down to the kitchen.
She poured water in the pan, and then hastily
Added the rice to cook the morning congee.
Turning around she wished her mother-in-law
Good morning, taking tea and water to her room.
But wishing her mother-in-law a good morning,
Her mind was on that immoral Zhang Wanliang.
"In which little detail have I ever offended you?
For three years you let me guard an empty room!
I won't blame you for not entering our bedroom,
But you cannot beat me and curse me each day!
Each three or two days you beat me and curse me,
Shouting with every word that you want to divorce me.
Outside the house you can banter, you can laugh,
But once back home your face is covered by frost.
Now if I, Dingxiang, were a loose woman,
I could not complain if you cursed me and beat me.
But considering that I have not made any mistake,
I wonder what the reason is why you mistreat me.
You may have no feelings, but I know my duty;
You refuse me as wife, but you are my husband.
If you, my husband, indeed are a faithless fellow,
I must blame myself for overlooking that failing.
Today I will prepare you a meal by cooking
A bowl of thin Dragon and Phoenix noodles,
And when I hand you these fine noodles,

I will question you to get to the bottom of this.
I cannot believe that your heart is made of stone,
That you are not a human raised by his parents."

She scooped up one ladleful of snow-white flour,
Which she poured out into a big golden bowl.
Then she ladled up *rengui* water from the North,[126]
Which she sprinkled on Dingbao's white gown.[127]
She stretched out her pair of bodhisattva hands[128]
And busily kneaded and kneaded the dough again.
The first time: may you achieve first rank at court!
A second time: may Liang and Zhu's love last forever![129]
A third time: the triple oath in the peach orchard!
A fourth time: the four lucky signs, as you wish!
A fifth time: may five sons all gain first place!
A sixth time: six times six—may all go smoothly!
A seventh time: seven stars honor the Northern Dipper!
An eighth time: eight trigrams determine yin and yang!
In the wink of an eye the dough has been mixed
And placed on the smooth table-board of Lu Ban.[130]
Press it once, press it twice: it's as big as cups;
Press it three or four times: brighter than the moon!
Taking the big cudgel of the Monkey King in her hands
She rolls out and flattens the dough till it extends far.[131]
When the dough has been rolled out till it is as thin as paper,
It is folded for Student Zhang so he can write his letters.[132]
Taking the huge sword of Lord Guan in her hands,[133]
She cuts the dough again and again, long and short.
The long noodles measure one rod two feet;
The short ones still measure a full eight feet.
The thick ones resemble a one-third thread;
The thin ones resemble a hair on the head.
Whether they are long or short, thick or thin,
Each and every noodle incorporates sugar.
Raking up the *bingding* fire from the North,[134]
She burns Little Prince Chai below the pot.[135]
The water is singing of Dragon and Phoenix:
Dingxiang keeps busily stirring the noodles.
First she downs the heads and then the tails:
Like a silver dragon crossing the three rivers!

At the same time she takes a million onions
And carefully removes all the First Emperors.[136]
Now she adds two full spoons of rich man Oil
And takes two pinches of that little King Yan.[137]
A translucent bowl of finest Yangzhou china
Is lightly set down on the stand for the pots.
She grabs the Immortal Maiden's skimmer
And takes out the substance, not the fluid.
With ivory chopsticks, matching yin and yang,
She stirs the noodles thrice, lets them sit thrice:
The Dragon heads rise high on the edge of the bowl;
The Phoenix tails soar up against the side of the bowl.
Dingxiang picks up the Dragon and Phoenix noodles
And brings them with slow lotus steps to his study.[138]
She calls to her husband, "Please wash your face;
Your wife is bringing you here a bowl of noodles.
Allow me to ask you: when last night you returned,
Why was your raging fury that extremely strong?
Could it be that you had had too much to drink?
Could it be that you had lost money gambling?
Could it be that you someplace had suffered a fright?
Could it be that your soul had been left in far lands?
If there is some explanation, please let me know it,
As we should share worries and sorrows together."
Dingxiang had carefully phrased her questions;
She hoped to move the heart of Zhang Wanliang.
All was still fine when no questions were asked,
But Wanliang exploded in rage on hearing them.
Pointing at her, he stamped his feet, red-eyed,
And the first curse he shouted was "Rotten slut!
I, Wanliang, am disgusted to see your features,
So fuck off and go back to that room of yours.
Gather together all your broken-down rubbish.
Fuck off and go back to Guo Family Village!"
As she heard this, he raised the rod in his hands
And used this staff to administer a beating to her.
With the first stroke, he disordered her hairdo;
With the second stroke, he beat down her jewels.
After the third stroke she fell down on the floor;
He hit the porcelain bowl, overturned his food.

Dingxiang wept in a heart-wrenching manner:
"Today I need to hear an explanation from you.
I have been married to you for a full three years
But I never experienced a single pleasant day!
Where, after all, might I have made a mistake in
Managing the household, serving your mother?"
"You dare say that you never made a mistake?
Just think a little to remember your three faults!"
"Could it be that my hands were too clumsy
And that I damaged those new clothes of yours?
Could it be that my language was too clumsy
And that I offended the neighbors on both sides?
Could it be that my person has been too lazy
So I've been negligent in serving your mother?
If it hasn't been this and it hasn't been that,
There is one thing, my husband, I must ask.
When that day you said you'd collect the rent,
How come you came home carrying candy?
Lately also, rumors have been circulating about
One or another cousin-in-law Wang Miaoxiang.
It can't be that you have fallen in love with her
And therefore want to divorce Guo Dingxiang?"
On hearing this Wanliang laughed heartily.
"You truly are an expert in solving riddles!
The one I am in love with is cousin Wang,
And I cannot bear the sight of you, you slut!
That cousin-in-law has a beautiful figure;
From birth she is blessed with good fortune.
I want to be able to marry that cousin-in-law,
Bring her good luck to Zhang Family Village!
Prospering men and goods, plenty of children—
She can provide the Zhangs with a son and heir.
Each year one son—that she won't promise,
But two in three years seems a fair estimate."
Once she heard that Wanliang loved Miaoxiang,
Dingxiang could not stop herself from crying.
But speaking again, she addressed Wanliang:
"I urge you, my husband, please listen to me.
When eating food, the best is homemade food;

When wearing clothes, the best is plain cotton.
It's your wedded wife who knows your needs;
A 'midway marriage' cannot last till the end.
When husband and wife are living together,
A chicken and pheasant are not the same kind.
Beat a chicken twice and she will stay around;
Beat a pheasant but once and she'll fly away!
Let me, Dingxiang, tell you the real situation:
That Miaoxiang is some gold digger for sure!
Now that the Zhang family has come into money,
Beware of people who are out to harm you!
Talk about that Miaoxiang, your cousin-in-law:
Why didn't she love you, Wanliang, in the past?
Now that today the Zhang family has become rich,
She hopes to push the phoenix from her nest."
When Wanliang heard this, the fire-star shone,
So his two eyes displayed a murderous glare.
Like a turtle that swallowed balance weights
He steeled his heart and he steeled his guts.
"Now if I today don't settle accounts with you,
How can I tomorrow marry Wang Miaoxiang?"
Thinking of that romantic Wang Miaoxiang,
He vilified Dingxiang again as a rotten slut.
"You even dare compare yourself to a phoenix?
You're not aware of how hideously ugly you are.
You are a pheasant hen from behind the hill;
It is I, Wanliang, who is the golden phoenix!
If the phoenix has wings but cannot soar up,
It's because you, a pheasant, are tied to its legs.
Even a weasel will not steal a breeding hen—
Pheasant and phoenix sharing a nest is improper!
You are a tiny cloud at the edge of the sky;
I am the brightly shining moon up in the sky.
If the eastern wind doesn't scatter the clouds,
Black clouds will cover and darken the moon.
The fortune teller has told me my fortune,
And a physiognomist has also read my face:
While your fate is Water, my fate is Fire:
Water conquers Fire, so Fire meets disaster.

From outside, you have a peach-blossom face
But it hides a cinnabar mark, a horse-tying pole.
The red cinnabar mark will undo your husband;
The horse-tying pole will undo my old mother.
Now I have woken up from a three-year dream;
As of today you and I will go our own ways.
Run away as quick as you can! Go and fuck off;
It's better to run away than to be squeezed out!"

Wanliang cared only to keep on cursing her;
He cursed her out till her heart grew frigid.
"My husband, still your rage and listen to me:
When acting as a human, don't be so absurd.
With every word you claim I harm my man,
With every sentence that I harm your mother.
These three years the Zhangs have prospered—
I cannot see how I may have caused harm!"
"Dingxiang, you are such a rotten woman
That you still dare defend yourself cleverly.
You have been at our place for three years
But how come you haven't yet borne a son?"
"As long as you did not bring up that issue—
If you raise that issue, you anger my heart!
In these three years since we were wedded,
You have lived outside, never coming home!
During the three happy days of the wedding
You did not sleep with me for a single night.
During the day you drank till drunk as a skunk,
And at night you disappeared to a gambling den.
You may deceive your mother in the high hall
With the excuse that you're away at the academy.
As you hung around outside these three years,
How could I ever bear you a son and heir?
Gourds may grow on their own, and melons,
But there are no babies that grow by themselves.
Melons that grow by themselves may be sweet,
But a baby that comes by itself is a disgrace!"
"Now if that is indeed the argument you make,
You and I will sleep together tonight for once.

And when I will have shared your bed tonight,
You'll carry my baby in your arms tomorrow!"
"My husband, you're someone who has studied;
I hadn't thought you could produce such words!
You say that if we will sleep together this night,
You'll have me carry a baby in my arms tomorrow!
Even if we would want to carve a baby of wood,
We would have to hire a wood-carver tomorrow!
And even if I would show you one made of clay,
I would have to wait till dawn for the sun to rise.
Let me today give you this single seed kernel;
Then tomorrow I can demand a sprout from you,
And the day after, you then can harvest the rice—
How can I have a baby after only a single night?
Let me today give you this one pit of a peach;
Then tomorrow I can demand the peach sprout,
And the day after, you can harvest the peaches—
How can I have a baby after only a single night?
Let me today give you this one chicken egg;
Then tomorrow I can demand a pullet from you,
And the day after, you will have a hatching hen—
How can I have a baby after only a single night?
When you speak as a man, it must make sense;
What you say will be evaluated by other people.
If you as a man speak only such shameful words,
Your study of the Classics has all been in vain."
"Dingxiang, don't persuade me with clever words;
I have steeled heart and guts to divorce Dingxiang.
If in this one year I do not divorce you, Dingxiang,
The grass may not sprout and trees may be barren.
If in these two years I do not divorce Dingxiang,
My mother in the high hall will encounter disaster.
If in these three years I do not divorce Dingxiang,
The male and female servants may all run away.
If in these four years I do not divorce Dingxiang,
The cattle of the Zhangs may all suffer from ulcers.
If in these five years I do not divorce Dingxiang,
Relatives and neighbors may refuse to see me.
If I today do not divorce you, this Dingxiang,

I, Zhang Wanliang, will die within three days.
When you have caused the death of Wanliang,
You can beat your drum to show off elsewhere."

When Dingxiang heard these heartless words,
It seemed as if thunder resounded below a clear sky.
This Wanliang was indeed a most faithless fellow;
She had lost all hope for a harmonious marriage.
Dingxiang might have a nature burning like fire,
But alas, Wanliang had a nature frozen like ice.
If he today abandons me, this Guo Dingxiang,
He must have drunk some soul-seducing potion!
Suppressing her tears she again implored him,
Saying, "My dear husband, please think again!
Overgrown mountains hide tigers and leopards;
Hearts blinded by profit house foxes and wolves.
The Zhang family has lately grown prosperous,
So jealous people are out there to set a trap for you,
Hoping to catch oyster and snipe like the fisherman,[139]
Eager to incite discord between mandarin ducks.
Why didn't they compute your fate at an earlier date?
Why didn't they read your face at an earlier date?
They waited until the Zhangs had grown wealthy
To pour that soul-seducing potion down your throat!
Don't believe that false talk, don't believe ghosts—
If you believe those ghosts, you will be bamboozled.
But as long as you will believe the words I told you,
Your family will prosper, people living in harmony!
Even if I, Dingxiang, may have had any failings,
How can you forget these three years of your life?
A good husband should not betray love and duty,
And a good man should not ignore his conscience."
But Wanliang was incapable of listening to her:
"You whore! You bitch! Don't have any thoughts!
I, Wanliang, already have made up my mind,
And I am disgusted having to hear your crap!
A four-in-hand cannot retrieve a spoken word.
The Long River has no wave that flows back;
If you want Zhang Wanliang to retain you,
You must wait for the sun to rise in the West!"

"If you are determined to divorce Dingxiang,
I, this weak girl, will display my divine power.
If you divorce me, Dingxiang, in a side room,
She who later lives there will not enjoy peace.
If you divorce me, Dingxiang, in the stable,
I must fear our horses and mules will all die.
If you divorce me, Dingxiang, in the high hall,
Disaster is bound to strike my mother-in-law.
If you divorce me, Dingxiang, in the kitchen,
I fear that a lightning strike will set it on fire!"
"This cannot happen, no, this will not happen.
I will drag you, Dingxiang, down to the courtyard.
There in the courtyard I'll divorce Dingxiang,
And affix to the writ the seal of hoof and hand.
Take whatever you want of the household wealth,
From horses and mules, and from pigs and goats."
This one writ of divorce was a thousand pounds:
Taking it into her hands, she was awash in tears.
"I want nothing of the millions of your family
Because each coin carries the surname Zhang.
But get that one old oxcart of mine from storage
So I can take my old clothes back home with me.
That oxcart originally belonged to the Guos,
So you should hand it back to the Guo family."
Turning away, Dingxiang ascended the hall
And knelt down to leave her mother-in-law.
"Wanliang in his cruelty has divorced me,
So from now on, Mother, I depart from you.
Even though these three years have been short,
Your love and affection for me are everlasting.
I leave for the edge of the sky, the board of the sea,
So I will not come and serve my mother-in-law—
Who will bring in the morning your washing water?
Who will spread in the evening your bed for you?
Who will sleep with you, Mother, in the same bed
To warm the blanket in winter, fan you in summer?
Who will accompany you when you have to work,
Weaving cotton in fall, picking mulberry leaves in spring?
Who will repair your clothes when they are worn?
Who will wash your coverlet when it is soiled?

And when you, Mother-in-Law, catch a disease,
Who will then concoct the medicines for you?
When you love to eat Dragon and Phoenix noodles,
Who will make you Dragon and Phoenix noodles?
This unfilial wife of your son has to leave today;
I wish you, Mother, a happy and healthy old age.
Mother, there's no need to keep thinking of me;
Just consider your son's wife one who has died.
Mother-in-Law, please forget all about Dingxiang
And consider me only a dream you once had."
She made three bows and again three bows;
She grieved three times and again three times.
She kowtowed once to show her filial piety;
She kowtowed twice to stop the funeral cortege.
She kowtowed thrice to support the coffin
And smash the old bowl in the graveyard.[140]
On seeing Dingxiang there awash in tears,
The old lady was involuntarily filled with grief.
She cursed out Wanliang: "You little beast,
Bereft of all feeling and bereft of conscience!
Dingxiang has been your wife for three years,
Spending her days in bitter toil and hard work.
Diligent and capable, and also nimble handed,
She restored the Zhang family to its former glory.
For a hundred miles you cannot find a smarter girl!
What kind of mistake may she have committed?
But this day you beat her, that day you curse her,
And each word you say is 'I divorce Dingxiang.'
He may divorce Dingxiang but I don't do so;
I will keep you, Dingxiang, here by my side.
I will grab the dragon-headed staff in my hand,
And curse out that miscreant, again and again.
If he mentions the word 'divorce' one more time,
Old as I am, I will grapple with him, fight it out!"
Dingxiang hurried to calm down the old lady,
And, holding her by the hand, she said again,
"My husband has broken with me without love.
I don't carry a grudge against you for this divorce.
You, Mother, have treated me with greatest love,
Which I will never in my life be able to forget."

One heartbroken person faced another one;
One tear-covered face looked at another one.

Having said goodbye to her mother-in-law, she turned around
And gazed at each and every place in the house of the Zhangs.
The god of the sky, the god of the earth, the gods of the
    house,
The lords of the gate and the lord of the room: she bowed
    to all.
"I lived here in the house of the Zhang family for three years,
But enjoyed only peace and health because of your protection.
Today I have been divorced and will leave all alone;
I, Dingxiang, may be strong but my fate is not strong.
Whatever is my prosperity should come along with me;
Whatever is Zhang prosperity should stay with young Zhang.
Let me open the chest and let me open the boxes;
Little packs are spread out in the middle.
Let me collect my old things,
Let me pick out my old clothes.
As long as I hadn't opened the boxes, I still could manage;
Now that I have opened the boxes, tears gush forth.
This vest of mine does not have a collar;
These pants of his do not have a belt.
There is this newly stitched pair of cotton shoe soles:
The soles have been stitched but the sides are lacking.
Three years as husband and wife is actually quite short,
But without any love or taste they were as cold as ice.
I will take an axe in my hand, curved like a moon sickle,
Because I want to destroy this beautiful trousseau.
First I will split the chest and then split the boxes,
And next wreck that eight-jewel, four-poster bed!
That precious bed was made for me to sleep in;
How can I leave it here for that crab apple flower?
Thinking it over from all sides, it's over, it's over—
Love has been ripped apart—we each go our way."

## 22. *Laments at the Ten Miles*

The sky fears black clouds, the earth fears a drought;
Flowers fear blowing winds, grasses fear the frost.

It was because Dingxiang's fate was so unfortunate
That the weak maiden had met a heartless husband.
When the oxcart had been packed in the right way
She led the old ox out to harness it before the cart.
She pulled once and pulled twice: the ox didn't move;
She pulled three and four times: the ox only stared.
The old ox moved slowly, found it hard to move,
As it did not want to leave Zhang Family Village.
The ox gazed at her and she gazed back at the ox,
And on both sides, tears gushed down in streams.
The old ox also understood feelings and decency,
As an animal still outshining Wanliang in all respects.
Having walked three steps, they retreated three steps,
Walking forward, going backward, and gazing again.
With both hands folded, she bowed and bowed again
To take her leave, take her leave of the Zhang farm.
The buildings on all sides had been built by Dingxiang,
So she bowed to the fine buildings on all four sides.
She bowed to the pigpen and Grand Marshal Pig,
She bowed to the chicken run and King Phoenix,
She bowed to the horse stable and Brother Horse,
She bowed to the goose run and to Childe Goose.
She bowed to the good neighbors on all sides,
She bowed to the aunts and to all the big sisters.
She could not leave through the Zhang main gate
Because a divorced person does not add luster.

The tiny little locust with its yellow belly skin
Flies from the southern farm to a northern farm.
When it feels hungry, it eats a sprout of grass;
When it feels thirsty, it drinks a droplet of dew.
The busy, so busy, locust is as happy as can be,
But where will busy, so busy, Dingxiang end up?
Through the back gate she drives the old oxcart,
Taking her leave from the Zhang family farm.
"Zhang family farm, dear Zhang family farm,
For three years on, you accompanied Dingxiang.
Each brick and each tile was bought with sweat,
Each bird and each beast was raised by my hands;
Each silk worm, each grain was fed by my blood,

Each sprout and each plant was cared for by me!
The wind-blown willow strands drift and dance;
The mulberry fruits turn yellow, thanks to the sun.
The farm is still as before, but I have to depart—
The dream still unfinished, awakened by thunder!
Three years of care and three years of labor
Have acquired me only this writ of divorce:
This writ of divorce resembles a millstone
That is crushing my organs as well as my innards;
This writ of divorce resembles an earthen mound
That buries a true maiden, Guo Dingxiang!
As of now Dingxiang will hide her name,
Afraid of the gossip if she shows her face:
A killed donkey is unwilling to pull the mill;
A divorced wife cannot be able and virtuous.
Even if I would have the three rivers' water,
It cannot wash away the injustice I suffered!
The main road is rocky, bumping the cart;
The unending grief of separation is killing!
The edge of the sky or the end of the earth—
Where should I go and where should I hide?"

When the cart arrived at the one-mile hall,
That one-mile hall was filled with a crowd.
There were not only many boys, but also girls—
Old and young, boys and girls, all were happy!
When the cart arrived at the three-mile field,
It was filled with chickens, ducks, pigs, and goats.
Chickens, ducks, pigs, and goats were so happy—
Only Dingxiang there was filled with gloom.
On the five-mile ridge grew mulberry trees;
The sprouts had been planted by Dingxiang.
Now it had all turned out to be only a dream—
Only in death does a cocoon complete its thread.[141]
When the cart arrived at the seven-mile pond,
A boat was drifting and bobbing on the water.
A drifting boat still can be tied up at the bank,
But where would the drifting Dingxiang go?
When the cart arrived at the nine-mile bridge,
Drums and pipes resounded against heaven.

Four carriers carried a wedding sedan chair;
The wedding guests forming a long procession.
The booming drums urged on the marriage;
Calling up memories they increased her pain.
In the past she sat in that wedding sedan chair,
And sitting in that chair she had only thought,
"I do not care whether those Zhangs are wealthy;
I only care that my groom will have a good heart.
If a man respects his wife, she will respect him;
With marital concord, mutual love will last long.
I never thought that today I would be divorced,
That I, Dingxiang, would have been dreaming.
Now that I today pass by this place, I feel so lonely,
So lonely and alone that it increases my grief."
When the cart arrived at the ten-mile archway,
There was a school there in that very ward,
And from inside that school, voices resounded,
Reciting their text: "Zhao, Qian, Sun, and Li."[142]
"All people have the ambition to climb higher;
It's only me who is fated to meet with misfortune."
And from her bosom she took the writ of divorce;
Once again she carefully read this writ of divorce.
It said that Dingxiang was without any breeding,
Incompetent in receiving people, treating guests.
It said that Dingxiang behaved most improperly,
Standing outside the gate, displaying her charms.
It said that Dingxiang was very lazy by nature,
Visiting neighbors left and right, engaging in gossip.
It said that Dingxiang was fated to be childless,
Unable to conceive and to raise any offspring.
She didn't read to the end, didn't look further—
This writ of divorce filled her heart with anger.
She folded the writ of divorce and put it away,
And urged on the ox to follow the road ahead.
That oxcart resembled the fate of Dingxiang:
Bumping up and down, nowhere an end in sight.

The wheels of the cart rattled on, crossing the ridge:
She could see her natal home, Guo Family Village.
She could hear the dog barking in front of the farm

And saw the cooking smoke rising in a sunset sky.
Could her father be standing in front of the gate?
Could her mother be busy in the kitchen in the back?
Could her brother be carrying firewood and straw?
Could her sister-in-law be out sunning the garments?
"That yellow dog is welcoming me back to the farm;
The cooking smoke beckons me to go to the kitchen.
I would like to drive this cart to my mother's home,
But I cannot, I cannot—it is absolutely unbearable!
I would go home and meet with Father and Mother;
What can I say when I see my father and mother?
Dear Mother, Dear Father,
Dear Father, Dear Mother!
Dingxiang is too ashamed to be able to meet you!"
But in her heart she still thinks of her parents.
"My parents' love and affection is unforgettable,
Their deep concern for Dingxiang unforgettable!
I remember that time when the sun had highly risen
But I, Dingxiang, was too lazy to get out of bed.
My father then came up to my upstairs room
And took me downstairs, carrying me on his back.
When Mommy saw that, she pointed at us and said,
'Aren't you resembling an old monkey carrying a little
    monkey on its back?'
That phrase of my mother, borne out of love for me,
Made the whole family collapse in loud laughter.
Their love for their daughter was without limit;
How would I ever be able to forget that affection?
Dear Father! Dear Mother!
The proverb says it, the old proverb says it well:
The tiger out on the plain looks for the deep hills;
The dragon caught on the shoals hopes for the river.
The sovereign in trouble looks for a great commander;
The minister in trouble sets his hope on his emperor.
Today I, Dingxiang, have landed in great trouble,
And in my heart my hopes are set on my parents.
My parents may be close by, but I cannot see them—
That breaks the heart of this miserable Dingxiang!
Your daughter Dingxiang now is a divorced wife,
So how could she have the face to see her parents?

This writ of divorce is a merciless sword, cutting
The endless love of mother and daughter asunder!"
Swallowing down a flood of heartbreaking tears,
She urged the ox to pull the cart down the hill.

As the sun set on western hills and evening fell,
The Sang River blocked her from going forward.
As she lifted her head, she sighed to Blue Heaven,
But black clouds surged before its Southern Gate.[143]
Those black clouds stretched across the wide sky
As a wild wind howled and rolled up the earth.
With loud peals, lightning flared again and again;
With a booming sound, thunder exploded doubly:
A sudden outburst of rain came bucketing down,
Cutting down and soaking that Guo Dingxiang!
There was no road she could follow forward;
When going back again, she reached no village.
When she called on Earth, Earth stayed silent;
When she called on Heaven, it did not respond.
"Old Heaven, if you want to send down something, don't send
    down rain!
You had better send down swords and lances on me!
Those swords and lances may kill Dingxiang—
Don't let me live any longer here in this world!
Water of the Sang River, Sang River's water!
How often have you fallen, how often risen again?
I, Dingxiang, have grown up drinking your water,
And today I will borrow you to bury my body.
I, Dingxiang, was born into a decent family,
But suffering injustice, I have no other way out.
I must steel my heart—so be it, alas, so be it—
And in one jump throw myself into the river!"

## 23. *The Rescue*

One strand of black hair floating on the waves,
Two peach-pink cheeks bobbing on the water,
Three souls and six spirits leaving and returning,
As the beauty's seven orifices show signs of life.[144]
When Dingxiang ever so slowly opened her eyes,

She saw a young man who stood before her.
He was dressed in short pants, torn and worn,
And from top to toe he was soaking wet.
His load of firewood placed in front of the cart
Marked him at first sight as a dirt-poor fellow.
He showed an honest and utterly innocent face
And slowly and haltingly started to speak.
"Big Sister, you woke up, so please tell me
From which village you are, which township?
What kind of mean injustice had you suffered
That you here all alone sought to end your life?"
Dingxiang on the ground forced herself to sit up,
And her tears gushed down along with the rain.
When she spoke, she didn't blame anyone else,
But she blamed that fellow: "You should not,
You should not have saved this poor-fated girl,
Wasting all your good time while you did so!"
The young man on his side replied to her thusly:
"Big Sister, you should not talk in this manner!
A real man in this world has to do his duty:
Not saving a person in danger of dying is wrong.
Even ants know to cherish and cling to their life;
Staying alive is always much better than dying.
You should follow this excellent advice of mine
And not concern yourself about anything else!
Don't give in to sadness out in the open field:
Rein in your horse when approaching the brink.
Forget for the moment whatever may pain you;
The wind is too chilly by the side of this river!
Make haste to come with me to my cold hovel;
In that cold hovel my old mother is waiting.
She will cook you a bowl of heartwarming rice
And give you a set of dry garments to wear.
When tomorrow morning we get up at dawn,
I'll see you off on your road going back home."

Rain descended from heaven, flooding the earth,
Putting this lonely girl Guo Dingxiang on the spot.
She eyed that young man three times from the left;
She eyed that young man three times from the right.

Dingxiang was of a mind to go along with him
But couldn't wade through the dense fog of her mind.
She was of a mind to jump into the waves once again,
But wouldn't she then betray his good intentions?
Heaven and earth were limitless, wide and large—
Why was there not a place for her, Guo Dingxiang?
Having thought to this point, her innards broke,
And wiping away her tears, she spoke again.
"Brother, now you had better go to your home,
While I will rest here by the side of the Sang.
I, Dingxiang, am the daughter of a poor family;
I can withstand storm and wind, sleet and rain."
When the young man heard this, he smiled;
Reporting his own status, he urged Dingxiang,
"I understand, I know what you are thinking.
You have some reservations concerning me.
But I am a stalwart seven-foot fellow, so please
Don't misunderstand Third Son Fan's intentions!
Weak as you are, you can't stand this violent rain;
How can you, alone, endure the chilly night wind?
You go by the shortest way to my cold hovel,
And I will take care of the ox and guard the cart.
When tomorrow morning the sky has cleared,
You can drive your cart wherever you want to."
When Dingxiang heard him give this speech,
She suddenly felt a rush of hot blood in her heart.
That there could be such kindhearted people—
So when she answered him, she spoke warmly.
"I cannot out in the open spend the night here,
But how can I let you keep guard here all night?
I will come along with you to your cold hovel,
So put your load of firewood on top of the cart."

Third Son drove the cart and went on ahead
While Guo Dingxiang followed behind him.
When the two of them arrived at his hovel,
Fan's mother immediately set out to work.
First she handed Dingxiang a set of dry clothes,
Then cooked some noodle soup for Dingxiang,
And she asked her, "My girl, where do you live?

And how did you end up here in these parts?"
Dingxiang first wiped the tears from her eyes,
And then she replied to her: "Kind Mother,
If you ask for my home, you can't say it is far;
It is Guo Family Village by the side of the hill.
My father by others is called Rich Man Guo;
My mother lives at home as a pious Buddhist.
They do not have that many sons and daughters;
It was only the pair of my elder brother and me.
I am called Big Sister Guo
And my brother is known as First Son Guo.
Three years ago I left my home to be married,
And my husband was named Zhang Wanliang.
It turned out that he was a licentious rake
Carrying on an affair with his cousin-in-law.
That cousin-in-law named Wang Manxiang
Was one bellyful of rotten, poisonous water!
She caused the lack of harmony in my home;
Because of her I had to guard an empty room.
But that Manxiang was only a minor problem:
She had a younger sister, blooming crab apple!
This vixen showed off her glamorous features
To seduce my husband, that Zhang Wanliang.
Again and again he found fault with me, and
Divorcing me, he chased me from his house.
I have no place to go on the whole wide earth,
And I also cannot hide myself at my mother's.
I, Dingxiang, have become a divorced woman,
Lacking the face to go on living in this world.
Concluding that I had come to my road's end,
I threw myself into the river to seek my death.
But fortunately I was then saved by Third Son,
And now, Mrs. Fan, I also enjoy your kindness."

When Mrs. Fan had heard the tale of Dingxiang,
She accompanied Dingxiang in her sad grief.
"Now if you don't mind that we are so destitute,
You can stay for a while with us in our hovel.
I will treat you as my own dear daughter,
And Third Son will be your elder brother."

Hearing this, Dingxiang fell down on her knees
And addressed her reverentially as "Mother."

## 24. *Bringing Prosperity to the New Family*

In the sky, the sun squeezes out the moon;
On earth a loving girl loves a loving man.
In the wink of an eye three months had passed:
Dingxiang never left the side of Third Son Fan.
Third Son was a diligent, hardworking man,
Honest and fair, sincere and good-natured.
His mother, too, was a kindhearted woman,
Treating Dingxiang better than a daughter.
Thrice good, twice good: united in goodness—
One happy event followed another happy event.
As a couple, in a pair, they ascended the hill to cut firewood:
Money and treasure descended the hills in flood upon flood.
As a couple, in a pair, they went down into the garden to pick
    mulberry leaves:
Gold and silver flowed into their house like a torrent.
The magpies in the trees shouted out their calls;
The Sang River's flowing stream roared loudly.
You are filled with desire but you do not speak;
I am filled with desire but keep my mouth shut.
You are filled with desire and I am quite eager:
Facing each other in silence, linked by long love.
The Fan family's old mother knew what to do,
And as a matchmaker brought about a marriage.
One couple of red candles were the decorations
As mandarin ducks united behind happy curtains.
While the old mother sat at the head of the table,
Third Son and Dingxiang bowed down in the hall.

After the Fan family had married Guo Dingxiang,
The wormwood was discarded, replaced by honey!
When husband and wife had slaved for three years,
The cold hovel had become the Fan family farm.
The homestead was surrounded by a deep ditch,
And the buildings were all covered by black tiles.
In front of the eastern rooms: firewood and straw;

In front of the western rooms: the abundant grain.
In the high woods of the southern hills they grazed horses
    and mules;
In the low grass of the northern slope they released oxen and
    sheep.
The five grains produced a rich harvest, so all people
    prospered;
One month ago they were blessed with the birth of a son.
Third Son was so happy that he laughed out loud;
Dingxiang was so happy that she laughed out loud.
The mother-in-law happily recited Buddhist scriptures,
Burning incense to express her gratitude to Guanyin.
Relatives and neighbors all around offered their
    congratulations:
Quite a crowd gathered at the Fan family farm.

## 25. *Begging for Food*

The amaranth is brightly red, the prickly ash yellow:
People in this world are divided into evil and good.
Imitate the amaranth and remain red till old age;
Don't imitate the prickly ash with its black heart!
A few lines of idle words do not make for a song—
I urge all those now alive to do good and act well.
If you as a human ever committed a shameful deed,
Retribution will sooner or later descend on your head.
I'll tell you about that young master Zhang Jinyu:
Having drunk his cousin-in-law's soul-seducing brew
He divorced his virtuous wife, that Guo Dingxiang,
And then married an evil wife, Wang Miaoxiang!
She loved to eat and drink, schemed for jewelry,
And, idling about, she only visited the neighbors.
At midnight, in the third watch, stewing silver-ear,[145]
She caused a fire—it burned down the Zhang farm.
When this merciless fire engulfed the Zhang farm,
It burned down the house and killed many people.
In her side room Miaoxiang lost her life in the fire;
In the high hall his old mother was burned to death.
Wanliang lost his sight in both his eyes in that fire:
Holding a staff he begged for food as a poor beggar.

On his head he wore an old felt hat full of holes;
He was dressed in a worn gown with many patches.
With his left hand he leaned on a dog-beating staff;
In his right hand he carried a worn willow basket.
When the basket was empty, he was forced by hunger
To stamp the earth with his staff, crying all the way,
"Dear Brother, Dear Sister, please show some charity;
Honored sir, honored lady, show some grace to me.
Please have pity on this poor man who lost his sight
And for three days and nights hasn't tasted any rice."
Going back and forth as he called, he was ignored,
And speaking to himself he bemoaned his poor fate:
"When I, Wanliang, in the past enjoyed high status,
Everyone would show me a smile on meeting me.
Everyone would show me a smile on meeting me,
Because they hoped to share in Wanliang's glory!
I had thousands of friends loving my wine and meat—
Once I landed in trouble, none has come to my aid.
How foolish I was in those days of great wealth!
I wasted money like water—that was my style!
During the day I spent money in gambling dens,
And at night I slept with flowers in willow lanes.[146]
Each day I dined thrice on meals of wine and meat:
Finest dishes from mountain and sea held no taste.
The slop I poured out was still brimming with oil:
Handed out to the poor, it was a nourishing soup.
Today I don't have the luck to eat rice or noodles;
When I smell wild greens, it's the fragrance of pork!
Begging for one mouthful of leftover cooking sop,
Good women and good men, I cry myself hoarse!"

While Wanliang was lamenting his own bitter fate,
He had to run into a party of organized beggars.
They grabbed Wanliang and gave him a beating,
Hitting him with their staffs all over his body.
"Let us ask you, aren't you that mean fellow,
That Zhang Wanliang without love or shame?
In the past when rich you showed us no love,
And you treated us beggars with utter disdain.
Let's forget that you refused to make any gifts,

But you also would tie people to trees or posts.
In the summer they were scorched by the sun;
In the winter they were stripped down buck naked.
Now that today you have fallen here into our hands,
We'll have you, scum, have a taste of the same."
Wanliang knelt down and bitterly implored them,
"Respected fellow beggars, honored teachers,
I have already met with Heaven's retribution:
The fire of Heaven has come down on my head.
For a blind man like me it's hard to find his way;
If you break my legs too, there's no hope for me.
Have pity on me, Wanliang, who soon will die—
Suffering hunger and thirst, I won't make it long.
If you want to beat me, please beat me to death,
And leave my dead body on the charnel grounds."
Among that group there was a big-bearded guy
Who was the king of this swarm of beggars.
"Let's take him for a fart and let's set him free;
We should make sure to get in time to the Fans'.
Over at Fan Family Village that Rich Man Fan
A month ago was blessed with the birth of a boy.
That Fan family loves to practice good deeds,
And now they are even more magnanimous.
Poor people who go there receive rice and noodles;
Beggars who go there will be given food and soup.
It's getting late, so we should hurry to go there
So as not to be late for the hour of distribution."

All of them thereupon hurried in that direction,
Followed from behind by blind Zhang Wanliang.
Having heard that over there he'd get food to eat,
He stumbled and crawled and pushed himself.
He threw down his basket, threw down his bowl;
He fell so often his body was covered in wounds.
For better or worse, he had to keep up with them
And arrive together there at Fan Family Village!

At Fan Family Village there was quite a crowd;
One heard only little dogs barking and snapping.
They didn't bark at the coming and going guests;

They snapped only at the beggar king in his rags.
Then one heard someone who loudly shouted,
"Beggars, line up in a row to receive your food!"
The blind Wanliang was slow in turning around
And found himself standing at the end of the row.
Food and soup were doled out from the row's head,
And when they got to Wanliang, all was finished.
When the second time Wanliang squeezed in front,
They had reversed the order of handing out food.
From the back to the front they doled out portions,
And when they reached Wanliang, all was finished.
The third time Wanliang stood right in the middle,
But now it had changed to starting from both sides.
They handed out food from the head and the end,
And on reaching Wanliang, the food was all gone!
Overcome by hunger, Wanliang was so at a loss
That he sat down on the ground, starting to weep.
"It is not people who destroy me, but it is Heaven!
Heaven and Earth destroy and punish Wanliang!
What human eyes fail to see, Heaven's eyes see:
If one commits evil deeds, there is no happy end.
When I received blessings, I failed to enjoy them,
But practiced criminal acts, acting most foolishly.
I divorced a virtuous wife, that Guo Dingxiang,
To marry a baleful broom-star, Wang Miaoxiang!
In the wink of an eye, blessing turned to disaster,
And I, a young master, became a poor beggar.
When I go from door to door begging for food,
I don't know where I go, a blind beggar begging.
People may say that Heaven always leaves hope,
But I fell into Heaven's snare for my own sins.
Alas, so be it! So be it, alas!
I awoke from the bitter wine that I drank myself!"

## 26. *Questioning Her Husband*

While Wanliang was giving vent to his laments,
Dingxiang appeared from her room in the back.
Seeing this crouching beggar in front of the gate,

So hungry he barely was able to breathe, she said,
"Right now it is not the time for doling out food,
And we also haven't any food or any soup left."
On hearing this, the beggar sighed and begged,
"Good lady, please save me, Zhang Wanliang!"
When Dingxiang heard this, it gave her a jolt;
She could not but halt her step and look closely.
She looked once: he indeed resembled Zhang Jinyu;
Looked again: he still resembled Zhang Wanliang!
Was it Zhang Wanliang? Was it Zhang Jinyu?
What would be the harm in asking the question?
"Mr. Beggar, please tell me who you are indeed.
What place and what region may be your home?"
When the beggar heard this, he heaved a sigh.
"Dear lady, as you don't know, please listen to me.
My family is established here in this location, in
Zhang Family Village, across the hill and the river.
My surname is Zhang, I'm called Zhang Jinyu;
And I go by the social name of Zhang Wanliang.
A demon seduced my heart so I fell into evil,
And I divorced my good wife, Guo Dingxiang,
To marry a cousin-in-law, Wang Miaoxiang,
Also known as the blooming little crab apple.
She craved food and drink, she loved jewelry;
Loafing around, she only visited the neighbors.
At midnight, in the third watch, stewing silver-ear,
She caused a huge fire that burned down the farm.
The Zhang family originally was worth millions
But that one big fire cleared me out completely!"
When Dingxiang heard this, her heart was pained:
He was indeed her fated enemy Zhang Wanliang!
"You traitor! You cheated me that time long ago,
When you secretly committed those heinous deeds."
Dingxiang's heart was beset by questions and doubt:
"Today I will have him tell me the story in full!
Mr. Beggar, dear Mr. Beggar,
On seeing you I am overcome by uneasy feelings.
Please tell the whole story from beginning to end
Of what happened to you in those former days.

If you tell it properly, I will surely reward you,
Reward you with rice, reward you with soup."

The beggar thereupon heaved a long, heavy sigh,
Saying, "Dear lady, please listen to the full story.
I, this beggar, had a cousin-in-law surnamed Wang;
That cousin-in-law's name was Wang Manxiang.
From the time that I was studying at the academy,
We already had an ongoing long-lasting relation.
After I had married that woman Dingxiang,
My cousin-in-law conceived an evil design.
When I went there to congratulate my aunt,
She, Manxiang, set a poisonous snare for me.
She hired a physiognomist to read my face—
That was a scheme to harm me, Zhang Wanliang!
He said that I, Wanliang, had a promising face
But never should have married Guo Dingxiang.
Dingxiang belonged to Water and I to Fire;
Fire is conquered by Water: I would meet disaster.
Dingxiang was originally a baleful broom-star
Who could not conceive and could not give birth.
Behind her left ear she had a red cinnabar spot;
Behind her right ear she had a horse-binding pole.
That red cinnabar mark would make her barren;
That horse-binding pole would harm her husband!
Once husband and offspring had been harmed,
She would afterward bring harm to my mother!
If I would not divorce Dingxiang in three years,
The whole Zhang family would suffer disaster!
Because I believed the words of that soothsayer,
I drank my cousin-in-law's soul-deluding brew.
My cousin-in-law suggested I marry her sister;
Her younger sister was named Wang Miaoxiang.
Miaoxiang's features were quite beautiful,
So she was called blooming little crab apple.
I, Wanliang, was seduced by that foxy girl,
Divorced Dingxiang and married Miaoxiang."
Dingxiang on her side smiled sardonically.
"You truly were, I see, a black-hearted wolf!
The proverb says, 'Without venom no real man!'

You divorced a woman like changing clothes.
You didn't care that the old clothes protected against the
    cold,
But were completely seduced by the new clothes' better looks!
You swore an oath to push Dingxiang out of the house
And were determined to marry that blooming crab apple."
When Wanliang heard this, he was quite shocked.
"Good lady, you have seen right through Zhang Wanliang!"
"What happened when you married that Miaoxiang?
Did excellent fortune descend on the Zhang family farm?"
Wanliang once again heaved a heavy sigh.
"Good lady, please be patient and let me tell.
After I married that woman Miaoxiang,
She was completely different from Dingxiang.
Dingxiang was truly a smart and virtuous woman;
She knew the Three Mainstays and Five Constants.
The Zhang family turned from poor to rich,
In all respects sharing in Dingxiang's glory.
That Miaoxiang was a dissolute ne'er-do-well
Who had been pampered and had been spoiled.
When she said 'one,' it never became 'two':
She became the queen of the Zhang family farm.
She was incompetent in needlework and cooking,
She could not fire the stove and prepare the food,
But she loved to wear the finest silks and satins,
Loved to eat delicate dishes, drink fresh soups.
One night at midnight as she stewed silver-ear,
The star of fire set fire to the Zhang family farm:
It burned down all of the hall and the courtyard;
It burned down all of the house and possessions.
It burned to death my mother in the high hall,
It burned to death Miaoxiang in her side room.
I, Wanliang, lost my sight in both eyes in the fire
When I crawled through the dog hole to escape.
When the Zhang family farm was engulfed by flames,
No one came to the rescue, no one cried alarm,
Because I, Wanliang, had done such shameful deeds;
I had offended friends and relatives and all neighbors.
Ever since I had divorced that woman Dingxiang,
The neighbors pointed at me behind my back;

Ever since I had divorced that woman Dingxiang,
The relatives did not come to visit me anymore.
I was hated by others because of my lack of virtue,
And so I landed in this terrible situation of today.
In the past I was a young master who lived it up;
Today I beg for my food like a common beggar.
Begging for food, I don't dare beg close to home
As I have no good story and don't have a good tale.
But I heard that a son was born to the Fan family—
At the Full Month they invited all quarters to enjoy happy
    noodles.
Good lady, dear madam, please show some mercy,
And give me some food to save me from starvation."

When Wanliang had told his whole story,
Dingxiang on her side did not know what to do.
Today Wanliang had told her a true account,
So Dingxiang only now knew the full truth.
She suppressed the tears of injustice in her heart,
But involuntarily they gushed out in streams.
Alas, that Wanliang had shown remorse too late
And all that good time had been wasted!
His remorse came too late, the time was passed—
A withered flower opening again was an illusion.
She wanted to grab a club and chase him away,
But how could she show such a violent nature?
He might be detestable for his utter lack of morals,
But she pitied him for ending up in this terrible mess.
Why not give him a little bit and let him move on?
Let him leave this place and try his luck elsewhere.
So she said, "Mr. Beggar, please come over.
Have a little bit of good food to eat in the kitchen."
She filled a bowl of Dragon and Phoenix noodles,
Pulled out a gold hairpin and put it atop the bowl.
That golden hairpin had been a symbol of faith,[147]
Which she now returned to that faithless fellow,
Saying, "Mr. Beggar, now please listen to me:
When eating, chew carefully and savor the taste."

When Wanliang had received this bowl of noodles,
He didn't use chopsticks but gulped it down in one go!

"Carrack!" his teeth sounded [as they hit the hairpin],
And he spat that golden hairpin out on the ground.
It hurt him so much that Wanliang rubbed his mouth.
"That was quite a big piece of bone, a true cudgel!"
When Dingxiang saw him behave in this manner,
She was involuntarily deeply saddened in her heart.
"You unfeeling and shameless arrogant fool!
In the wink of an eye you have turned into a beggar.
Even a cat eating fish will still savor the aftertaste,
So how can you have degenerated to such a state?"
Dingxiang pulled out one black hair from her head,
And once again filled a bowl with noodle soup.
"Beggar Zhang, now make sure to listen to me.
Eat one more bowl but don't eat it in such a hurry.
Taste it carefully, savor it carefully, and then tell
What kind of noodle soup these noodles may be."
On receiving the bowl, Wanliang tasted the noodles,
And upon tasting the flavor, he spoke as follows.
"I have tasted this carefully, savored it carefully:
This is Dragon and Phoenix thin noodle soup.
This one bowl is filled by only nine noodle strings:
Nine dragons surrounding a pearl follow the rim.
The thickest strings resemble a one-third thread;
The thinnest strings are thinner than a human hair;
The longest strings measure one rod two feet in length;
Even the shortest ones are more than eight feet long.
Let's not consider thick or thin, and long or short;
Each string is filled on the inside with crystal sugar.
Good lady, you are truly an expert in making noodles;
They simply are exactly the same as hers!"
While Wanliang was eating these noodles,
Tears gushed forth from his eyes in streams.
"Today eating Dragon and Phoenix noodles again,
I cannot but remember my wife, Guo Dingxiang.
Dingxiang was such a smart and virtuous woman,
An expert in all aspects of needlework and cooking.
Ever since I divorced my wife, Guo Dingxiang,
I haven't had Dragon and Phoenix thin noodles."
While Wanliang was eating, he wept and sighed,
But then he found his lips were troubled by a hair.
When Wanliang stretched out his hand and caught it,

Dingxiang on her side addressed him once more.
"Allow me to ask you: what's that in your food?"
"It seems to be a hair, but one that is quite long."
"Who, let me ask you, has hair of three feet long?"
"That would be my divorced wife, Guo Dingxiang."
The more she heard, the more offended she was.
"So you still can remember that Guo Dingxiang!
Oh Guo Dingxiang, Guo Dingxiang—
Dingxiang's nature was strong but not her fate!
Dingxiang was a woman predestined for misery;
Dingxiang did not have the face to bear offspring.
She belonged to Fire and you belonged to Water:
Water douses Fire so you will meet with disaster.
Behind her left ear she had a red cinnabar mark;
Behind her right ear she had a horse-binding pole.
The red cinnabar mark would harm her children;
The horse-binding pole would harm her husband.
And when children and husband had been killed,
She would afterward kill Her Ladyship your mother!
If the Zhang family would not divorce Dingxiang,
All maids and farmhands would be struck by disaster;
If the Zhang family did not divorce that Dingxiang,
Oxen and horses and mules and goats would all die!
On top of that, Dingxiang was a low-class woman
Whose face displayed all those features of a whore.
Out in the ox-grazing field she'd spread a blanket
To engage in lechery with the crowd of hired hands.
She was a pheasant hen from behind the mountains,
Whereas you were a golden phoenix atop the hill.
She was only the tiniest speck of cloud in the sky,
Whereas you were the bright moon up in heaven.
How could the bright moon be matched to a cloud?
How could a pheasant hen be matched to a phoenix?"

Not yet having heard this, Wanliang was still fine,
But once he had heard this, he became annoyed.
"It all happened because my cousin harmed me;
She most bitterly harmed me, Zhang Wanliang!
If only that Dingxiang had still been at my house,
I would never have ended up in this terrible mess!

None of the hundred medications in this world
Can cure my hurt, except a medicine for remorse!
But, good lady, please allow me to ask a question:
How come you're so informed about my situation?"
Dingxiang heaved a long, a very long, heavy sigh.
"I sigh for you, this blinded Zhang Wanliang—
Good and evil in this life are in the end rewarded,
So today retribution has descended on your head.
In the past you hated and rejected Guo Dingxiang,
But this day has delivered you before her eyes.
You address her with every word as 'good lady';
You address her serving maids as 'young ladies.'
So Dingxiang today can only heave a heavy sigh,
Sighing for you, this lamentable Zhang Wanliang.
From the very beginning you have been blind in both eyes,
Not distinguishing between black and white, red and yellow!
You clearly treated good and noble as evil and bad;
You secretly treated evil and bad as good and noble.
Today both your eyes may have gone blind for real,
But inside your heart you see more brightly than ever.
More brightly than ever, more brightly than ever before:
Today it turns out to have been only one single dream!
You miserable Wanliang, you muddle-headed fellow,
Old Heaven's retribution is always right on the mark.
If Heaven didn't send retribution, it would not be fair:
Heaven cleansed injustice on behalf of me, Dingxiang!"

## 27. *Jumping into the Stove*

When Wanliang heard this, his heart was shocked;
It seemed as if five thunders crashed above his head:
The woman standing before him was Dingxiang;
Wanliang received his retribution before her eyes!
"Dingxiang recognized me, this faithless traitor,
But I, Wanliang, did not recognize Guo Dingxiang!
No wonder she could cook Dragon and Phoenix noodles;
No wonder she allowed me to eat that noodle soup!
No wonder she let me find that single black hair;
No wonder she discussed with me those details!
She caused me, Wanliang, to remember the past,

She caused me, Wanliang, to think matters over.
She blamed me, Wanliang, for my black heart
That treated honey and sugar as purest arsenic.
I divorced that Dingxiang to marry Miaoxiang;
I welcomed a crow and squeezed out a phoenix.
What kind of nonsense did I talk in those days
When I said she couldn't conceive or give birth?
Once she arrived at the Fans', she bore them a son—
I deserve indeed to be slapped in the face!
I, this immoral and shameless Zhang Jinyu,
Am too ashamed to face Guo Dingxiang.
I, this Wanliang, face Dingxiang in shame—
How can I undo this in a coming existence?
I would like to fly up to the celestial river
To wash away my shame, but I lack the wings;
I want to descend to the hells to redeem my sins,
But the road to the underworld is distant and far.
Go three steps forward and I've no place to hide;
Go three steps backward—no place to seek cover.
There's no place to hide, no place to seek cover,
So let me smash, headfirst, into the southern wall!"
Who knew he would not smash into the southern wall
But smash straightaway into the belly of the stove?
Dingxiang rushed forward to pull him out again,
But how could she ever pull Zhang Wanliang out?
She rescued one scrap of his clothes as big as a hand:
Later people still use it to wipe the stove's sides;
She rescued one thigh bone that looked like a poke:
Later people still use it to stir the stove's belly.

## 28. *Visiting the Underworld*

Gods vie over offerings, buddhas vie over incense;
A man relies on his face while alive in this world.
Wanliang, having lost his face, jumped into the stove,
And, once dead, his soul drifted off to the underworld.
Two underworld runners escorted him there
By an iron chain that was fastened around his neck.
The first one addressed him as "Zhang Jinyu!"
The second one as "Zhang Wanliang" [and declared],

"Your sins in the world of light merit punishment,
So we will go to the earth-prison of purifying fire."
One of them went ahead, pulling him by his chain;
The other one had a steel fork and struck his back.
Murderous gods, most evilly, shrieked and cried;
Some of them pushed him and others slapped him.
Pushing and slapping they entered the Gate of Ghosts;
Once inside the Gate of Ghosts he saw ghastly sights:
Somber, so somber, the underworld realm was pitch dark;
Cruelly, so cruelly, the chilly winds pierced one's bones.
The piteous wailing of the ghosts resounded from all sides
While flickering will-of-the-wisps produced a green light.
In groups of three and five, disorderly ghosts passed by,
Displaying ferocious appearances with their hanging hair.
Some of them were in shackles and carried long chains;
Some of them were losing fresh blood from their heads.
Some of them had mouths ripped open beyond their ears;
Some of them had cut-open bellies, dragging their guts.
Now he saw a ghost of one who died of starvation:
His skin was sucked into the space between his ribs.
Next he saw a ghost of one who died from hanging:
His tongue stuck out of his mouth for more than a foot.
Now he saw a ghost of one who had craved riches:
String upon string of copper cash pierced his backbone.
Next he saw a ghost of one who had been a sex fiend:
All over his body, from top to toe, flesh had rotted away.

Ahead of them they arrived at that bridge across the Alas:
When one is forced to see it, one is filled with fright.
The face of the bridge is oh so narrow—a tangled mess;
Below the bridge the black stream rushes so loudly!
Scorpions and centipedes crawl all over that bridge;
Poisonous insects and snakes wind around its pillars.
When a good-hearted person will cross that bridge,
The vermin and centipedes will move to the sides.
When an evil-hearted, bad person crosses the bridge,
Centipedes, scorpions, and snakes with gaping maws
Push you off the bridge into the black stream below,
Where they clean your bones of your skin and flesh.
When Wanliang saw this, he was filled with fear,

And bowing down he begged the two ghost kings,
"Ghostly runners, dear brothers, show some mercy,
And please take another route, away from this place!"

In the wink of an eye they arrived at the heated oil ward:
The oil in the vats there was seething over a huge fire.
Traitorous thieves and evildoers were burned to death:
Pushed down into the vats of oil, they were deep-fried.
In the wink of an eye they arrived at the killing mill:
The ultraheavy millstones resounded like the thunder.
Con men who trap the innocents, men without virtue,
Are thrown into the eye of the stone, crushing blood.
In the wink of an eye they arrived at the sawing shed,
Where one huge saw was handled by four ghosts:
Deceitful people who buy and sell without wares
Are placed below the saw and cut into two halves.
In the wink of an eye they came to the sword hall;
Criminal souls and ghosts were lined up in two rows.
Those in one row in the world of light had been thieves:
Bellies were opened, hearts scooped out, chests cut open.
Those in the other row in the world of light had been
    extortionists:
Eyes were gouged out, tongues cut out, teeth pulled out.

The more Wanliang saw, the more his heart shivered;
As he stood to one side, his legs were winnowing chaff.
"While in the world of light I committed evil deeds,
And now do not know what my punishments will be.
I, Wanliang, am a person who deserves punishment
As I behaved in a faithless manner toward Dingxiang.
That lovable Dingxiang was so diligent and careful!
That lovable Dingxiang was so good and so noble!
That pitiable Dingxiang was so kind and so friendly!
That pitiable Dingxiang was so forgiving and nice!
Why did I have to frequent gambling dens outside?
Why did I have to hang out with those prostitutes?
Why did I have to hatch such a venomous scheme?
Why did I have to commit a wrong without reason?
Why did I have to make her guard an empty room?
Why did I have to beat her and curse her out daily?

Why did I have to squeeze her out of the house?
Why did I have to chase her away with nowhere to go?
I treated Dingxiang without any love or decency,
But what was Dingxiang's attitude toward me?
When I came begging for food to the Fan family,
How did Dingxiang then treat me, Wanliang?
Each and every action showed her old feelings;
Each and every word displayed her friendliness."
Hundreds of words of sorrow, thousands of complaint:
Each and every syllable betrayed his deepest emotion.
"What kind of human being am I, Wanliang?
In which aspect can I ever face Dingxiang?"
Wanliang had arrived in the underworld,
But he still could not forget Guo Dingxiang.
"Dear Mr. Runners, please show me some mercy:
Let me have a look from Home-Gazing Terrace."

## 29. *Gazing Home*

When Wanliang had mounted Home-Gazing Terrace,
He directed his gaze at his own Zhang family farm.
He didn't see any movement of people at his place;
He didn't see the fine house and farm of the Zhangs.
He didn't see the thousand willows before the gate;
He didn't see the countless mulberry trees in the back.
The farm of the Zhang family had been turned to ashes,
A sight that filled the heart of Wanliang with emotion.
When he turned his gaze toward the farm of the Fans,
He succeeded in seeing his former wife Guo Dingxiang.
Brought down by disease, she was lying on her couch;
Tears coursing down from her eyes, she called her man.
She said to him, "Third Son, my dear man and master,
There is one thing for which I beg your forgiveness.
Why did I so suddenly come down with this disease?
This must have been caused by a divine intelligence.
A blind man begging for food jumped into the stove;
His death caused me calamity so I met with disaster.
If you would want to know who this blind man was,
He was my own former husband, Zhang Wanliang.
Even though Wanliang lacked all love and decency,

I found it impossible to forget we were married once.
So when he died here today right before my eyes,
I was involuntarily overcome by sadness and hurt.
I beg you to be kind enough for the sake of your wife
To provide him with a coffin in which he can be placed."
Third Son answered her thusly: "This is well spoken;
Your goodness and nobility of heart are hard to find.
But you should not be too much saddened by this—
If people have died, they cannot come back to life."

"There still is something else I would like to suggest,
But I don't know whether it is proper to do so or not.
Wanliang has ended up as an orphaned soul and ghost;
Jumping into the stove, he burned to death inside the stove!
How can I bear to see him depart without any clothes?
So I think I would like to make him a full set of clothes."
"My wife, your proposal in this matter is quite proper,
But there's no need to weary yourself out on this task.
We have plenty of satin and cotton right here at home,
So I will give the order and all will be perfectly done.
Your most important task is to take care of yourself!
The whole family hopes to see you recover your health."
"I am grateful, my husband, for your kindness to me;
Throughout my life I will never be able to forget it.
But as your wife I still feel that this disaster this day
Cannot but be a sign that spells little good fortune for us.
On the occasion of the Full Month, we donated rice,[148]
And I noticed my former husband, Zhang Wanliang.
I gave him a bowl of Dragon and Phoenix noodles,
And eating them, he guessed that I was Dingxiang.
Wanliang was in dire straits, as he lacked ambition;
I told him so, but that was the wrong thing to do—
I shamed him so much that he jumped into the stove;
I was the cause of that blind fellow losing his life.
Now Wanliang has died, but his soul has not scattered;
The ghost of the dead man is wildly showing its shape.
A whirlwind was whirling all day outside the gate:
That ghostly soul is pestering me, Guo Dingxiang!
Not a hundred medicines can cure my disease;

Dredging the moon from a stream would not help.
I fear that it will be impossible to preserve my life
And that our marriage bond will not last for long.
Now it doesn't matter that I will return to heaven,
But I cannot repay the love and kindness of the Fans.
You, my husband, treated me in a broad-minded way;
My mother-in-law treated me like my own mother.
The one I find hardest to abandon is my darling son,
So there is something that I want to say about this.
My son has been born to a fate that is most bitter:
His mother gave birth to him but cannot feed him.
My husband, in case that I will now lose my life,
You must make sure that my baby will have a ma.
You are quite young, so you must marry once more,
So you must marry once again with a second wife.
When you have brought a stepmother into the house,
Don't change your attitude toward this little child.
Whenever you beat the child, suppress your rage,
And do so out of consideration for me, your wife.
Apart from a mother, a child also needs a father;
Only if you remain a father will it have a mother.
Don't look on this child as if it had sneaked away,
Because that would sadden me below the earth."
When Third Son heard this, he wailed sadly
And, weeping, spoke: "My dear wife, Dingxiang,
The Fan family cannot exist without you here!
Any disease can be cured—don't think otherwise.
I will dig up the divine fungus from western hills;
I will beg the dragon-spittle brew from eastern seas;
I will pray to Guanyin in the southern convent, and
In his northern temple implore the Jade Emperor.
As long as you but recover from your disease,
I, Third Son, will be happy to pledge my life!"
"My husband, you should take a broader view;
Don't be too much saddened because of me.
Don't blame your wife for being too cruel—
Our karmic bond is fated to last only this long."
As she was speaking, her situation deteriorated:
Her inhalations were short, her exhalations long.

Dingxiang's five senses had lost their functions;
Her eyes lost their spirit, their light was gone.

When Wanliang saw this, tears covered his face:
This was all due to him—he had killed Dingxiang!
Wanliang still wanted to gaze down at the world,
But he suddenly heard his ghostly escorts shout,
"Come down from that terrace, come down quickly,
To receive your punishment in Mean Dogs Village!"

## 30. *A Meeting of Souls*

When Wanliang left the Home-Gazing Terrace,
He again followed the runners on their way ahead.
From far away he already saw Mean Dogs Village,
Where those vicious dogs were barking and baying.
When Wanliang said that he would not go there,
The runners stretched out their hands, wanting silver.
Wanliang could not help but smile bitterly:
The underworld and the world of light were the same.
"I am the ghost of a beggar who died of starvation;
How could I be carrying any silver on my person?"
In a moment those vicious dogs came running over,
Closely surrounding Zhang Wanliang on all sides.
A black dog came forward and bit him on his arm;
A white dog came forward and pulled at his clothes.
Brown dogs and spotted dogs in limitless numbers
Attacked him left and right, showing their madness.
Wanliang suffered so much that he shouted from pain,
Having no way to run off, having no way to hide.
This is how you'll receive your retribution below
If you have committed evil in this world of light.

When Wanliang was at a total loss to know what to do,
He suddenly heard someone softly calling, "Zhang"!
Following the sound, someone approached quickly—
Behind her the two Impermanences, black and white.[149]
Upon her arrival, that person chased the dogs away,
And in a moment that pack of dogs had disappeared.
Only then could Wanliang fix his eyes to have a look:

It turned out she was his former wife Guo Dingxiang!
Dingxiang was of course a soul without any crime;
On seeing her, these mean dogs fled in all directions.
Wanliang crawled over to her as fast as he could,
And holding on to Dingxiang, he refused to let go.
"I, Wanliang, was a man with a heart that was black,
So I cannot complain that on death I fell into hell.
But for what reason did you come to the underworld?
I am not worthy that you come to the shades for me!"
"Young Zhang, you died because of me when you,
Overcome by shame, jumped into the belly of the stove.
Because of me, Dingxiang, you became a lonely ghost,
So I came to keep you company at the Yellow Springs."[150]
While Wanliang and Dingxiang were talking together,
The black and white Impermanences informed them,
"You two souls, Guo Dingxiang and Zhang Wanliang,
Quickly return to Fengdu in order to see King Yama!"[151]

## 31. *Appointment as the Stove God*

Somber, so somber, Fengdu in all four directions;
Frightening the chilly winds, endless the thick fog.
Iron gates and stone wall rise to a height of many rods;
Bronze nail heads as big as bowls strengthen the gates.
In this underworld city there are inns and shops;
One sees ghosts coming and also ghosts leaving.
Everywhere one hears the cries of wronged souls,
Persistent ardent voices fueled by ardent rage.
Some are elderly people seeking their children,
Some are sons-in-law seeking their fathers-in-law;
Some are wives who are seeking their husbands,
Some are children who are seeking their mothers.
Wanliang and Dingxiang followed the runners,
Behind them the Impermanences, white and black.
Not entering the gate of King Yama's first palace,
They also didn't enter King Yama's second palace.
Passing through the third and fourth palace gates,
They straightaway came to the fifth palace hall.
Oxhead and Horseface stood to the left and the right,
Ghostly runners and associate judges on both sides.

There were those dressed in green and those in black;
Then there were those who did not wear any clothes.
His Majesty King Yama was girded with a horn belt;
A high scarf, wide sleeves—his body wrapped in yellow.
Behind his desk, he held in his hand a written register,
And, pointing to an associate judge, he spoke thusly:
"The two souls that have been brought here today
Are named Zhang Wanliang and Guo Dingxiang.
These two souls do not fall under our jurisdiction,
As their files are kept in the offices in high heaven.
You, associate judge, are assigned to escort them
And hand them over to the queen of heaven Wang."

Her Majesty the Queen-Mother was seated on her throne:
Her eyes were jumping, ears burning; she felt ill at ease.
Inside her sleeves she bent her fingers and computed
That Golden Page and Jade Maiden returned home.
Golden Page was Zhang Jinyu;
Jade Maiden was Guo Dingxiang.
Three hundred years ago they offended a celestial rule
And were banished to earth to atone for their crime.
For seven lives in the human world they were no pair;
Their karmic bond of seven lives did not make a couple.
Now that the term was fulfilled, they resumed their
    functions;
Each would be given one bowl of soul-awakening brew.
On drinking the brew, their minds would be enlightened
And only then would they know what had happened before.
"You were never that Guo Dingxiang,
And he is also not Zhang Wanliang:
You are in origin Golden Page and Jade Maiden,
Who on serving their term now return to heaven."

On hearing this, Dingxiang didn't touch her bowl;
On hearing this, Wanliang didn't taste the brew.
The two of them both knelt down on their knees
And implored the Queen-Mother of Heaven thusly:
"We do not desire the joys of the celestial halls;
We long only for a lasting mutual love on earth.
Wanliang still owes a debt of conscientious life

And swears he will treat Dingxiang most kindly."
Dingxiang also implored Her Majesty, saying,
"I will happily be a ghost to be with Wanliang."
The Queen-Mother smiled and nodded her head.
"We already have made a decision in your case.
You have served seven lives of disaster on earth,
So it would not be right to be reborn as mortals.
For the celestial Golden Page and Jade Maiden
It also would be an injustice to make you ghosts.
As you can become neither humans nor ghosts,
There is a good place for you in the divine realm.
There you can achieve your wish and desire
To live forever as husband and wife, as a pair!"
She then ordered Golden Page and Jade Maiden
To receive her edict and accept their appointment.
"The god of the stove was earlier surnamed Li,
But from now on his name is changed to Zhang.
Wanliang, you are appointed King of the Stove;
Her Majesty Queen of the Stove will be Dingxiang.
Miaoxiang also is a maiden dispatched by Heaven,
So she will be appointed your concubine as well.
Every family reveres the Stove image in the kitchen;
The three of you will be depicted in that image.
The Stove image is also called the Stove print:
Each year each family will put up a new image.
Wanliang and Dingxiang will occupy the center
And Miaoxiang has her position in the margin.
This reflects your relationship while on earth,
A karmic connection forged in the hall of gods."

Ever since then, people revere the Stove King;
The one they revere is that Zhang Wanliang.
Ever since then, people respect the Stove Queen;
The one they respect is that Guo Dingxiang.
The tale of Dingxiang is preserved on earth;
Thousands transmit it, ten thousands sing it.
Carpenters sing to the stove *Guo Dingxiang*:
This Stove Book will be transmitted forever!

# The Textualization of *Guo Dingxiang*

## The Short Edition of 1981

All publications on stove tales and stove plays stress that, tradition-ally, the genre was orally transmitted and no texts were available. To what extent the performers were illiterate is a matter of some dispute. Whereas earlier articles tend to stress the illiteracy of all performers, some later publications admit that at least some master carpenters had "quite some ink in their bellies" and are also willing to admit to interac-tions between performers and educated members in their audiences.[1] But traditional performances would appear to have become a thing of the past when Cao Jiazhen started his collecting activities. In the late 1970s, Cao was a cultural cadre in his midthirties with a background in composing folk-style materials, and he was eager to find a subject that would enable him to produce a major work. He left us a description of his motivation and the circumstances at the time in a little essay that is included in the 2017 reprint of the "complete edition":

> In 1978 I was employed by the District Cultural Office, and or-dinarily I also liked to engage in amateur literary creation, writ-ing such things as song verses [*changci* 唱词], fast-paced ballads [*kuaiban* 快板], stories [*gushi* 故事], and other literary items [*wenyi*

*jiemu* 文艺节目]. One day, my good friend and colleague Li Haihua told me that in his home village there were people who sang
"stove tales" about Zhang Wanliang and Guo Dingxiang. I asked
him, "Are they obscene?"[2] and he said, "They aren't obscene, but
it still makes for very good listening and the people in the village
all love to listen."[3]

Cao Jiazhen at that time was on the lookout for materials he could develop into a major publication, and when his mind was set at ease as to
the contents of these "stove tales," he teamed up with his friend Li Haihua
and visited his home village. When he heard the elderly carpenter Qian 钱
sing some fragments, he was immediately captivated by the lyrics. Real-
izing that they had heard only snippets of a much larger work, Cao and
Li teamed up with a third friend, Peng Huahou, to extend their collection
activities. Under the most primitive circumstances, they traveled from informant to informant, and eventually they collected three thousand lines
of verse, on the basis of which the threesome produced the 1,350-line version that they submitted to *Minjian wenxue*. Unfortunately, Cao Jiazhen
and his friends were not professional folklorists and so failed to properly document their sources, and Cao Jiazhen lost his original field notes
when he was asked to submit them to the editors of *Minjian wenxue*, who
wanted proof that his submission was based on authentic materials.[4]

Every textualization of oral materials unavoidably carries the imprint of its time and place. When we compare the 1981 edition of "Guo
Dingxiang" not only with the later editions but also with the extensive
summary of the tale in the article by Yang Xianru, this becomes very
obvious. To the extent that Cao Jiazhen was acquainted with folklore
studies, it would have been the Marxist version of the 1950s and early
1960s, which prescribed that folklorists were to raise the level of the materials they had collected among the masses before returning them to
the people in improved versions that reflected the people's "true" aspirations. In the Chinese case, this usually meant removing any elements
that were deemed counterrevolutionary, superstitious, or obscene, and
strengthening or inserting positive elements such as respect for hard
work, true love, and revolutionary struggle.[5] The Cultural Revolution
(1966–76) had further condemned the use of members of the elite as
protagonists. In these kinds of Marxist folklore publications, "editing"
often was more important than "collecting," and one can only assume
that Cao Jiazhen and his colleagues did not just feel at liberty to edit
the materials they had collected but actually felt it was their duty to do

so. A lack of data, of course, makes it impossible to establish exactly to what extent Cao, Li, and Peng edited their materials.

Now it is obvious that in other versions of their tale, Zhang Wanliang and Guo Dingxiang both belong to elite families, but that aspect is toned down and removed from the 1981 edition. As for Guo Dingxiang, the 1981 edition says not a word about the elaborate wedding preparations that take up many sections in the 2007 and 2009 editions of *Guo Dingxiang*. As for Zhang Wanliang, the 1981 edition removes any reference to his status as a student at the southern academy, even though Cao Jiazhen, when recording his first encounter with the tale in his essay of 2017, explicitly mentions "The Second Absence from the Academy," an extensive episode in the 2007 and 2009 editions. When reading the sections on Guo Dingxiang and Zhang Wanliang opening wasteland and on the hard work of Guo Dingxiang and her second husband, Fan Sanlang, one is immediately reminded of the *yangge* 秧歌 play *Brother and Sister Clear Wasteland* (*Xiongmei kaihuang* 兄妹开荒) that was such a hit in Yan'an,[6] but in Yang Xianru's summary there is no reference to physical labor on the part of Guo Dingxiang and her first and second husbands.[7]

Yet another episode in which we may suspect the intrusion of the editors is the meeting of Guo Dingxiang with her second husband. When Yang Xianru summarizes that episode, she tells us that Guo Dingxiang, upon her divorce, leaves her old home riding an oxcart, determined to settle where the ox would halt. When the ox stops in front of the hovel of a poor woman and refuses to move any farther, she insists she will stay there despite the poor woman's protests:

> But Dingxiang said, "As the spotted ox has pulled me to your house, I will stay for a while at your place." As she was saying this, she was hurt at heart and involuntarily her tears fell to the ground. Come to tell of it, a miracle happened: When her tears fell on the ground they crystallized and gave off a light! When they removed the earth, they found a pile of gold and silver! From that day on, she renovated the house of the Fans and opened a tofu shop, so the family increased in wealth by the day.[8]

Following this, she also meets the poor woman's son, whom she soon marries. But in the version published by Cao Jiazhen, Peng Huahou, and Li Haihua in 1981, a desperate Guo Dingxiang, after leaving the Zhang manor upon her divorce, tries to commit suicide by jumping into the

Sang River, only to be rescued in the nick of time by a handsome and honest poor peasant called Fan Sanlang 范三郎, who takes her home with him to his mother. She is taken in by the family and joins the young man in cultivating the fields, and she cannot help but fall in love with the hardworking young peasant. They soon are married, and thanks to their common exertions, the family becomes prosperous.[9] A most likely (direct or indirect) source for the version by Cao Jiazhen and his collaborators is the Liuqinxi 柳琴戏 Opera *Young Zhang and Dingxiang* (*Zhanglang yu Dingxiang* 张郎与丁香), by Wang Guiyin 王桂银, first performed in 1956. Liuqinxi is a genre of local opera popular in northern Jiangsu, southern Shandong, and eastern Henan. In its traditional adaptation of this legend, *Young Zhang Divorces Dingxiang* (*Zhanglang xiu Dingxiang* 张郎休丁香), the divorced Dingxiang, as in the summary provided by Yang Xianru, settles at the hovel of a poor woman when her ox refuses to go any farther, and she decides to marry the woman's son without ever having seen him. Following the marriage, she has her new husband dig up a number of buried pots filled with silver, so the family suddenly is extremely wealthy.[10] In Wang Guiyin's rewriting of this old play, however, the poor woman's son saves a desperate Dingxiang from drowning (after she has accidentally fallen into the water and cries for help), and she eventually falls in love with him when she observes his honest character and love of physical labor. Such a scenario of a high-born young woman falling in love with an honest, hardworking, handsome peasant and sharing in his physical labor conforms very closely to the rewritings of folktales in the 1950s.[11] Prosperity in such adaptations is supposed to be the result of hard work, not of some miracle. Wang Guiyin's *Young Zhang and Dingxiang* enjoyed considerable success and was revived after the Cultural Revolution had come to an end.[12]

It would appear that miraculous elements were removed as much as possible by Cao Jiazhen and his collaborators. Yang Xianru and the 2007 and 2009 editions describe in great detail a precious gown embroidered by Guo Dingxiang's mother that Guo Dingxiang places over her husband on their wedding night to protect him against the cold, and that he then burns because he thinks she is trying to murder him—in a drunken dream he believes that the pythons on the gown threaten to devour him. This detail does not appear in the 1981 version. Nor does the episode of venerating the stove and all of the scenes that are set in heaven or the underworld, which are found in the 2007 and 2009 editions. In this latter case, one may wonder to what extent Cao Jiazhen and his friends were limited by their sources. For stove plays we know that following the formation of the people's communes in 1958, scenes after Zhang Wanliang's death were not performed anymore, and few if any could perform these scenes by the end of the last century.[13] According to the editions of 2007 and 2009, Zhang Wanliang's soul is taken to the underworld after he has jumped into the stove; there he witnesses the punishments of sinners in the various sections of hell. From the terrace for looking back home, he observes how a bedridden Guo Dingxiang sees to his own proper burial. Upon the death of Guo Dingxiang, their two souls are reunited in the underworld, but their case is reassigned to heaven.[14] They refuse to take up their original positions there, whereupon they are appointed as the stove god and his wife. If censorship made it impossible to perform these scenes in the years from 1958 to 1976, elderly performers who still had a very lively memory of the Cultural Revolution may well have felt reluctant to narrate them in its immediate aftermath, and that may also have applied to the scenes set in heaven and the opening scene of the veneration of the stove, as found in the later versions.[15]

## The Reading Edition of 2007

Following the publication of the 1981 edition, Cao Jiazhen continued to be active in cultural work in Gushi. Together with Li Haihua, he published yet another stove tale, "Liu Yingchun" 柳迎春, but this text did not attract the attention that "Guo Dingxiang" had earlier.[16] Cao claims that he continued to remain interested in the tale of Zhang Wanliang and Guo Dingxiang and to collect relevant materials whenever he encountered them,[17] but he once again became more actively involved in the collection of materials on the tale of Zhang Wanliang and Guo Dingxiang only in 2003. This time he was not merely a private individual but a member of an official project, as work began on the protection of China's intangible cultural inheritance and the leadership of the National Folk Artists Association raised the issue of the advanced exhumation and editing of the stove tale *Guo Dingxiang*, making it a matter of importance for the province, the city, and the district. By this time Li Haihua had passed away, as had most of the original informants, but Cao and Peng, together with a certain Wu Zengming 吴曾明 of the district cultural bureau, continued the further collection and editing of *Guo Dingxiang*. Fortunately they also located some new informants:

> We discovered the old artist Liu Yuwu 刘玉武, Guo Zhenduo 郭振铎 (currently a provincial-level transmitter of the performance of

stove tales), Pan Jing'e 潘景娥 (currently a provincial-level transmitter of stove plays),[18] and old lady Guo 郭, who all her life had
been an avid audience for stove tales (at that time she was eighty-
six and blind in both eyes; her life had been one of lonely struggle,
and, according to her own words, all her life she had found the
strength to go on living only by listening to stove tales and being
stimulated by Guo Dingxiang).[19]

In their epilogue to the 2007 "reading edition" of *Guo Dingxiang*,
the responsible bureaucrats from the Xinyang city government and the
Gushi district government provide a self-congratulatory survey of the
process leading up to the "materials edition" prepared for the application for stove singing's status as an intangible cultural heritage.[20] This
materials edition then served as the basis for the reading edition. Again
the epilogue goes to great length to stress the care with which that edition had been prepared:

> To safeguard the quality of this published *Guo Dingxiang*, the re-
> sponsible comrades of the Henan Federation of Literary and Arts
> Circles, of the Federation of Literary and Arts Circles of Xinyang
> City and Gushi District, and of the publishing company time and
> again held discussions in order to determine the principles and
> methods of editing and copyediting. . . . What we publish this
> time is a reading edition of the long poem *Guo Dingxiang*. Basing
> itself on the principle of safeguarding the original truth of folk
> literature, this edition has conducted a screening and selection
> of variants. . . . In the transition from oral performance to writ-
> ten text, suitable revision and editing were unavoidable. . . . We
> have preserved without any changes all cases of divergence, cru-
> dity, superfluity, omission, and vulgarity that are found in this
> long poem. We have also preserved dialect expressions and added
> pronunciation notes and explanations to lines that are hard to
> understand.[21]

The responsible comrades naturally felt very proud of their accomplish-
ments, but they did not neglect to voice an appropriate measure of
modesty, while at the same time announcing further plans:

> This reading edition of *Guo Dingxiang* prints 4,838 lines altogether,
> and among the many editions that are currently in circulation, it
> can be called the most unabridged and most systematic one; it is
> also the edition that contains the most lines. Hemmed in by the

conditions of time, energy, and level, however, the work of collecting, editing, and publishing cannot be called perfect yet. . . . The
[story of] *Guo Dingxiang* that has been transmitted to the present
in the prosimetric format of stove tales has very many folk editions, song-sections [*changduan*], and sung verses [*changci*].[22] When
the conditions are ripe, we will also publish a "documentary edition" of *Guo Dingxiang* that will include the materials of field research and print the different editions, with song-sections and
verses side by side, and we will also record videos.[23]

Reflecting developments in folklore scholarship in China of the
1980s and 1990s, the editors firmly stress how they have stuck to the
original words of the performers in producing their edition, and they
mention the names of the performers who have provided them with
most of the new materials. Still, they do not specify which sections
derive from which performer. They have incorporated almost all of the
edition of 1981, but their Zhang Wanliang and Guo Dingxiang are now
reincarnations of a Golden Page (Jintong 金童) and Jade Maiden (Yunü
玉女) who have been banished from heaven for a timid display of passion. On earth, they are the single children of high officials who have
been promised to each other in marriage by their parents even before
their birth. While the 1981 edition provides an extensive description
of the beauty of Guo Dingxiang, we now also have a long description
of the handsome but lazy Zhang Wanliang and his infatuation with
his cousin-in-law Wang Manxiang 王满香. The wedding negotiations
conform to the 1981 edition, but these are now followed by extensive
description of the lavish wedding preparations and wedding rituals.
On the wedding night, Zhang Wanliang now burns the precious gown
embroidered by his mother-in-law. A long chapter ("Returning Home"
[Huimen 回门]) is dedicated to Guo Dingxiang's return to her parental
home on the third day after her wedding, when her mother finds out
about the unhappy start to her marriage. Upon her return to her marital home, Guo Dingxiang sets out to restore the fortune of the Zhang
family as she did in the 1981 edition, but when Zhang Wanliang cannot
stand the hard work anymore, he now returns to the academy,[24] whereas
in the 1981 version he simply runs off with all the money he can find.

Three years later in the story, when the family fortune has indeed
been restored, Zhang Wanliang in the 1981 edition returns home because his money has run out, but in the 2007 edition he returns home
from the academy because Guo Dingxiang has sent him a (false) letter
stating that his mother is seriously ill. When Zhang Wanliang is invited

to visit his aunt, Guo Dingxiang embroiders a beautiful vest for him in both versions, but the 2007 edition goes into much greater detail about its decoration. In both versions, meeting with Wang Manxiang again, Zhang Wanliang is led to believe by a physiognomist that Guo Dingxiang is infertile, and in both versions Wang Manxiang urges him to divorce Dingxiang and marry her younger sister Wang Miaoxiang 王妙香. In the 1981 edition, Zhang Wanliang proceeds to do so when he comes home, but in the 2007 edition the process is much more complicated. In "The First Beating and the First Divorce" (Yida yixiu 一打一休), Zhang Wanliang tries to incite Guo Dingxiang into a fight (so as to have a pretext for a divorce) by insisting that they compare the wealth of the Zhang and Guo families. This is an episode that traditional performers considered one of the most beautiful pieces (because of the parallelism of the matching lines), so it is quite remarkable that it is missing from the 1981 edition—but it is clear that it would not work in that edition in view of the background of the protagonists.

Following his failure to incite Guo Dingxiang into a fight, Zhang Wanliang in "The Second Beating and the Second Divorce" (Erda erxiu 二打二休) visits Wang Miaoxiang the next day to assure her that he will divorce Guo Dingxiang (after which they make love), and on his way back he meets with a blind soothsayer who refuses to confirm the predictions of the physiognomist. These scenes also have no counterpart in the 1981 edition.[25] After Guo Dingxiang's attempts to woo her husband with her cooking have failed, we return to the storyline of the 1981 edition. Following her departure from the Zhang family, Guo Dingxiang is overcome by shame and jumps into a river, but she is saved by a young man who takes her home and whom she soon marries, bringing fortune to his home. Zhang Wanliang's suicide is followed in the 2007 edition by the scenes in the underworld and in heaven, concluding with Zhang's and Guo's appointments as, respectively, king and queen of the stove.

## The Complete Edition of 2009

In many ways, the 2007 edition of *Guo Dingxiang* can be seen as a product of the more liberal atmosphere of the beginning of the twenty-first century. But despite its warm reception, apparently not everybody was pleased with that edition. One of the agencies that was responsible for the 2007 edition, the Gushi Cultural Bureau, produced a new edition in 2009. In his introductory essay to that edition, Gao Tianxing 高大星, a

professor at Zhengzhou University and an authority on folklore studies, writes, "The publication of the reading edition of *Guo Dingxiang* has
drawn the attention of the leadership at all levels and of scholars, but
the book still did not completely live up to one's expectations. Readers
hoped they could have a better text of the long poem that could preserve the original flavor and that could preserve its authenticity to satisfy their needs and desires; scholars also hoped to be able to see more
materials about this long poem and a complete text."[26]

Those who have read the epilogue to the 2007 edition will be somewhat surprised by the statement in the epilogue to the 2009 edition
that its predecessor was produced in great haste and therefore contained many mistakes: "The 'materials edition' and the 'reading edition' were in origin materials attached to the recommendation of
"transmitters"; these editions had not been carefully edited and revised
and were printed in great haste, whereupon it was discovered that their
contents contained many omissions, divergences, and logical contra-
dictions." According to Gao, these issues could be solved only by collecting more materials, and this had been undertaken by the Cultural
Bureau of Gushi District in the period from fall 2006 through winter
2007. Gao claims that many new materials had been found by not only
locating (former) performers but also by locating members of the audience with good memories: "For instance, old Mrs. Guo who is approaching ninety, a villager from Wangliuzhen, had listened all her life
to *Guo Dingxiang*, and even at present is still able to recite lines from it;
she is able to recite several sections of *Guo Dingxiang* without any inter-
ruption, and when we carefully listened and carefully recorded this, it
was more than two or three hundred lines."[27] The insistence here on the
importance of audiences in the reconstruction of the text constituting
an original breakthrough in the collection of materials is quite surpris-
ing, since according to Cao Jiazhen, Mrs. Guo was also already a major
new informant in the preparation of the 2007 edition!

Gao Tianxing saw the draft of the 2009 edition (the fourth version
of *Guo Dingxiang*) and believed its text still presented many problems,
so he voiced his opinions to its editors. He claimed that that draft still
exhibited eight kinds of defects, but in his introductory essay he unfortunately does not specify which kinds. After another three months, Cao
Jiazhen and Wu Zengming came up with a revised edition that reflected
at least some of the suggestions of Gao, who expressed his appreciation
of the 2009 edition as follows: "Later, after detailed and serious analysis
and discrimination, and spending more than three months, they edited

the current fifth text of this long poem, which reaches a length of more than 6,600 lines. They have handed it to the Henan People's Publishing House to publish as the complete edition of *Guo Dingxiang*, a long narrative poem on the social customs of China's Han nationality, hoping that this book, as a long narrative poem on the age-old social customs of the Han ethnic group, can be protected and preserved in order to enrich the intangible cultural heritage of our fatherland!"[28] Echoing the opinions of Gao Tianxing, the official epilogue to the 2009 edition also claims that it presents a near-perfect edition of the song.

What are the improvements to this 2009 complete edition when compared with the reading edition of 2007? First of all, the 2009 edition has indeed tried to remove some inconsistencies that are encountered in the 2007 edition. One clear case concerns the absence of Guo Dingxiang's elder brother and his wife in the 2009 edition. The 2007 edition clearly suggests in the opening chapters that Guo Dingxiang is her parents' only child, but when the wedding ritual prescribes that the bride be carried by her elder brother from her upstairs room to the wedding sedan chair, she suddenly turns out to have an elder brother, and when she comes back to her parental home on the third day after her marriage, he is also very much present, together with his wife. For the description of the wedding ritual, the 2009 edition replaces the elder brother with a cousin who has been invited to fulfill the role of an elder brother on this occasion. In the 2009 edition there is no mention of the elder brother in the description of Guo Dingxiang's return home on the third day after the wedding, but this means that we also miss the 2007 edition's description of the spunky sister-in-law. But would it be impossible for readers of the 2007 edition to assume that Guo Dingxiang's parents had decided to adopt a son sometime after her birth?

Another case concerns an awkward transition in the 2007 edition. Immediately following the scene of Zhang Wanliang burning the precious gown on the wedding night, we encounter the newlyweds side by side on the bank of a pond: Guo Dingxiang believes she sees a hoard of silver in the pond and asks her husband what he would do with the money. Zhang Wanliang's and Guo Dingxiang's different proposals clearly illustrate their contrasting characters, and there are later references to this episode too. The 2009 edition has removed this episode and deleted all later references to it, even though the problem here is not any inconsistency but the rather awkward placing of the episode.

Of the many small and large additions of the 2009 edition, the most conspicuous are those passages that delve into the inner life of the characters and explain their motivation.[29] For instance, when, following her divorce, Guo Dingxiang has been rescued by a young man named Fan Sanlang 范三郎 and follows him home, she very quickly marries him in the 1981 edition, and in the 2007 edition, his mother serves as matchmaker. In the 2009 edition, the mother makes sure to invite a matchmaker, and Guo Dingxiang is psychologically prepared for the decision to remarry by an extensive new chapter, "A Sent Dream" (Tuomeng 托梦). In this chapter, a full translation of which is included in appendix II, the god of the soil is ordered to appear in a dream to Guo Dingxiang, who feels still bound by her earlier marriage to Zhang Wanliang. Her parents (the god of the soil and his wife in disguise?) then appear to her in a dream and tell her that she is not bound in any way by her earlier marriage because of Zhang Wanliang's amoral behavior.[30] Even so, the next chapter, "Bringing Prosperity to the New Family" (Wang xinjia 旺新家), which basically follows the outline of the chapter of the same title in the 2007 edition, contains a long passage in which Guo Dingxiang struggles with the question of whether or not it is proper for her to marry Fan Sanlang.[31] In other places, too, this edition pays more attention to Guo Dingxiang's inner life than any other edition; in the chapter "Instructing a Daughter" (Jiaonü 教女), we encounter her remembering her youth and worrying about her future marriage to Zhang Wanliang, and in the chapter "Meeting Again" (Zaiyu 再遇), we witness her hesitation before she decides to question the beggar Zhang Wanliang.

One of the other characters who has benefited from this greater attention to motivation is Wang Manxiang. In the chapter "The First Absence from the Academy" (Yi xiaxue 一下学), we encounter not only a passage in which Zhang Wanliang, while at the academy, is obsessed by her but also a long passage in which Wang Manxiang is basically described as a nymphomaniac. And in the chapter "Offering Birthday Congratulations" (Baishou 拜寿) we find a long passage about Wang Manxiang's decision not to divorce her own husband and marry Zhang Wanliang but rather to have her younger sister marry him. While it is of course not impossible that such extended passages on the inner life of characters as they are confronted with major choices are also found in contemporary performances, one cannot escape the impression that such passages have been very much influenced by modern fiction, which demands psychological realism. Such psychological realism is hardly encountered, however, in traditional folk literature.

Some of the additions in the 2009 edition add little to the plot or the characterization of the protagonists but may well have been included for their own entertainment value. We encounter such passages especially in the chapters dealing with the wedding preparations and the wedding ritual in the first part of the text. In the section "The Match-makers" (Shuomei 说媒), the 2009 edition includes a long, humorous passage (included in appendix II) in which Guo Dingxiang's maid ponders the qualities of an ideal husband as she goes upstairs to inform her mistress that her parents have agreed to the wedding proposal of the Zhang family.[32] When it comes to the description of the wedding day, the 2009 edition includes a completely new section titled "Doing Up the Bride's Hair" (Shu xitou 梳喜头), which is almost completely dedicated to the interaction between Guo Dingxiang's mother and the specialized hairdresser who is brought in to style the hair of the bride.[33] A translation of this section has been included in appendix II, along with a translation of the greatly expanded description of the activities of the master of ceremonies during the "disturbance of the bedroom" (naofang 闹房) in "Praising the Room" (Songfang 颂房, the counterpart to "The Wedding Room" [Dongfang 洞房] in the 2007 edition).[34] The master of ceremonies in the 2009 edition recites an elaborate song while scattering sweets and also praises the food that is served to the guests.[35]

Last but not least, it should be mentioned that in the complete edition of 2009, each chapter is preceded by an "outside-the-picture folk song" (huawai shange 画外山歌) made up of five lines of seven syllables each. For instance, the first chapter is preceded by the following poem:

Coarse grain and fine grain both are grain;
A straw-thatched house and a tile-covered house both are houses.
Man here on earth is only a passing guest:
Riches and nobility, poverty and low status all are common—
Why should one be too detailed in one's schemes?[36]

粗粮细粮都是粮
草房瓦房都是房
人是世上一过客
富贵贫贱都平常
何必算计太周详

While these thirty poems well may be local folk songs collected in the course of gathering materials for *Guo Dingxiang*, the reader is nowhere informed about their origin or their function in the performance of stove tales, if any.

## The Fragments and the Whole

In folklore studies, scholars have long debated the best way to record the songs and stories they encounter during their fieldwork, and some of them have devised elaborate procedures to set down not only the text but also other aspects of the performance, and to document as much of the context as possible. The increased awareness of the role of the scholar in the creation of the folk text has also resulted in greater attention to the ways in which scholars of earlier generations had shaped the text they edited. The way the Grimm brothers repeatedly revised the text of their fairy tales has been studied a number of times and has shown how they increasingly adapted their materials to the German bourgeois morality of the nineteenth century. In the case of epic studies, the Lord-Parry theory of oral composition long held sway during the second part of the twentieth century. This theory focused on the ability of epic poets in oral traditions to create the texts of their performances on the spot with the help of formulas and set scenes, and it also pointed out that no two performances were ever the same, even when the performer claimed they were so. Scholars of ancient written epics often were more interested in arguing that these epics had originally been orally composed than in recovering the process by which originally oral works had been written down. In more recent decades, it has especially been the work of the Finnish folklore scholar Lauri Honko (1932–2002) that has revived interest in the process of textualization of epics. Honko's writings on the subject were inspired both by his historical studies on the growth of the *Kalevala*, the Finnish epic that was composed in the nineteenth century on the basis of a living tradition of short epic songs, and by his own experiences in South India recording a local folk epic. His publications have stimulated scholars all over the world to reconsider the way in which the texts of epics have come into being.[37]

Scholars in the China field nowadays are also taking a close look at the process of textualization when dealing with epic texts as published in China since 1949, whether they are dealing with epics of minority ethnic groups or long narrative poems of the majority Han ethnic group.[38] Perhaps the most important finding of these textualization studies is that in the past and the present, the factors affecting textualization are many and highly divergent and that these by their nature differ from case to case. And while the use of modern recording devices has created new possibilities, it has also created new dilemmas.[39] The rich paratextual materials accompanying the three printed editions of *Guo Dingxiang* allow us to scrutinize their editors' understanding of their aims and methods as expressed in their own words. These texts range from Cao Jiazhen's lively memories of his early involvement in the collection of materials on *Guo Dingxiang* in the immediate post–Cultural Revolution years to the turgid bureaucratic prose of the early twenty-first century, when such materials were collected in the context of national government programs. This in turn allows us to gauge how the self-understanding of the persons involved shaped the texts they published.

In the case of *Guo Dingxiang*, all editions that have been produced are based on disparate, fragmentary materials originating with different performers.[40] As such, the published texts may all be characterized as "composite" texts;[41] there is no single text that can be identified as a main text or master text to which excerpts from other performances have been added, as no informant would appear to have provided more than a few hundred lines of text.[42] This makes it difficult to believe the strong assertions of the editors of the second and third editions that their texts are fully based on authentic verse lines collected out in the field. Their descriptions of their editorial activities make it clear that they made substantial additions in order to come up with one long coherent text. In the case of the 1981 edition, these editorial additions and changes may have been even more important.

The 1981 edition and the 2007 and 2009 editions are separated by more than twenty-five years, a period when Chinese society and culture witnessed drastic changes. Even so, one person, Cao Jiazhen, was involved in all three editions of *Guo Dingxiang*. The 1981 edition was produced by him and his friends without any outside interference, even though it clearly shows the impact of internalized norms. The preparation of the later editions was supervised by committees, whose members clearly did not see eye to eye on many issues. Some of them apparently were convinced that with more research, enough materials might be retrieved to allow for the reconstruction of a text that would be both internally consistent and fully authentic. Cao Jiazhen remained convinced that in view of the fragmentary nature of the materials collected from a wide variety of performers, each with his or her own conception of the story, it is impossible to come up with a text that is both fully authentic and fully consistent at the same time. In his little essay that appears at the end of the 2017 reprint of the complete edition of 2009, he summarizes his conclusions as follows:

> We can fully confirm that the stove tale *Guo Dingxiang* is the sung verse [*changci*] as originally created, in its original manifestation. It belongs to the oral literature of the folk and could be transmitted only by the hearts and mouths of the folk carpenters. Because these carpenters all were different in their cultural level and power of expression, they all made their personal improvements, additions, extensions, and cuts in the process of transmission. Therefore the sung verse could not be unified at the highest level; at the same time, there is not a single person who could sing the complete sung verse from beginning to end. What we have collected are only single boards, bricks, and shards. But the main plot of the story is to a large extent unified. Matters of detail may be completely different in their concrete expression, and it is impossible to come up with a standard text [*changben* 唱本].[43]

This means of course that any edition of *Guo Dingxiang* is at best a compromise between those who want to document a living oral tradition and those who want to produce a reader-friendly text that will throw a positive light on the local community and its administration. As a result, these texts will probably be unable to satisfy the demands of all users. Pursuing an integral, internally consistent text, editors may want to drop scenes that in their opinion do not belong in the "original" story; they also may add passages to create an internal consistency that never was there. In recording the text in a language that may appeal to an audience outside the local community, many dialect expressions must be sacrificed. And in a publication that is published under the auspices of the local government, the hint of obscenity of course had to be avoided at all cost: despite Li Haihua's assurance to Cao Jiazhen that he did not have to worry in this respect, the tale of Zhang Wanliang and Guo Dingxiang apparently allowed for some saucy bits, which had been scrupulously edited out.[44]

When preparing her 2018 master's thesis, Liu Wenwen 刘文文 spoke not only to Cao Jiazhen but also to some local performers, and she summarized their opinions on the available editions of stove tales as follows:

> Through discussions with scholars of stove plays and transmitters, the author learned that these later editions all, to a different

degree, display re-creation. First, there is the loss of part of the contents. For the sake of the integrity of the text, some of the transmitters and artists have engaged in re-creation of the text. Second, content that is too vulgar has been suitably prettified. Stove plays are originally performed in the local dialect of Gushi, and some dialect expressions that are hard to understand have been adapted to the standard of the modern written language, and there are also some saucy pieces that have been suitably changed and adapted. This has resulted in the loss of text of stove plays, and there are doubts as to whether some parts are authentic.[45]

For scholars outside China who work on Chinese folk literature and base their work on published texts, these are chastening words. Even the best texts never tell the full story.

## Epic or Long Narrative Poem?

In their epilogue to the 2007 edition of *Guo Dingxiang*, the editors of that edition discuss the classification of the text, and it is clear that they prefer the categorization of "epic":

On the question of the position and nature of *Guo Dingxiang*, opinions differ. Those who are involved in music say that it is a folk song; those who are involved in literature say that it is a narrative poem; those who are involved in the minor performance arts [*quyi*] call it a script; and those who are involved in traditional drama say that it is a folk play. There are people who call the stove tale *Guo Dingxiang* "a long narrative poem on the folk life of the Han nationality of China," but there are also specialists who call it "an epic on the folk life of the Han nationality of China." There also are people who call it "a long poem of folk love." Mr. Bai Gengsheng in his preface to this book firmly determined its position as "an epic on the folk life of the Han ethnic group of China." We will at a suitable date convene a conference on *Guo Dingxiang* to study and discuss these questions and compile a collection of articles.[46]

The announced conference has, to the best of my knowledge, not yet taken place, but in the 2009 edition of *Guo Dingxiang*, the work has lost its status as "epic" (*shishi* 史诗), despite its increased length, and is instead identified as a "long narrative poem" (*xushi changshi* 叙事长诗). And thereby hangs a tale.

*Shishi* 史诗 (a poem on history) in the sense of "epic" is a neologism in China. When Chinese intellectuals at the end of the nineteenth and the beginning of the twentieth centuries encountered the academic disciplines of literary history and comparative literature, these were very European disciplines indeed. Historians of (Western) European literatures traced the development of the national literatures back to the ancient literatures of Greece and Rome, in which the epic as a genre played a predominant role, whether in the form of the *Iliad* and the *Odyssey*, which were believed to have originated in oral compositions, or in the form of Virgil's *Aeneid*, which had been composed in writing. These works that told of the noble deeds of great heroes on the battlefield or while traveling were not only seen as the product of specific nations but were also seen to have created them. "Both Giambatista Vico and G.W.F. Hegel," notes Haun Saussy, "maintained that epic enables nations to discover their freedom to act in the world. Epic founds the 'we.' "[47] In reconstructing national histories, too, the romantic scholars of the nineteenth century gave pride of place to the epic in the origin of national literatures, greatly raising the status of (the often only recently rediscovered) *Beowulf*, *Chanson de Roland*, and *Nibelungenlied*. The rule that any major literature originated in a founding epic would appear to be further substantiated by the position of the *Mahābhārata* and the *Rāmāyana* in South Asia.[48]

Reading these Western studies, China's modern intellectuals of the first half of the twentieth century could conclude only that despite the long duration of the Chinese written tradition, it did not originate in an epic, and so it did not conform to what seemed to be a universal pattern. Concluding that China had no epic, they set out to explain its absence, finding a cause in the practical nature of the Chinese mind from earliest times or in the limitations imposed by the Chinese script. Other Chinese scholars, considering it unthinkable that the Chinese literary tradition would not have originated in an epic, suggested that China of course had had its oral epic once upon a time but had never committed it to writing, while still others argued that the narrative songs in the Book of Odes about King Wen and King Wu and their ancestors could have provided the materials for a "Weniad," an epic about the foundation of the Zhou dynasty.[49] Even though nowadays our knowledge of the existence of long heroic poems all over the world has greatly increased, few scholars would argue that all major literary traditions originate in epic (as obviously some do not). But the influence of nineteenth-century thinkers such as Hegel (who claimed that the Chinese never had a national epic) and Marx (who claimed that the epic was the product of a primitive stage in the development of art) is still very strong in the People's Republic of China, and the opinion that China lacks an epic is still widespread among scholars of Chinese literature. It should be stressed, however, that when these scholars claim that China lacks an epic, they actually intend to say that it has no epic as the foundation of the Chinese literary tradition and the Chinese nation.

If the epic is associated with an early, formative period in the development of a nation (the age of barbarism, in the words of Lewis H. Morgan [1818–81]),[50] it comes perhaps as no surprise that Chinese scholars as a rule are willing to accept that many of the minority ethnic groups in the People's Republic have an epic tradition. While the long narrative songs on great warriors of central Asia (the Gesar epic of Tibet, the Kyrghyz epic of Manas, the Uyghur epic of Oghuz Khan, the Mongol epic of Janggar) easily fit the model of the heroic epic, Chinese scholars coined the term "creation epic" to characterize the long narrative songs encountered among the many ethnic groups of southern China that describe the origin of the cosmos, the divine pantheon, and the first generations of mankind finding their home.[51] Studies of the epic in the People's Republic of China are overwhelmingly devoted to the two traditions of the heroic epic and the creation epic among the minority ethnic groups in China.[52]

Surprisingly for an outside observer, however, Chinese scholars rarely if ever classify any of the many, many thousands upon thousands of oral and written, verse and prosimetric narratives that circulated among the Chinese-speaking population (the Han ethnic group) throughout the imperial period and beyond as epics, even though many of these works focus on the founding of China's dynasties and feature China's most famous heroes.[53] One reason may be that many Chinese intellectuals first met such tales in the shape of the vernacular "novels" that have been printed in increasing numbers since the sixteenth century; another may be the strong association between the epic and orality among Chinese folklore scholars; yet another reason may be the traditional elite's disdain for the popular nature of such genres of literature, which is still observable in the limited space devoted to popular literature in the teaching of Chinese literature in Chinese schools. But even if there are plenty of Chinese works that meet the formal requirements of the epic, admittedly none of these ever became foundational to Chinese elite culture.

Especially since the years of the Cultural Revolution, Chinese scholars have become increasingly aware of the persistence among the Han Chinese in rural areas of living oral performance traditions of long verse narratives. In scholarly literature, the preferred term for these verse narratives has become "long narrative poems."[54] Occasionally when such a long narrative poem deals with the creation of the world or a local rebellion, it may be hailed as an "epic of the Han ethnic group,"[55] because the term "epic" obviously is more prestigious, and the discovery of a "Han epic" frees the Chinese from the shame of lacking an epic. *Guo Dingxiang* undeniably is a long narrative poem. But while it deals with the origin of a minor divinity and his wife, it is difficult to qualify it as a "creation epic," and the bickering between husband and wife does not qualify as heroic action, so if one wants to raise the status of *Guo Dingxiang* to that of an epic, one has to identify yet another type of epic. This has resulted in the invention of the category "epic on folk life," but notwithstanding the academic and political clout of Bai Gengsheng, that term so far has failed to catch on.

# APPENDIX II

# Selections from *Guo Dingxiang* (the complete edition, 2009)

## "The Servant Girl Evaluates Possible Husbands"

(From "The Matchmakers")

> I, Meixiang, I am the serving girl in this house;
> A serving girl I am, and I am called Meixiang.
> Ever since I came to the Guo family manor,
> I've accompanied the young lady night and day.
> She orders me to serve her tea, bring her water;
> I wash her clothes, sweep the floor, make the bed.
> The young lady treats me as her younger sister;
> I want to serve the young lady with all my heart.
> The young lady is eighteen, and I am sixteen,
> So there is a difference of only two years in age.
> Now that the young lady is promised in marriage,
> Let me also think a little bit about a husband.
> The young lady is promised to a single person,
> But I would like to marry eight different men.
> That first husband will carry the surname Hot,
> The second husband will carry the surname Cold;
> The third husband will carry the surname Rice,

The fourth husband will carry the surname Soup.
The fifth husband will carry the surname Pork,
The sixth husband will carry the surname Lamb;
The seventh husband will carry the surname Drug,
The eighth husband will carry the surname Ginger.
Then when I feel cold I will seek that Hot,
And when I feel hot, I will seek that Cold;
When I feel hungry, I will seek that Rice;
When I feel thirsty, I will seek that Soup;
When I want something fat, I will find Pork,
When I want something lean, I will find Lamb;
When I have a disease, I will take that Drug,
And for a snack, I will find me some Ginger.
But alas, as a serving girl I suffer a bitter fate:
I'll never be able to marry the husband I want.
That guy Hot is hot in summer but not in winter;
That guy Cold is cold in winter, not in summer!
That guy Rice is now too dry and now too thin;
That guy Soup is now too hot and now too cold.
That guy Pork I will as a rule only rarely meet;
That guy Lamb, when we meet I can't say a word.
That guy Drug pierces my heart with his pain,
And that guy Ginger will make my eyes water!
Too bad! Too bad!
I will not think any further, not daydream at will—
A serving girl has to accept a serving girl's fate,
So I'll hurry to her room to invite the young lady!

## "Doing Up the Bride's Hair"

Encountering happy events, people are bound to feel better;
On the fifteenth of the month, the moon shines brightly.
The fifteenth day of the Eighth Month is Mid-Autumn Day;
Today is the day that Dingxiang will be the new bride.
When a girl leaves to be married, her face will be epilated;
When her face has been epilated, her hair will be done up.
Epilating the face and doing up the hair tell a story:
The new status of the new bride is shown on the face.
The face must be epilated till it feels quite smooth;
The hair must be done up so it gleamingly glows.

The black tresses like clouds now display a bun;
Gold pins and silver needles add flowers and gold.
Even though she may not be wearing a phoenix crown,
She'll be more stunning than if she were wearing a phoenix
    crown.
But if you want the new bride's hair done up properly,
You have to hire a specialized hairdresser for sure.
The lady hairdresser who does up buns has her craft,
And of all eighty-eight crafts hers is the best by far:
With stretched-out hands she can stroke the bride's head—
Which other craft would dare compare with this one?
The lady hairdresser's mouth enjoys great blessings:
In each house she is the first to taste the wedding wine.
Having drunk the happy wine, she looks even happier,
As she needs a happy face to do up the bride's hair.
The lady hairdresser of buns enjoys great prosperity;
The hire for the day all depends on what she demands.
However much she may want, none contradicts her—
If you do, she will not come—you're not magnanimous!
When the lady hairdresser enters the gate of the house
It cannot be allowed that a small dog would snap at her.
In case it would happen that a dog would bark at her,
The marriage of the new bride would not be blessed.
The lady hairdresser's water for washing her hands
Has to be made up of two-thirds hot and one-third cold.
Only Chenxiang soap provides freshness and fragrance,
And the towels provided had best be two feet in length.
Out of her loving concern for Dingxiang, the old lady
Of course had prepared everything in perfect order,
In order to please the lady hairdresser she had engaged,
So she would do a fine job in doing Dingxiang's hair.
Because this was the concern of the old lady,
She went in greatest haste to the upstairs room:
She took two strings of big coins in her hands
And she also took out one pair of silver ingots.
She took two pieces of fine silk and fine satin
And three rods of coarse linen and fine linen.
She took one bundle of red thread and silk thread;
She took one pair of cotton thread and tassels.
She took two bedsheets made of coarse cotton;

She took four pairs of socks made of wool.
This thank-you gift was made up of eight articles,
And all articles were placed on a carrying plate.
But who could know she would be one step late,
So the hairdresser was venting her dissatisfaction?
"As a lady hairdresser I am aware of my worth;
It is not so easy to master this craft really well.
I hope with my comb to earn my daily keep;
I hope with my comb to make some money.
When I do up the hair at some rich family,
I make one bushel of grain and one of chaff.
When I do up the hair at a carpenter's house,
I will earn a chest or it may be a box.
When I do up the hair at a painter's house,
It's a painting or a calligraphy to hang in the hall;
No one may be as poor as a vegetable peddler,
But they give a basket of greens or of radishes.
But who of them is like the Guos, these people,
Where I do not see anything white or yellow!"
When the old lady heard this unseemly chatter,
She hastened her steps to come to her side.
She said, "Dear Sister, please don't be offended.
Because of this wedding, everyone is occupied.
We've been so busy that I only now had the time
To prepare this little gift to express our respect.
This meager gift is made up of household goods.
Dear lady hairdresser, don't think them useless.
If you agree to accept them, it will be my honor;
If you don't accept them, you make me lose face."
When the lady hairdresser had accepted the gift,
Each and every article was of the finest quality.
The gift was made up of eight different articles,
Of which four were so-so but four were better.
To call this a generous gift would go too far;
To call this a small gift would be an injustice.
She looked them over and made up her mind
And said in reply, her face wrapped in smiles,
"My thanks, Lady Guo, for such a generous gift.
I would not dare accept all of these fine articles.
I will take one-half of these eight presents, and

The four remaining articles I will return to you.
Let that count as a small token of my appreciation;
I'll leave them for the girl to add to her trousseau."
As the lady hairdresser spoke these modest words,
Her two hands were at work, picking and choosing,
Stuffing the copper coins and silver ingots into her sack
And putting the pieces of silk and satin on top of them.
The coarse and fine linen she pushed at the sides,
And wrapped all things up in those two bedsheets.
The remaining articles she picked up one by one
And then put them all back on the carrying plate.
Repeatedly she said, "Add it to your trousseau!"
But the result was an empty show of liberality.
Mrs. Guo understood this only too well
But it would not be fitting to speak the truth.
"People say it is hard to find the right person.
It was my bad luck to hit upon this creature.
Originally these things were all our own stuff,
But giving them to that bitch I let her show off."

## "Praising the Room"

Men and women, old and young, were filled with joy;
Surrounding the bride they entered the wedding room.
Above the door to the wedding room hung a couplet,
A wedding couplet in bright red that was quite bright:
"May Golden Page and Jade Maiden both be satisfied;
May this wonderful marriage last for a hundred years!"

The serving girl rushed ahead in her haste and hurry
To arrive first in the room and make the wedding bed.
She spread out the red coverlet with stitched flowers
And she arranged the pair of mandarin-duck cushions.
The embroidered cushions should be placed together,
But she had placed them quite some distance apart.
The serving girl could only secretly laugh at herself:
"We'll see who of you is the first to feel the itch of lust.
Who feels that itch will be the first to move the cushion:
Who first moves the cushion is the most amorous person.
Your brothers-in-law will listen outside the window

And lick a hole in the window paper to watch the bed.
Seeing you perform the play of moving the cushions,
They will spread a big basket of jokes all around!"
The serving girl gave bride and groom a naughty wink
And used this chance to deliberately entice the groom.
Having made the bed properly, she called them inside:
"Please let the newlyweds enter the wedding room!"
According to ritual, Dingxiang sat down on the bed,
While her head was covered by a veil on all four sides.
Peeking through the veil, she took in her surroundings:
What first caught her eyes were the red gauze bed-curtains.
The bed-curtains made of red gauze were as thin as paper;
The golden hooks hung aslant and the tassels were long.
The coverlet embroidery showed a Dragon and Phoenix,
And double-headed lotuses were depicted on the cushions.
In the middle of the bed had been placed seven dates,
And five peanuts had been positioned to one side.
The peanuts and the dates had their explanation:
A lucky omen for the speedy birth of noble sons,
Seven sons who return home as Dragon and Phoenix;
Five sons who pass the exams as the Top-of-the-List.
Four radishes were placed at the bed's four corners;
An earthen brick had been put in the bed's center:
These radishes like pimples have ample offspring—
Might each of these sons be as strong as bricks!
Red lanterns and wax candles shone brilliantly,
Illuminating the new room, arranged to perfection.
The bride stepped onto the red carpet on the ground.
Her steps were an uneven, never an even, number:
If her steps were uneven, she would first have a son;
If they were even, she would first have a daughter!
Four colorful lanterns hung in the four corners
And each of those lanterns came from a fine shop.
The first lantern had been fashioned quite artfully,
Showing An'an delivering rice to the temple;
The second lantern had been fashioned quite well:
With a slice of her liver Haitang saves her mother.
The third lantern had been fashioned quite artfully:
Guo Ju buries his son and receives Heaven's boon;
The fourth lantern had been fashioned quite well:
Wang Xiang lies down on the middle of the ice.

The two newlyweds entered the wedding room,
And everyone was eager to "disturb the room,"
But the master of ceremony first gave a speech,
And he coughed three times to clear his throat.
"May this one burner of incense rise to heaven,
So a fine marriage descends to the Zhang home.
'Following the examples' you enter the room;
'Isn't this a joy': we congratulate the groom.
'Like friends from afar': such is your meeting;
'Thrice scrutinize yourself': I'll say a few words.
As master of ceremonies I have little learning,
But my classical scholarship still has its pattern,
And as master of ceremonies I must give a speech,
So as master of ceremonies I'll admonish the bride.
Yesterday, new bride, you were still at your home,
And in front of your mother you were a young lady;
As a young lady you were a chrysanthemum girl,
And no one dared speak any coarse words to you.
If anyone spoke uncouth words in your presence,
He was a glib-tongued bare stick or rude vagrant.
Carried in the sedan chair, you arrived at this manor,
And now the young lady has become a wedded wife.
Young lady and wedded wife are separated by a ditch:
The two sides of that ditch are quite different indeed.
Coarse words and fine phrases you both will hear;
You must show yourself magnanimous to all people.
Today friends and relatives come to disturb the room;
Their aim is to have some fun, to have a good time.
In case they speak flippant words or serious phrases,
You cannot let those enrage you—just let it pass!
Only on the third day old and young are separated—
Without the disturbance, a wedding lacks all glamour.
If I as master of ceremonies don't tell you so clearly,
Each and every one will say that I don't know my job.

A wedding couplet in bright red adorns the wedding room;
Men and women, old and young, are all filled with joy.
Everybody is happy at this happy event at the Zhangs',
But without the disturbance a wedding lacks all glamour.
Praising the room and disturbing the bride must be lively,
But the disturbance should be civilized and normative:

Disturbing the room relies on the master of ceremonies,
And you all have ceded leadership in this affair to me.
Even if I were to say that I am incapable of such a job,
You all would insist that I am an expert in this work.
The groom himself bowed to me, and even kowtowed,
Insistently requesting I should help him out in this case.
As a master of ceremonies I may perhaps pass muster,
But I completely depend on the support of you all.
First, I have never studied with an experienced teacher;
Second, I've never studied with an experienced mistress.
I've never recited the Five Classics and the Four Books,
Haven't learned the Three Mainstays or Five Constants.
I don't recognize the character 'one' in the carrying pole,[1]
And I could not even pretend to be an illiterate pedant!
And then the master of the house came to talk to me—
If a carp has swallowed the hook, he can't spit it out!
Now that the matter has come to this, I cannot step down,
So I will raise my spirits and gather some courage.
I need two men to be in charge of the wax candles:
You will take up positions in the highest place.
I need two men who will carry the tobacco pouch:
You will take up positions on both my sides.
I need two men to carry the plate with fruits:
You will follow behind me, close on my heels.
When I tell you to offer tobacco, you offer tobacco;
When I tell you to scatter sweets, you scatter sweets.
I am in charge here of the disturbance of the room,
But I depend on you in helping me out in this mess.
A single person cannot have the intelligence of ten;
A single hand cannot produce any sound in clapping.
I will go in front and establish meter and tempo,
But you must follow behind and continue the tune.
When I say something well, don't praise me for it;
When I say something wrong, please do forgive me.
If I mess up the tune and don't stick to the tempo,
I can only beg you to quickly continue the tune.
Three times three makes nine: I've explained all,
But there is still one matter that must be arranged.
If I do not take care of relatives and friends, you'll say

That I as a master of ceremonies don't know my job.
Those who are advanced in years, please sit down,
Have a smoke, drink some tea, and have a nice chat.
Chat about the Former Tang as well as the Later Han;
Chat about the Eastern Capital known as Bianliang.
Those who are younger in years may praise the room,
But don't have any weird thoughts ogling the bride.
On the day when your wedding has been arranged,
I'll also come and praise the wedding room for you.
When you middle-aged men come to praise the room,
I will place you on top of the southern blunderbuss:
Your fine vocation is the farmwork in the fields,
So you will harvest lots of wheat when fall arrives.
When you middle-aged women come to praise the room,
I will assign you your place in the eastern kitchen,
To help in the kitchen choosing onions and garlic,
To assist the servants in serving tea to the guests.
When you middle-aged brothers-in-law arrive,
I'll have you carry green hats on your heads,[2]
And when your wives will try to take them off,
Each of their ten fingers will grow ulcers.

Now that I have settled this in a few words and phrases,
Praising the room proceeds to the scattering of sweets.
Heaven opens a yellow road, sending down blessings;
The music of bells and drums resounds, filling the hall.
The old man in the moon manages the marriage files:[3]
Heaven matches a virtuous maiden to a fine groom.
Dragon and Phoenix today are tied together as a couple;
Mandarin ducks today are matched together as a pair.
This one marriage bond makes two families happy;
Three cups of wedding wine ensure four seasons of health.
Five blessings descend on this house, six blessings follow;
Seven times a lucky karma brings glory on all eight sides.
Nine generations live together as one bustling crowd;
Tenfold complete and perfect, status and fortune will last!

Now that I carry this oh-so-little wedding plate in my hands,
I'll explain the background of this little wedding plate.

This wedding plate is made of the wood of the sal tree
That grew in the palaces of heaven on that old moon.
When Zhang Ban and Lu Ban passed through the moon,
They cut down the red osmanthus tree with their axes.
They hacked and they hacked, they planed and planed:
The outside was lacquered, the inside inlaid with gold.
Even though this oh-so-little plate may not be that big,
It still can contain all the many fruits you can imagine.
The peanuts have been hidden inside the red bed-curtains;
The dates have turned red, a red that is brilliantly red.
The seeds of the ginkgo are bright and shining;
The sesame seed cookies are gloriously yellow.
Chestnuts are best when they have been cooked;
Melon seeds are most fragrant when they're fried.
I cannot enumerate the hundred kinds of fruits;
I'll scatter them handful by handful across the bed.

This first handful of fruits I will scatter all over heaven
So sun and moon and all the stars will spread their light.
A celestial immortal has descended to the mortal world
And is united in wedlock with the young master today.
The new bride and the new groom are united in wedlock:
May this marvelous marriage last for one hundred years!

The second handful of fruits I will scatter over the earth:
May gods of the earth and ancestors protect our well-being.
Today they happily tie the fine knot between Qin and Jin;[4]
The family tradition of Odes and Rites will remain strong;[5]
If a family lives in harmony, all its businesses will prosper,
Continued by sons and grandsons for five grand generations.

This third handful of fruits I will scatter across the fine hall;
A happy pair of Dragon and Phoenix is hanging in the center.
Tea stands, tables, and chairs are arranged in one straight row;
Calligraphies and paintings by celebrities give a golden glow.
Carved beans and painted pillars resemble the realm of fairies;
Pavilions and buildings of jade surpass the halls of heaven!

This fourth handful of fruits I'll scatter in the wedding room,
A wedding room that is arranged in a quite spectacular way.
The trousseau of the bride fills the whole room to the ceiling;

The boxes provide the floor, and the chests come in pairs.
Each kind of furniture is there in many kinds of styles;
Each and every piece is set out in the proper manner.

The fifth handful of fruits I will scatter all over the couch:
The couch of the new bride is a grand eight-step bedstead.
Suzhou and Hunan embroidery, bed-curtains of gauze silk;
The mandarin ducks lie down on gold-rimmed cushions.
When these two people this evening doze off to sleep,
They will sleep together on this one single cushion.

This sixth handful of fruits I will scatter over her head:
The bride's hair has the smell of osmanthus flowers.
If you do not believe the words that I spoke just now,
I will ask the new groom to help me out in this matter.
I will ask the groom to go over to the bride and ask her
Whether those are honeybees that descend on her hair.

This seventh handful of fruits I'll scatter on her cheeks:
The bride's cheeks are powdered with white-jade frost.
If you do not believe the words that I spoke just now,
I will ask the new groom to help me out in this matter.
Let the new groom stroke the cheeks of the new bride
To see whether or not he'll find some white-jade frost.

This eighth handful of fruits I will scatter on her waist:
The new bride's willow waist that sways in the wind.
When her mother-in-law sees it, she cannot but smile;
When the groom sees it, flowers blossom in his heart.
Let me ask the new bride to take a few steps to show
How, when walking along, she moves just like a willow.

The ninth handful of fruits I´ll scatter over her hands—
The fingers of the new bride resemble onion stems.
She excels on the zither, in chess, in wielding the brush;
Her skills in embroidering dragons are even greater.
New bride, please pick one of your handkerchiefs
To let us see which famous firm embroidered them.

The tenth handful of fruits I´ll scatter over her feet—
The small feet of the bride are truly a perfect muster.

Some people may say they measure five inches five,
But I say that her feet are only three inches in length.
To find out once and for all how small her bound feet are,
I'll take off her embroidered shoes to look for myself!

Opening the red bed-curtains with both my hands,
I'll display the red silk that covers both the beds.
When I carefully inspect those silk coverlets,
The embroidery patterns give off a bright light.
The first picture is dragons meeting like wind and clouds;
The second picture is phoenixes settling on wutong trees.
The third picture is tree peonies and herbaceous peonies;
The fourth picture shows cape jasmines and crab apples.
The fifth picture is a carp jumping across the Dragon Gate;
The sixth picture shows Weaving Maiden meeting Oxherd.
The seventh picture shows a tomcat catching a mouse;
The eighth picture: the Eight Immortals crossing the sea.
The ninth picture shows Chang'e carrying the jade hare,
And the tenth picture shows lotuses filling tank and pond.
Having observed the ten kinds of design on the coverlets,
They are tenfold complete and perfect, blessing the room!
Let me with both hands pull aside the red silk coverlets
So husband and wife may sleep here as mandarin ducks.
If husband and wife sleep together as mandarin ducks,
They'll hold a little baby boy in their arms next year.

Pair upon pair of wax candles, a joy that is boundless.
Praising this room I could go on praising till midnight.
But bending my body, I will take my leave with a bow,
And having made my bow, I will continue my oration.
The master of the house has set out a wedding banquet,
So please follow me all together to the painted hall.
Let us all drink some wine to celebrate the wedding,
Wishing that husband and wife share a lasting love.
Those who love to smoke should enjoy a smoke,
And tea will be served to those who do not smoke.
Those who want to have a drink should follow me,
And those who don´t want to drink may have a chat.
Little kids with balls should go home, go to bed,
Because if you sleep too late, you may wet the bed.

Outside the wedding room, take the flower path:
The wind-carried fragrance fills the courtyard.
This shows the sophistication of the Zhang family:
A little courtyard resembles a fine flower garden.
In spring the butterflies sport amid the peonies;
In midsummer honeybees crowd the crab apples.
At Mid-Autumn the osmanthus spreads its fragrance;
In winter months the whole prunus turns yellow.
As we take in the scenery, we keep on walking,
And after a turn in the path we reach the kitchen.
Above the door to the kitchen we see a couplet,
And that couplet is phrased most appropriately:
'Soy sauce and vinegar can well adjust the taste;
Cooking and steaming must be done with care.'
In the storeroom we also may see a couplet;
If I recite this couplet, it has the smell of ink:
'The wedding wine has its smell, the grape wine is green;
Chrysanthemums are brilliant, osmanthus flowers yellow.'
Now if we focus our view on the eastern kitchen,
We see that two tables are set out: one dry, one wet.
Fresh fruits have been placed on the dry tabletop;
Pork and lamb have been placed on the wet table.
What should be cut is cut; what chopped, chopped;
What should be hot is hot; what chilled, chilled.
Onions and leeks, mustard and garlic all are fresh;
Chicken and duck, fish and meat all smell great.
Cooked and fried on a big fire, boiled on a small fire—
Prepared over a slow simmering fire are fine soups.
The first bowl: fresh phoenix, tasting excellently;
The second bowl: dragon-bricks, floating on the river.[6]
The third bowl: sweet potatoes pulled into strings;
The fourth bowl: deep-fried prawns that are yellow.
The fifth bowl: meatballs that are turning around;
The sixth bowl: cooked eggs following the waves.
The seventh bowl: slices of belly fat, fragrant and thin;
The eighth bowl: fried wontons giving off a fine smell.
The ninth bowl: simmered greens, fresh and tender;
The tenth bowl: braised pork in little square blocks.
The eight small plates are divided into spicy and bland;
The ten big bowls of fish are served in sequence.

Even if all say that the cook has done a great job,
I will say that the chef is only a mediocre fellow.
His steamed and baked pastries don't have any taste;
His cooked and fried dishes don't have any fragrance.
His bland soup is so bland that it tastes like water;
I don't dare try his salty soup, as it is way too salty!
This cook, this chef, has not made any effort at all—
He should not place his fingers on his waistband.
These few words of joking are nothing but a joke,
So, chef, don't pay any attention to these phrases.

Dear guests, please follow me to the painted hall,
The hall where wedding candles shine brilliantly.
The couplet on both sides of the gate to the hall
Has been executed in the calligraphy of a master:
'A talented man of the eastern capital: a poem of a thousand
     words;
A beautiful lady of the southern garden: a hairdo of rarest jewels.'
In the gatehouse one sees a matching couplet
That is also a fine piece of writing for all eternity:
'They have sons, they have grandsons; grandsons have sons,
Enjoying blessing, enjoying longevity; longevity and health.'
On the lintel over the gate the four characters
'A heaven-ordained union' are a fitting match.
In the hall, 'Heaven, Earth, State, Parent, Teacher'
Is matched by the couplet hanging on both sides:
'Heaven is high, Earth is fruitful, the State's bounty great;
The Ancestral virtues and Teacher's example last forever.'
Let us in the hall happily drink the wedding wine:
May this union of man and wife be amply blessed.
Let us in the hall happily drink the wedding wine:
May husband and wife all their life stay together!"

## "Sending a Dream"

One day in the halls of heaven only feels short,
But in the mortal world one full year has passed.
While the gods pass one day of pleasure and joy,
Human beings suffer a year of storms and frost.
Golden Page and Jade Maiden, banished to earth,

Had ended up in this world to experience its misery.
In the blink of an eye, twenty-one years had passed:
Only three times seven rolls of the Celestial Drum.
On this day the Jade Emperor was seated on his throne,
Attended on both sides by the gods and immortals.
The high god in charge of affairs loudly announced
That Guangzhou's god of the soil submitted a report.[7]
When the Jade Emperor opened the report for reading,
Each word and each phrase was written quite clearly:
"In front and in back of Mt. Sang there are two families.
The first one is called Guo, the other is called Zhang.
Golden Page was born in the Zhang family manor
While Jade Maiden was born in Guo Family Village.
The two of them tied the knot at the age of eighteen
When Zhang Jinyu was married to Guo Dingxiang.
This doomed karmic bond united Water to Fire:
The wedding ritual did not lead to consummation,
And after three long years of collisions and fights
The two of them live at present in separate places.
Golden Page has been married to his new love;
Jade Maiden has found shelter with young Fan.
Young Fan would like to marry this Guo maiden,
And she would very much like to marry this boy.
But in the world of men there are Norms and Values,
So these two people cannot tie the marriage knot:
A good horse will not carry a pair of saddles, and
A good woman will not marry a second husband!
Dingxiang is by nature a loyal and filial maiden,
With 'wisdom' and 'virtue' engraved in her heart.
If she were to marry that young man of the Fan family,
This loss of Norms and Values would ruin her name.
If she does not marry that young Fan family fellow,
She will have nowhere to go and no place to hide.
Dingxiang accumulated good deeds here on earth,
So she should not lose her life without any guilt.
As the local god of the soil, this is my responsibility,
So I submit this case to Your Majesty, Jade Emperor.
Consider how obedient she was in the celestial halls,
And issue an edict summoning her back to heaven."
Having read this report, the Jade Emperor thought,

"This report of the god of the soil really makes sense.
As she has the exalted status of a celestial divinity,
She should maintain the morals in the world of men.
I very much would like to summon Jade Maiden home,
But I'm afraid the Queen-Mother might be an obstacle.
In days past it was she who decided on their banishment,
So it would be best if she today, too, made the decision."
Having reached this conclusion, he turned to her
And suggested that she should read this memorial.
When the Queen-Mother had finished reading the text,
She addressed him, unhurriedly, without undue delay:
"Jade Maiden from birth has been a seed of passion,
So of course these male souls jump onto her body.
Seven lives of divorces and unions and still not liberated—
Drowning herself in a river she meets young Fan!
Today I grant her yet another half lifetime of marriage
And allow her to give birth to a son in the mortal world.
When she has left behind this root of passion on earth,
I'll summon her back to heaven when the time has come."
On hearing this, the Jade Emperor stroked his beard
And smilingly asked the queen to think once again:
"Dingxiang is a girl who sticks to the proper rules,
In all her actions conforming to Norms and Values.
How can she in a second marriage marry young Fan
As long as she has that writ of divorce in her hands?"
The Queen-Mother answered, "This is easily fixed!
One's fortune in the world below depends on Heaven.
Order the local god of the soil to return to the world
And have him at night deliver a dream to Dingxiang.
Let him tell her that young Fan is one of the stars
But has been dispatched to earth to live there awhile.
In high heaven you have the right status and position,
So to marry him now is only the proper thing to do.
Moreover, that Wanliang showed no feeling or love,
So this is no case of a loving husband losing his life.
When a loving husband dies, one should maintain chastity;
If he had no love, marrying again conforms to the Norms."
The Jade Emperor thereupon issued a celestial edict,
Ordering the god of the soil to transmit his command.

Using his magical powers he had to deliver a dream,
Making Dingxiang realize she should marry young Fan.

Green, so green, the wutong trees rise three rods tall;
After the autumn storms, the leaves turn to yellow.
Those yellow leaves come down in large profusion:
Having nowhere to settle they drift in the winds.
Dingxiang was mending clothes sitting at the gate;
Observing those yellow leaves she was hurt inside:
"My fate is as bitter as that of those yellow leaves;
There's no place for me in this whole wide world.
My parents are still alive, but I don't dare see them;
Young Fan has a good nature but I cannot love him.
Most unfortunate and most miserable is a divorcee—
If she remarries, people curse her out as shameless!"
The more she thought, the more upset she became,
And in her misery big tears gushed from her eyes.
But while Dingxiang was so overcome by her grief,
She suddenly saw an explosion of light before her eyes.
That bright light enveloped the body of Dingxiang
And she was against her will carried off by the wind.
Drifting and floating, she went outside through the gate;
Blurry and misty, her eyes lost all sense of direction.
She only heard the winds roaring past her ears
And smelled the fragrance of mountain flowers.
Dingxiang was, after all, not a girl of this world,
So she maintained her calm, steadying her mind.
She thought that immortals came to her rescue;
She thought she was summoned back to heaven.
While she was guessing, she touched the earth
And walked with both feet on a mountain road.
The mountain road curved around the mountain;
From behind the hill, her two parents approached.
Her old father's white beard drifted on his chest;
Lifting his feet, moving forward, he staggered.
Her old mother was stooping and hunchbacked;
Walking unsteadily, she was supported by her staff.
Looking for their dear daughter, these old people
Had left home, crossing mountains and ranges.

Observing these two, a pain stabbed her heart
And her tears gushed down like a cloudburst.
She rushed forward and fell on her knees to bow:
"How ashamed I am to meet my parents like this!"
And she said, "That I was divorced by the Zhangs—
I bear my shame filled with rage at this injustice!
But afraid that I might hurt my parents' heart,
I did not go home to see my father and mother.
I caused the two of you to look for your daughter,
Wearying yourself on the road, suffering the cold.
I beg you to kindly forgive your unfilial daughter
And consider your daughter one who has died."
When the old mother had embraced her daughter,
She urged her daughter not to be so sadly hurt.
"Your parents left the house to look for their child
Because your dear father has some words for you.
That you have been divorced by the Zhang family—
Your father and mother already know all the details.
But because we had not yet seen you face to face,
We could only store these words inside our hearts.
Now that today we meet you, Daughter, face to face,
Listen carefully to what your father will tell you."
Dingxiang walked over to her father's side
And helped her father to the side of the road.
By the side of the road was a long, flat rock
And she helped him as he sat down on the rock.
Then she turned around to assist her mother,
To assist her as she sat down next to her father.
As her father sat down, he panted somewhat,
Lightly coughed once and then started to speak,
Saying, "My dear daughter, Big Sister Guo,
Now listen to what your father will tell you.
As you have been divorced and chased away,
There is no way to turn that situation around.
Dear Daughter, you shouldn't be too saddened;
Let your old father give you words of advice.
Your father has lived now for several decades,
And crossed on his road more bridges than you.
What kind of situation have I not witnessed?
What kind of emotions have I not understood?

What kind of principle have I not grasped?
What kind of lawsuit have I not experienced?
I've seen through true and false in this world,
And I know hot and cold in the affairs of men.
My daughter, now that you have met this disaster,
I blame you only for focusing solely on goodness.
In this world, good and evil have always existed,
But good and evil should not be treated the same.
When meeting goodness, treat it with goodness,
And when meeting with evil, oppose it with evil.
If you rely on goodness when confronting evil,
The evil people will win and engage in madness.
That evil young Zhang lacked love and affection;
Without love and affection he hurt his conscience.
How could he have any feelings of love for you
If he divorced you like he was tossing away old clothes?
But now you maintain chastity on behalf of him
And you refuse to remarry—that is too annoying!
One guards Norms and Values because of love:
Without any love, Norms and Values do not exist.
My daughter, you are a very intelligent person,
So I want you to carefully consider my advice.
You cannot hang yourself from a tree branch;
You cannot die by clinging till death to a pillar.
You cannot look at only one line of the sky;
You cannot die while leaning against a wall."
While Dingxiang was listening to her father,
She suddenly felt a great light in front of her.
Waking up with a start, she shivered—
It had all been a Southern Bough dream![8]
No shadow of her parents remained in sight—
Only the wutong leaves were rustling in the wind.
She was still sitting all by herself at the gate
With the half-mended old clothes in her lap.
Rubbing her eyes and refreshing her memory,
She pondered what she had seen in her dream.
"It is clear to me! It is now fully clear to me.
My parents sent me a soul-awakening brew.
For these many days here with the Fan family,
I broke my head: Should I leave? Should I stay?

If I were to leave, I would not be able to endure it,
But if I were to stay, I would have no clear reason.
Pasting the door gods upside down, I was in a quandary;
Confronted with this dilemma, I was filled with sorrow.
My old father poked a hole in the window's paper
And so shed light in the dark recesses of my heart.
Now this hanging heart has fallen into my stomach—[9]
True love, a sincere intention: I'll marry young Fan!"
Her face now was wrapped in a rarely seen smile;
The bitter brew that filled her mouth became sugar.
She rushed outside and knelt down on her knees to bow,
Kowtowing with a bang toward Guo Family Village.

# Notes

## Introduction

1. On the origin and the cult of the god of the stove in China, see Chard 1990; Chard 1994; Chard 1995; Chard 2000; Landsberger 1996-97; Yang Fuquan 1994. The tale of Zhang Wanliang and Guo Dingxiang, which occurs in many variants, is only one of the many legends on the origin of the stove god that have been recorded in the twentieth century.

2. For brief introductions to stove tales, see, for instance, Zhang Lingyi, Liu Jingliang, and Li Guangyu 2007, 168-70; *Zhongguo quyi zhi: Henan juan* 1995, 113-15. For surveys of research, see, for instance, Duan Jinlong and Zhang Rui 2020; Gao Tianxing 2009.

3. Bo Songnian 2021; Po Sung-nien and Johnson 1992, 23-59.

4. Confucius 1979, 69 (book 3, chap. 13). The commentators disagree about the meaning of this exchange. The southwest corner may have been the location of the ancestral tablets.

5. Translation quoted from Chard 1995, 6.

6. Chard 1994.

7. Zhou Ruchang 1974, 241-42. In southern China, the stove god was sent off to heaven on the twenty-fourth of the last month, but in Northern China on the twenty-third of that month.

8. Zhou Ruchang 1974, 241-42.

9. Chard 1995, 21-55. Also see Chard 2000 and Graham 1930 for more (partial) translations of such texts.

10. Some modern scholars argue that the god of the stove in early times was believed to manifest itself in the shape of a cockroach or a toad. Yang Fuquan 1994, 44-53. It may be noted that in modern times, some texts on the stove god called their protagonist Zhang lang 张郎 (young man Zhang), which is homophonous to *zhanglang* 蟑螂, meaning cockroach.

11. Quoted in Chard 1990, 155.

12. Chard 1994; Yang Fuquan 1994, 53-67.

13. Gaomu Lizi 1999a, 1999b, 2000; Jiang Fan 2001. In a traditional arranged marriage, the groom and bride would meet for the first time on their wedding day, and the bride would remove her veil only after she and her husband had retired for the night to the wedding room.

14. Comparable tales about the origin of the stove god and his wife are found in many parts of China and have made "the stove god's wife" (or "the kitchen god's wife," in the title of Amy Tan's novel) a byword for the long-suffering wife of an unappreciative and at times abusive husband. In such tales the protagonists may have slightly different names.

15. Si Zhulin 2023, 69–71.

16. Wang Jiaju 2006, 151–52.

17. *Gushixian quyizhi* 1989, 75–76.

18. For a more detailed description of this particular type of drum, see Yang Xianru 1981. Yang calls the instrument a "divine drum" (61).

19. Cao Jiazhen has on various occasions downplayed the differences between the texts of stove tales and those of stove plays.

20. "Pan Jing'e" 2011.

21. Other examples of stove plays do show the inclusion of prose dialogue. See, for instance, Zou Zhenqi and Pei Shihu [1989?], 53.

22. Carpenters were not the only ones to put on such extended plays of the legend of Zhang and Dingxiang. In the middle region of the Huai River, groups of a particular kind of ritual specialists known as *duangong* 端公, who also performed plays, organized Dingxiang Companies (Dingxiang ban 丁香班) that exclusively performed plays on this topic—performances that might last for more than a month. See Anhuisheng wenhuashi 1959, 430.

23. Yang Xianru 1981, 61–62.

24. Yang Xianru 1981, 61–62.

25. The stove god was not the patron saint of carpenters. That was Lu Ban 鲁班, a legendary craftsman and inventor who is believed to have lived in the fifth century BCE. For a hagiography of Lu Ban from the early Ming dynasty, see Ruitenbeek 1993, 152–54.

26. "As three drops of water" is a local expression meaning "beautiful."

27. "Five-man cannons" are heavy cannons requiring five men to handle.

28. *Gushixian quyizhi* 1989, 85–86.

29. Yang Xianru 1981.

30. The name of the genre most likely derives from the fact that its most popular topic was the tale of the god of the stove and his wife. Another hypothesis is that the name derives from the fact that its most important audience was made up of women and girls who spent most of their lives in or near the kitchen, and yet another is that carpenters expressed with these songs their gratitude to the (god of the) stove of the house at which they were working.

31. When the ballad is described as an independent work or published as a book, I italicize *Guo Dingxiang*. The 1981 edition was published as one item in a journal, so I place the title in quotation marks in this case.

32. Cao Jiazhen, Peng Huahou, and Li Haihua 1981. In this version as well as the later versions of 2007 and 2009, only one rhyme (*-ang*) is employed throughout.

33. Cao Jiazhen, Peng Huahou and Li Haihua 1981, 29.

34. For a selection of studies on *The Legend of Darkness*, see Liu Shouhua 2015. An English translation by Zhang Liyu 张立玉, Zang Junna 臧军娜 and H. W. Lan of the version as edited by Hu Chongjun is included Hu Chongjun 2021, accompanying the Chinese text.

35. For a general study of "Wu songs," see McLaren 2022. In an appendix on "The Folk Epic of Fifth Daughter," McLaren presents translations of highlights of this long narrative song as performed by Lu Amei 陆阿妹 (1902–82), based on the original recordings of the early 1980s.

36. Cao Jiazhen, Peng Huahou and Li Haihua 1981, 29.

37. Bai Gengsheng 2007 supports this genre classification.

38. For instance, the text was reprinted as Cao Jiazhen, Peng Huahou and Li Haihua 1987; and as Cao Jiazhen, Peng Huahou and Li Haihua 2003.

39. *Gushixian quyizhi* 1989, 10–14 (nature and development of stove tales); 24–25 (*Guo Dingxiang*); 32–34 (music of stove tales); 75–76 (performance of stove tales); and 85–86 (veneration of the stove).

40. Zou Zhenqi and Pei Shihu [1989?], 51–61.

41. I have not seen this version. To judge from its name, it was made up of available texts but had not otherwise been edited.

42. Xinyangshi minjian wenhua yichan qiangjiu gongcheng gongguo weiyuan hui and Gushixian minjian wenhua qiangjiu gongcheng gongzuo weiyuan hui 2007a.

43. Henansheng Gushixian wenhuaju 2009a.

44. Dong An 2017.

### Guo Dingxiang

1. In late imperial popular literature, stories of tragic love may be linked into sets of seven stories, in which the protagonists in each story are considered to be reincarnations of the protagonists in the preceding story, repeating their tragic fate. One retelling of such a set as a traditional novel in twenty-four chapters is entitled *Husband and Wife through Seven Lives* (*Qishi fuqi* 七世夫妻). That set of seven tragic couples does not include the story of Zhang Wanliang and Guo Dingxiang. The next section contains a list of the tragic couples in the Gushi set of seven stories.

2. "As three drops of water" is explained as a local expression for a pleasing alternation of high and low.

3. "Five-man cannon" (*wuzipao* 五子炮) refers to a traditional type of cannon that requires five men to fire. The phrase *wuzi* can also be rendered as "five sons," designating the ideal number of sons.

4. "Gold and silver paper" refers to sacrificial money (often in huge denominations) that is burnt as an offering to the gods.

5. A bride wears a veil on the day of her wedding.

6. The Queen-Mother, also known as Queen-Mother of the West, is in late-imperial popular literature often depicted as the wife of the Jade Emperor, whose surname is Zhang.

7. The peaches of the Queen-Mother of the West ripen only once every three thousand years. Eating them confers eternal life.

8. In Chinese mythology, the inhabitants of heaven are expected to rise above all passion, so the behavior of Golden Page and Jade Maiden is scandalous and deserves punishment.

9. Meng Jiangnü's 孟姜女 husband Wan Xiliang 万喜良 is carried off on the day of her wedding to work as a construction worker building the Great Wall. When she later travels to the building site, she learns that her husband has died of exhaustion and that his corpse has been buried in the body of the wall. See Idema 2008.

10. Zhu Yingtai 祝英台 is a young girl who dresses up as a boy in order to be able to study away from home at an academy. On her way there, she runs into the student Liang Shanbo 梁山伯, who is on his way to the same academy, where they share a room. While Liang initially suspects that Zhu may be a girl, she manages to convince him that there are no grounds at all for his suspicions. She falls in love with him, and upon leaving for home hints that she is a girl after all, but he does not pick up any of these suggestions. She tells him to come and visit and ask for the hand of her sister. When Liang visits the Zhus after a while, he learns to his surprise that Zhu is a girl and that her parents have already promised her in marriage to another young man. The love-stricken Liang soon dies, and when the marriage procession of Zhu Yingtai passes by his grave, she steps down from her sedan chair and jumps into his grave, which has opened at her prayer. See Idema 2010a.

11. In a popular play, Qin Xuemei 秦雪梅 has been promised in marriage to Shang Lin 商林. When the Shang family falls on hard times, Shang Lin is allowed to study at the Qin manor, but when Qin Xuemei meets with him and declares her abiding love, her father chases Shang Lin away and tries to cheat him by dressing a maid up as his bride. Shang Lin dies from rage, whereupon Qin Xuemei insists on joining his family as a daughter-in-law in mourning and supervises the education of his son by a concubine.

12. In the drum song *Wang Hanxi Borrows Grain* (*Wang Hanxi jieliang* 王汉溪借粮), the impoverished Wang Hanxi borrows grain from the family of his fiancée, Li Aijie 李爱姐. When he and Li Aijie have sex on that occasion, they are discovered by her sister-in-law.

13. In a popular tale, the poor girl Lan Yulian 兰玉莲, while drawing water from a well, meets a rich student. They make an appointment to meet later that night, but when he is late, in desperation she commits suicide by jumping into a well. When he arrives and realizes she has died, he also commits suicide.

14. In the play *Bringing Fragrant Tea* (*Song xiangcha* 送香茶), Zhang Guizhi 张桂枝 and her brother flee their home because they cannot stand the abuse by their stepmother. When her brother is taken in by a mother and daughter, the latter brings him tea as he is studying and falls in love with him. The summaries of the plays on this topic that I have seen do not specify the fate of Zhang Guizhi.

15. "Citing one's age" (*gaolao* 告老) was a common way for elderly officials to request permission to retire.

16. The "yellow memorials" are prayers addressed to the celestial authorities and written on yellow paper. They are burned during a religious service.

17. The word Sang 桑 used as a place name is written with the character *sang* 桑, which also means "mulberry tree."

18. Mandarin ducks are believed to mate for life and are a symbol of marital concord (including good sex).

19. The Three Mainstays refer to the subordinate relations of father and son, ruler and subject, and husband and wife. The Five Constants refer to benevolence, righteousness, propriety, wisdom, and fidelity. Together these terms refer to the morality of traditional society.

20. Emperor Yang (r. 605–18) was the last emperor of the Sui dynasty. He was rumored to have murdered his father and was notorious for his voluptuous lifestyle.

21. From the narrative here and later, it appears that Wang Manxiang was married to a man surnamed Shi, so most likely a son of a sister of Zhang Wanliang's father.

22. In traditional Chinese literature, sexual activities are often described in martial terms.

23. Clear and Bright (Qingming) is a spring festival that is celebrated on the 105th day following the winter solstice. Family members gather to visit and clean the graves of their ancestors.

24. These four lines copy a well-known quatrain by the Tang dynasty poet Jia Dao 贾岛 (779–843).

25. Double Five refers to the fifth day of the Fifth Lunar Month. In many parts of China, the day is celebrated by dragon boat races.

26. A "shoe basket" contains the materials for embroidering shoes for a woman's bound feet. On the construction of such shoes, see Ko 2001, 77–95.

27. As part of the wedding ceremony, the groom and bride bow to the parents of the groom and to his ancestors who are venerated in the main hall of the house.

28. An eight-step bedstead (*babuchuang* 八步床) is a four-poster bed. It is large enough to spread the mattresses and also provide room for sitting.

29. In other words, it is a win-win situation.

30. The oil used for the lamps to provide light in the evenings.

31. "Disturbing the wedding room" (*naofang* 闹房) is an important aspect of traditional wedding customs. While the veiled bride is seated on the wedding bed in the wedding room, male and female relatives of the groom look her over and comment on her and on the trousseau she has brought along. Quite often the comments may be quite salacious.

32. During the wedding days, the norms of social interaction are relaxed, and order is fully restored only on the third day following the wedding.

33. Threefold obedience stipulates that a woman as a daughter has to obey her father, as a wife her husband, and as a widow her eldest son. Fourfold virtue refers to a woman's morals, speech, bearing, and work.

34. "Bare sticks" (*guanggun* 光棍) are young men who for one reason or another have not been married and are on the lookout for some action.

35. This line means that if a wife gets into a fight with her mother-in-law, all of the female relatives at her husband's place will take the mother-in-law's side.

36. The traditional Chinese mile (*li* 里) measures about one-third of an English mile.

37. *Zao* 枣 (date) has the same pronunciation as *zao* 早 (early, quick). *Huasheng* 花生 (peanut) contains the element *sheng* 生 (life, to give birth).

38. An'an 安安 is the name of a filial young boy who in a popular play delivers rice to the temple where his mother is staying after she has been divorced by his father, who was forced to do so by his mother. Eventually father, mother, and son are reunited.

39. In late-imperial China, it was widely believed that children could save diseased parents (including parents-in-law) by feeding them a piece of the children's own flesh or a slice of their organs. The parents should of course be unaware of the true nature of the medicine they were given to eat. Confucian scholars as a rule condemned the practice but praised the filial fervor that gave rise to it.

40. Guo Ju 郭巨 is one of the filial sons who is featured in the *Twenty-Four Exemplars of Filial Piety* (*Ershisi xiao* 二十四孝), a widely popular primary textbook in the Ming (1368–1644) and Qing (1644–1911) dynasties. Guo Ju is so poor that he cannot feed both his mother and his son, so he and his wife decide to bury their child. When they dig a hole, they find a pile of gold "for the filial son Guo Ju."

41. Wang Xiang 王祥 is another filial son who is featured in the *Twenty-Four Exemplars of Filial Piety*. When his cruel stepmother wants to eat fresh fish in the middle of winter, he lies down on a frozen river to melt the ice with the warmth of his body. Soon two large carps jump out of the water.

42. Each of these four lines starts with a quote from the *Analects* (*Lunyu* 论语), a collection of sayings of Confucius and dialogues between him and his students, which was widely used as a primary textbook in imperial China.

43. The "happy plate" is a plate filled with sweets.

44. The Dragon Gate is the name of rapids in the Yellow River. Carps jumping across the rapids when swimming upstream are an image representing a student passing the government examinations and entering a bureaucratic career.

45. Weaving Maiden is the name of the star Vega, Oxherd the name of Altair. These two bright stars are located on opposite sides of the Heavenly River (the Milky Way). Legend has it that these stars were separated by the emperor of heaven because the two of them neglected their duties following their marriage. They are allowed to meet once a year, during the night of the seventh day of the Seventh Month, when magpies form a bridge across the river. Idema 2009, 79–99.

46. Dragon-Tiger Mountain (Longhushan 龙虎山) in Jiangxi is the seat of the Heavenly Master, the hereditary head of the Zhengyi sect of Daoism. Here the term is used to refer to the steep mountains of the Deep South.

47. "His Lordship" here refers to Guo Dingxiang's father.

48. The group of Eight Immortals has been widely popular since the Song dynasty, but it took until the sixteenth century before the membership of the group became established. The adventures of the individual members of the group were narrated in *Journey to the East* (*Dongyou ji* 东游记), a vernacular novel of the sixteenth century that concludes with their common adventures on a trip by boat across the ocean in order to visit the Dragon King of the Eastern Sea.

49. Zhongli Quan 钟离权 is said to have lived during the Han dynasty (206 BCE–220 CE). Having lost a battle as general, he abandoned all worldly ambition and devoted himself to the pursuit of life eternal.

50. Lü Dongbin 吕洞宾 is said to have been a student from the Tang dynasty (617–906) who turned to religion when, on his way to the capital to take

part in the examinations, he experienced the vicissitudes of a full bureaucratic career during a dream while waiting for his meal to be cooked. Lü Dongbin is also the main character in many tales and legends that are not related to his membership in the Eight Immortals.

51. Zhang Guolao 张果老 is depicted as an elderly gardener.

52. The "fisherman's drum" is a musical instrument used by Daoist priests when engaged in popular preaching. It is made of a long bamboo tube covered with a piece of skin on one end.

53. Cao Guojiu 曹国舅 is said to have been a brother-in-law of the Song dynasty emperor Renzong (r. 1023–63).

54. Iron Crutch Li 铁拐李 is depicted as a lame beggar. He had been a teacher with many students, but his soul borrowed the body of a recently deceased beggar to come back to life when his students had buried his decomposing body after his soul had left it temporarily for a visit to heaven.

55. Lan Caihe 蓝采和 had been a performer in his youth.

56. Han Xiangzi 韩湘子 was a distant nephew of the famous Confucian ideologue Han Yu 韩愈 (768–824), who is said to have converted his uncle to the superior truth of Daoism when, in 819, the latter offended the emperor and was banished to the Deep South.

57. Maiden He 何仙姑 is the only female member of the Eight Immortals.

58. The bodhisattva Avalokateśvara (Guanyin 观音) has in China during the last millennium mostly been venerated in a female manifestation. Common illustrations show her dressed in white and seated on a lotus throne, holding a bottle of pure water in one hand and a willow wand in the other.

59. In the early chapters of the sixteenth-century novel *Journey to the West* (*Xiyou ji* 西游记), the Old Master (Laozi 老子) is depicted as an alchemist preparing the elixir of longevity.

60. Lü Dongbin is renowned as one of the masters of sexual techniques to achieve longevity. Such techniques are based on the absorption of the vital forces of one's sexual partner, who of course also may be a master of such techniques. One legend tells that Lü Dongbin lost out in this competition to the courtesan Baimudan 白牡丹 (White Peony).

61. The 2009 edition writes "Zong Erjie" 宗二姐 (Second Sister Zong) instead of "Song Erjie" (Second Sister Song). The annotations to the 2009 edition identify Zong Erjie 宗二姐 and Hu Yanzhang 胡彦章 as characters in local skits but do not provide more information.

62. The reunion at Broken Bridge is an episode from the legend of the White Snake. After the monk Fahai 法海 at Zhenjiang has alerted Xu Xuan 许宣 of the true identity of his wife as a white snake, Xu has returned to Hangzhou. Near the West Lake he meets his wife and her servant at Broken Bridge. The latter threatens to kill him for his infidelity, but his wife forgives him and the couple is reunited for the moment.

63. When the famous Ming dynasty painter Tang Yin 唐寅 (1470–1524) from Suzhou fell in love with the slave girl Autumn Fragrance 秋香, he hired himself out as a servant to her owner in order to be able to approach her.

64. In chapters 30–31 of the sixteenth-century novel *Water Margin* (*Shuihu zhuan* 水浒传), Yulan 玉兰 is an adopted daughter of Military Director Zhang,

who promises her in marriage to Wu Song 武松. That very night, Zhang has Wu Song falsely arrested for burglary. When Wu Song escapes from a murder attempt and returns to take revenge, Yulan is one of his victims. In later retellings, Yulan may be a willing or unwilling accomplice in the framing of Wu Song. In those versions that stress her innocence, she commits suicide to demonstrate her loyalty to Wu Song. Here Yulan is an emblem of a hardworking wife.

65. In traditional China, the night was divided into five watches of equal length. In cities the watches were announced by beating a drum on the drum tower.

66. "Revolving pavilion" is a literal translation of *zhuan loutang* 转楼堂. The expression occurs a number of times but makes no sense. Most likely it should be written as *zhuan loutang* 砖楼堂, meaning "brick pavilion." The next chapter writes *zhuan loufang* 砖楼房 (brick pavilion). In ancient times a prefect was entitled to a carriage drawn by five horses, so "five-horse" came to mean "high-status, luxurious."

67. King Yama is the highest judge in the underworld.

68. The Three Lords and Five Rulers reigned in a mythic past.

69. Yao 尧 ruled for many years and eventually ceded the throne to Shun 舜. Shun in his turn ceded the throne to Yu 禹, who became the founder of the Xia dynasty (the twentieth through the sixteenth century BCE). Tang 汤 was the founder of the Shang (or Yin) dynasty (the fifteenth through the eleventh century BCE).

70. King Zhou 纣王 was the evil last ruler of the Shang dynasty. He was overthrown by King Wu 武王, who established the Zhou dynasty (eleventh century BCE through 256 BCE). King Wu's father, King Wen 文王, had already obtained the allegiance of two-thirds of the empire by his virtue. Seeking an able minister, King Wen found Jiang Ziya 姜子牙, then a simple fisherman. Jiang Ziya would later assist King Wu in his campaigns.

71. During the period covered by the *Annals of Spring and Autumn* (*Chunqiu* 春秋; 770–425 BCE), the Zhou dynasty had lost much of its central power. The many small states that had existed earlier were gobbled up by seven large states that were engaged in intermittent but continuous warfare. From time to time, one of these sates achieved a hegemonic position. During the period of the Warring States (fourth and third centuries BCE), the state of Qin eventually emerged as the victor, and the king of Qin declared himself the First Emperor in 221 BCE.

72. Following the death of the First Emperor in 210 BCE, rebellions broke out all over the empire. Initially it appeared as if Xiang Yu 项羽 (232–202 BCE), who titled himself the Hegemon-King of Western Chu, was the strongest candidate in the ensuing struggle for power. He burned down the huge Epang Palace of the First Emperor, but in the end he was defeated by the low-born Liu Bang 刘邦 (d. 195 BCE), who founded the Han dynasty (206 BCE–220 CE).

73. In the period 9–23 CE, the Han dynasty was replaced by the Xin dynasty of Wang Mang 王莽. After several years of civil war, the Han dynasty was restored by Liu Xiu 刘秀, who claimed to be a member of the royal house. In the final years of the Han dynasty, the imperial court was dominated by

Cao Cao 曹操 (155–220) whose son would found the Wei dynasty (220–65), initiating the period of the Three Kingdoms (Wei, Wu, and Shu-Han).

74. During a campaign in the winter of 208–9 against the southern warlords Sun Quan 孙权 (182–252) and Liu Bei 刘备 (161–223), Cao Cao suffered a massive defeat in a naval battle on the Yangzi River at Red Cliff. Before the battle, Cao Cao had been led to believe that two of the commanders of his fleet were about to defect to his enemies when Jiang Gan 蒋干, making a pretense of surrendering, brought him a letter he claimed to have stolen in which these two commanders offered to turn sides. Cao Cao thereupon had executed these experienced commanders, and this decision contributed to his defeat.

75. Zhao Yun 赵云 was one of the generals of Liu Bei. When Liu Bei's army was badly defeated by Cao Cao's troops at Long Bank Slope, Zhao Yun saved the life of Liu Bei's infant son. Qin Qiong 秦琼 (d. 638; better known as Qin Shubao 秦叔宝) was one of the generals who supported Li Shimin 李世民 in establishing the Tang dynasty (618–906).

76. Emperor Yang (r. 605–17) was the bad last ruler of the Sui dynasty. He loved to visit the area of Yangzhou and is credited with the construction of the Grand Canal. Zhenguan 贞观 (627–49) is the name of the reign of Li Shimin, the second emperor of the Tang dynasty, who established a reputation for wise rule.

77. The period of Five Dynasties following the demise of the Tang came to an end with the founding of the Song dynasty (960–1279) by Zhao Kuangyin 赵匡胤 (927–60). Zhao served as a general of the Later Zhou dynasty (951–60). When he was about to set out on a campaign against the Liao, according to official historiography, at Chenqiao 陈桥 his soldiers spontaneously placed the imperial yellow robe on his shoulders because they feared that the ruling infant emperor lacked the strength to lead the country. In the eleventh century, Bao Zheng 包拯 (999–1062) established a reputation as a fair and accessible judge when serving as the metropolitan prefect of Kaifeng.

78. The Song dynasty never succeeded in subduing its northern neighbors. Among the generals who served along the northern border, the members of the Yang family stood out, especially Yang Ye 杨业 (d. 986) and his sixth son, Yang Yanzhao 杨延昭 (958–1014). In 1125 the Jurchen invaded the territory of the Song, eventually conquering all of northern China up to the Huai River. Later popular tradition held that the general Yue Fei 岳飞 (1103–42) had been on the verge of reconquering the lost territory when the Song prime minister (in the pay of the enemy) had him called back and murdered in jail.

79. The Sage is Confucius, who was revered in every school as the First Teacher.

80. A screen wall was a freestanding wall behind the entrance of a courtyard; it blocked people on the street from seeing what is going on inside the house in the courtyard. It also served to protect the house from ghosts, as these were believed to be able to walk only in a straight line.

81. Top of the List, Second Place, and Flower Snatcher are the designations of the three persons with the highest rankings in the final round of the metropolitan examinations.

82. "Old home" is a local expression denoting a painting on the back wall of the hall.

83. An eight-immortal table is an eight-sided table.

84. While Qin Xuemei is famous for her education of the adopted son of her deceased husband, it is the mother of the famous philosopher Meng Ke 孟轲 (Mencius) who is famous for instilling in her son the need for repetition in learning by cutting off the piece of cloth she was weaving. When she asked him when he returned from school how his day had been and he replied, "The same as always," she destroyed the piece of cloth that came about by the endless repetition of the same movement. Qin Xuemei is said to have used the same expedient.

85. These two lines describe two episodes in the saga of the Three Kingdoms. At the beginning of the sixteenth-century novel of the tale, the three protagonists—Liu Bei (161–223), Guan Yu 关羽 (160–220), and Zhang Fei 张飞 (d. 221)—swear brotherhood in Zhang Fei's peach orchard by sacrificing a horse and a bull. During the wars of their time, they suffer many defeats despite their personal bravery and come to realize they need the advice of an able strategist. And so they call on Zhuge Liang 诸葛亮 (181–234), who at that time lives in a thatched cottage as a farmer. Zhuge Liang refuses to receive them during their first two visits and agrees to see them only when he has become convinced of their sincerity by a third visit.

86. Both the pine and the crane are emblems of longevity.

87. The Chinese text writes *Zhaojun* 赵君 (lord of Zhao), which makes no sense in this context. The 2009 edition writes *Zhaojun* 昭君, which is the personal name of the famous beauty Wang Zhaojun.

88. One *qing* 顷 equals a hundred *mu* 亩 (roughly one-sixteenth of a hectare).

89. The moon is inhabited by a hare.

90. This describes Zhao Yun crashing through enemy lines when saving Liu Bei's infant son.

91. Second Son 二郎 is a well-known deity. One myth tells that he chased the superfluous suns that were scorching the earth and buried them below the mountains he carried in the baskets of his carrying pole.

92. The triple oath in the peach orchard refers to the oath of brotherhood sworn by Liu Bei, Guan Yu, and Zhang Fei.

93. When the famous historian Sima Guang 司马光 (1019–86) was still only a child, he saved the life of a little boy who had fallen into a huge earthenware water vat by picking up a brick and breaking the vat. He is mentioned here because the element *si* 司 in his surname has the same pronunciation as the word *si* 四 (four).

94. The Five Tiger generals of Western Shu are Guan Yu, Zhang Fei, Zhao Yun, Ma Chao 马超, and Huang Zhong 黄忠.

95. The seventh son of Yang Ye died when Yang Ye was trapped in a narrow valley by overwhelming numbers of enemy troops, and this seventh son was dispatched to ask the commander in chief for additional troops. The commander in chief hated Yang Ye and had his son tied to a stake and killed by a volley of arrows. Without outside help, Yang Ye preferred to commit suicide rather than surrender.

96.  In late-imperial China, the common currency was copper coins and unminted silver.

97.  Vinegar is an emblem of jealousy.

98.  The word I have translated as "trap" actually refers to battle array (*zhen* 阵). Traditional Chinese lore knows about many artfully set-out battle arrays a warrior cannot escape from once he has entered them. In the "wine battle array," the warrior is overcome by alcohol.

99.  Daji 妲己 was the beautiful woman who bewitched King You (r. 781–771 BCE). As a result of his downfall, the capital of the Zhou dynasty was moved from the Wei valley in the West to Luoyang in the East. Consort Yang 杨贵妃 was the favorite concubine of Emperor Xuanzong (r. 713–755) during the later years of his reign. She is held responsible for the rebellion of the Sogdian general An Lushan 安禄山 that almost brought down the Tang dynasty.

100.  To share in someone's glory means to benefit financially from one's relation to a rich or important person—"to share in the spoils."

101.  On the art of physiognomy in traditional China, see Wang 2020.

102.  The "three hills" here refer to the forehead and the cheekbones, while "virtue" denotes an inherent power. The "marchmounts" are the holy mountains that dominate the five directions (North, South, East, West, and Center).

103.  "The eight-bushels part" designates the highest possible score.

104.  "Left and right are cinnabar phoenixes" describes the eyes.

105.  The "eight characters" refer to the four two-character combinations of the year, month, day, and hour of birth. As part of the marriage negotiations, the two families exchange the eight characters of the prospective groom and bride so that professionals may judge whether the combination of the two sets of eight characters bodes well for the future.

106.  *Zi, chou, yin,* and *mao* are characters that belong to the ten Heavenly Stems and the twelve Earthly Branches that are combined in a series of sixty two-character terms.

107.  In the series of the Five Phases (Metal, Wood, Water, Fire, and Earth), the elements can not only "generate" each other but also "conquer" each other.

108.  The "flowing years" refer to the sequence of lucky and unlucky years.

109.  The Chinese term translated as "hitching post" is *jimazhuang* 羁马桩, which most likely is synonymous with *shuanmazhuang* 拴马桩 (hitching post), which also designates an accessory auricle, one that in men, at least, is considered an auspicious sign, promising a high office.

110.  The word "pheasant" (wild chicken) also means "prostitute."

111.  In traditional Chinese physiology, man was believed to have three souls and six spirits.

112.  The thin fleece around an egg below the shell, the eggshell membrane.

113.  The prunus flowers in winter and so may be covered by snow.

114.  A "chrysanthemum girl" (*huanghuanü* 黄花女) is a virgin.

115.  To be forced to call an unrelated person "Father" or "Mother" means utter humiliation.

116.  For "conceive and give birth," the text actually reads "give birth and feed" (*shengyang* 生养).

117.  "Broom-star" is the Chinese term for "comet."

118. "Hauling wave on wave" (*chelanglang* 扯浪浪) is the name of a children's game involving children holding hands and forming a long row.

119. Zhang Gong 张恭 (also known as Student Zhang 张生) is the protagonist of China's best-known love comedy, *The Story of the Western Wing* (*Xixiang ji* 西厢记), by Wang Shifu 王实甫 (ca. 1300). Staying at a monastery, Zhang Gong falls in love with Yingying 莺莺, who is also temporarily staying there with her widowed mother. When the monastery is besieged by rebels who claim Yingying, her mother promises to treat any man as kin who is able to save her. Zhang Gong thereupon writes a letter to a friend in the military, who indeed comes and lifts the siege. At the banquet that follows, the widow, against his expectations, does not allow him to marry Yingying but has her call him "Elder Brother." When later he tries to seduce her by playing the lute, she sends him a poem that he interprets as an invitation for a nighttime visit. In order to reach her room, he has to climb across a wall. When he falls down on the other side, he is berated at length by Yingying and leaves in frustration. After further complications, the lovers are eventually united in marriage. The play was adapted in basically all forms of performative literature in later ages.

120. King Wen was the father of the founder of the Zhou dynasty, King Wu. He is credited with arranging the sequence of the sixty-four hexagrams in the *Book of Changes* (*Yijing* 易经), which was widely used in divination throughout Chinese history. As many fortune tellers claimed the wisdom of King Wen, they sometimes adopted his name.

121. When using coins to consult the hexagrams, head and tail stand for broken and unbroken lines.

122. Triple Nine refers to the twenty-seven days following the winter solstice, the coldest period of the year.

123. *Jia, zi, yi,* and *chou* are all characters that belong to the ten Heavenly Stems and the twelve Earthly Branches that in combination make up a series of sixty two-character combinations.

124. A heaven-well courtyard is a small inner courtyard surrounded on all sides by rooms of the house.

125. In traditional China there were seven recognized reasons for a divorce: infertility, adultery, refusal to obey the parents-in-law, quarrelsomeness, stealing, jealousy, and an evil disease. A wife who had shared her husband's years of poverty could not be divorced by him when he had become rich. If Zhang Wanliang could incite Guo Dingxiang into a fight, he could claim that she was quarrelsome.

126. *Ren* 壬 is the ninth of the ten characters that make up the Heavenly Stems, and *gui* 癸 the tenth. Together they correspond to Water as the fifth of the Five Phases and to North as one of the five directions (North, South, East, West, and Center).

127. In popular fiction, Xue Dingshan 薛丁山 is the son of the Tang dynasty general Xue Rengui 薛仁贵 (614–83). Both generals are said to have fought their battles in white battle dresses.

128. The bodhisattva intended here will be Guanyin, who in her female manifestation was considered the acme of female beauty.

129. The surname Liang 梁 has the same pronunciation as *liang* 两 (a pair, two).

130. Lu Ban 鲁班 is the patron god of carpenters.

131. "The big cudgel of the Monkey King" refers to the dough roller. The Monkey King, Sun Wukong 孙悟空, accompanies the holy monk Xuanzang 玄奘 on his pilgrimage to the Buddhist paradise in the sixteenth-century novel *Journey to the West* (*Xiyou ji* 西游记). When defending the monk against the many monsters that want to devour him or sleep with him, the Monkey King's weapon is his cudgel that can take on any size he wants.

132. Student Zhang is Zhang Gong, the male protagonist of *The Story of the Western Wing*.

133. Guan Yu's favorite weapon was his huge crescent-moon blade.

134. *Bing* and *ding* are the third and fourth characters of the series of ten characters that make up the ten Heavenly Stems. Together they correspond to Fire as one the Five Phases and to South as one of the five directions.

135. The surname Chai 柴 has the same pronunciation as *chai* 柴 (firewood). Little Prince Chai, a young boy, was the last emperor of the Later Zhou dynasty and was deposed by Zhao Kuangyin when he founded the Song dynasty.

136. "First Emperors" (*shihuang* 始皇) is very similar in pronunciation to *sihuang* 死黄 (dead brown [leaves]).

137. King Yan 阎王 is King Yama. Yan 阎 has the same pronunciation as *yan* 盐 (salt).

138. The small bound feet of Chinese women of the Ming and Qing dynasties are often compared to golden lotuses.

139. In an old fable, when a snipe wanted to eat an oyster, the oyster closed its valves around the snipe's beak, hoping to kill the bird. As the two animals refused to let go of each other, a fisherman passing by caught both of them.

140. These kowtows replace the ritual duties she would have to fulfill as a daughter-in-law upon her mother-in-law's death.

141. The word *si* 丝 (thread) has the same pronunciation as the word *si* 思 (thinking, longing). The silkworm cocoon that keeps on spitting out thread until its death is therefore a symbol for undying love. The line is already encountered in a poem by Li Shangyin 李商隐 (813–58).

142. These four surnames form the first line of the *One-Hundred Surnames* (*Baijiaxing* 百家姓), a common primer in late-imperial China.

143. The Southern Gate is the entrance to heaven.

144. The seven orifices refer to the seven orifices of the head (eyes, ears, nostrils, and mouth).

145. Silver-ear (*yiner* 银耳; *Tremella fuciformis* Berk., white fungus) is a kind of champignon.

146. The "willow lanes" are the red-light district; the "flowers" are its prostitutes.

147. A wedding gift from the groom as a symbol of love.

148. The Full Month is the first full month after the birth of a child.

149. The Impermanences (Wuchang 无常) are the runners from the underworld who come to the world of light to fetch the soul of a person destined to

die. One of them is tall and thin and dressed in white; the other is short and fat and dressed in black.

150.  "Yellow Springs" is one of the oldest terms for the realm of the dead.

151.  Fengdu 丰都 (Prosperous Metropole) is another designation of the underworld. Here the term is used to indicate the capital of the underworld.

## Appendix I. The Textualization of *Guo Dingxiang*

1.  Henansheng Gushixian wenhuaju 2009b, 273.

2.  Cao Jiazhen's question would have been inspired by his awareness of the scurrilous nature of many nighttime entertainments in the countryside. As entertaining as such jokes and skits might be, they would not lend themselves easily to adaptation in a publishable form, certainly not in those years. Li Chen (2004, 11) discusses the presence of ribald plays in the late-night repertoire of rural shadow theater. She has also published translations of some of these skits (e.g., Li Chen 2009, 2010).

3.  Cao Jiazhen 2017, 291. While this essay devotes one line to the 2009 edition, one wonders whether it may originally have been written on the occasion of the publication of the 2007 edition.

A somewhat different account of Cao Jiazhen's first encounter with the genre of "singing the stove" and its tale of Zhang Wanliang and Guo Dingxiang is found in an interview published in the May 29, 2007, issue of *Henan Shangbao*, on the occasion of the appearance of the "reading edition" of *Guo Dingxiang*.

4.  Cao Jiazhen 2017, 292.

5.  Yen 1967.

6.  Holm 1991, 225–30.

7.  In southeastern Henan there also circulated folktales in which Zhang Wanliang is described as the poor son of a family that has been poor for generations. See, for instance, "The King of the Stove and the Queen of the Stove" (Zao wangye yu zao wangnai 灶王爷和灶王奶) in Chen Yongsheng 1992, 339–41. This tale was told by Yu Wenyao 余文耀, a sixty-two-year-old farmer. In his tale, the poor Zhang Wanliang marries the equally poor daughter of the Ge family 葛氏女. The couple starts a rice shop that prospers thanks to her hard work and honesty. Once they have become rich, Zhang Wanliang acquires a concubine named Li Manxiang 李曼香, who quickly incites him to divorce the daughter of the Ge family but equally quickly leaves him when he is reduced to poverty once again. In the meantime, the daughter of the Ge family, now dressed as a man, has opened a shop elsewhere and is prospering once again. When Zhang Wanliang has become a beggar and happens to pass by her place, he recognizes the food she serves him and remorsefully tells his story, whereupon the couple reunites to happily live together till a ripe old age and be venerated as king and queen of the stove upon their deaths. There is no indication that Cao Jiazhen and his collaborators were acquainted with this version. One may note that in this tale, as told by a farmer, riches do not come from working the land but from operating a shop.

8. Yang Xianru 1981, 61. A very comparable account of this episode of the legend is also provided in the *Zaojun chan* 灶君忏 (*Hymn for the god of the stove*), from the Jiang-Huai region (Zhu Hengfu and Huang Wenhu 2011, 194–218). This long narrative, in passages of seven-syllable verse alternating with passages of ten-syllable verse, dates from the late nineteenth century, at the latest. Despite the emphasis in the text on the miraculous origin of the wealth of Dingxiang (here surnamed Ge 葛) and her new husband, the introductory note still insists on the "hard work" (p. 194) of the couple. In this version of the legend, too, the ox that pulls the cart of the divorced wife determines her future by depositing her in front of the house of her second husband, whom she marries without further ado. This text is part of the repertoire of the *shenshu* 神书 (divine books) of ritual specialists in Liuhe (opposite Nanjing on the northern side of the Yangzi). The version of the ritual specialists to the north in Jinhu has a very similar plot (Jiang Yan, 2007, 138–160).

The story of young man Zhang 張郎 and Ge Dingxiang 葛丁香 as told in the *Zhaojun chan* also bears a striking similarity to the story as told in the anonymous *Zhang lang xiuqi—Ge Dingxiang jiezhi ji* 張郎休妻葛丁香戒指記 (Young Zhang divorces his wife—Ge Dingxiang: The tale of the ring) that has been preserved in a Shanghai lithographic edition from the early years of the twentieth century (*Zhang lang xiuqi* n.d.) that most likely is based on an earlier woodblock edition (on the first page of the text, the title is preceded by the two characters *xinke* 新刻 [newly cut]). This latter text is written primarily in verse but is made up of eight sections, each of which starts with a poem and a short introduction in prose. In these texts Dingxiang is described as an incarnation of the star of prosperity, while Zhang is said to be an incarnation of the star of eightfold bankruptcy. Zhang has no propensity for book learning but is addicted to hunting. Pursuing a white hare, he sees Dingxiang, who is enjoying herself on a swing with her maids. Her parents initially refuse a wedding proposal but give in when the go-betweens threaten to comment suicide. When Zhang wants to divorce his wife, he buys a knife and uses it to accuse her of intending to murder him. Following her departure from his home, she marries Fan Sanlang. Zhang remarries and is quickly reduced to begging. Following his encounter with Dingxiang, he jumps into the stove, whereupon Fan Sanlang and his mother commit suicide as well, followed by Dingxiang. Upon their deaths, all four of them receive divine appointments, but while Zhang is appointed god of the stove, Dingxiang in these texts is appointed the goddess of the toilet.

In the version of the legend found in Hu Yongliang 2013, the future god of the stove chases from his house not his wife but his youngest daughter, when she insists that her present prosperity is due to her piety in an earlier life rather than to her father. She entrusts her fate not to an ox but to a horse.

9. Fan Sanlang, as the son of a poor family, persists in his hard work, whereas Zhang Wanliang fails, one assumes because of his background as the pampered son of a once-rich family (even though such a background is not specified in the 1981 edition).

10. Shandongsheng xiqu yanjiushi n.d., 133–206. Also see Cai Yuyan and Gong Chuhan 2015, 1:424–25.

11. For instance, in the pre-1949 versions' legend of Dong Yong 董永, who sells himself into servitude to be able to provide his father with a fitting funeral, the heavenly maiden Seventh Sister is ordered by the Jade Emperor to assist this filial son for one hundred days by her weaving. In the post-1949 adaptations of the legend, Dong Yong's status is changed from student to poor peasant, and Seventh Sister falls in love with him when she observes his plight and flees from heaven to support him (see Idema 2015). The emphasis on mutual love as the basis of marriage (strengthened by the contrast with an arranged marriage that collapses) fits in very well with the PRC campaign for marriage reform in the early 1950s. In many parts of China, cultural cadres in the 1950s urged professional performers to bring their stories in line with the government policies of those days, but the existing scholarship on stove tales and stove plays does not mention such interference in the contents at that early date.

12. Cai Yuyan and Gong Chuhan 2015, 1:595. Wang Guiyin's rewriting of the play was part of a nation-wife phenomenon, during the years 1955–57, of rewriting traditional plays based on myths (*shenhua* 神话). Another, even more successful, rewriting of the legend of Zhang and Dingxiang, this time as a Luju 庐剧 opera from Anhui Province, was produced by Chen Zhong 陈仲 as *Xiu Dingxiang* 休丁香 (Cai Yuyan and Gong Chuhan 2015, 1:424). In this version (Anhuisheng wenhuaju 1959, 429–95), Fan Sanlang comes to the rescue of Dingxiang during a downpour after she has already made up her mind not to drown herself in the river. Chen Zhong's version includes a number of episodes that are also encountered in the 2007 reading edition of *Guo Dingxiang*. Cao Jiazhen and his colleagues may well have experienced such revised versions of more than twenty years back as authentic when they were revived after the Cultural Revolution.

13. Gaomu Lizi (Takaki Tatsuko) 1999a, 19. If cultural cadres in the early years of the PRC prohibited the performance of certain scenes, it is of course also quite thinkable that they insisted on certain changes in the episodes that could be performed. But so far I have not encountered any record of this in the publications by PRC scholars.

14. In the 2007 edition, Zhang Wanliang and Guo Dingxiang appear before King Yama, who notes that their files are kept in heaven and sends them off. In the 2009 edition, Zhang and Guo do not appear before King Yama but leave the underworld when informed that their case will be decided in heaven.

15. *Gushixian quyizhi* (1989) provides two different texts for venerating the stove, neither of which is identical to the corresponding sections in the 2007 and 2009 editions.

16. The Cultural Bureau of Gushi District in 1987 convened a roundtable discussion of research on stove singing to which some performers were also invited, but this did not result, to the best of my knowledge, in any publications. One wonders to what extent the comments of the cultural authorities may have influenced the later performances of the invited performers. Gaomu Lizi (Takaki Tatsuko) 1999a, 15.

17. Cao Jiazhen 2017, 292–93.

18. A brief biography of Pan Jing'e is found in the January 20, 2011, issue of the *Zhongguo shehui kexue bao* 中国社会科学报. Pan Jing'e attended primary and middle school and was trained as an actress. In 1988 she became a pupil of Ye Zhaoqun, training to be the first female performer of stove tales. She is reported to have memorized a version of *Guo Dingxiang* that ran to 4,231 lines.

19. Cao Jiazhen 2017, 293.

20. The colophon lists the bureaucratic agencies from Gushi and Xinyang as the responsible editors. The names of the persons involved are mentioned in very small type at the bottom of the reverse side of the title page.

21. Xinyangshi minjian wenhua yichan qiangjiu gongcheng gongguo wei-yuanhui and Gushixian minjian wenhua qiangjiu gongcheng gongzuo weiyuan hui 2007b, 265.

22. Strictly speaking, *Guo Dingxiang* cannot be characterized as a "prosimet-ric" text, as it is completely composed in verse. But the term *shuochang wenxue* 说唱文学 (prosimetric literature) is often used in a broad sense, also including long vernacular verse narratives.

23. Xinyangshi minjian wenhua yichan qiangjiu gongcheng gongguo wei-yuanhui and Gushixian minjian wenhua qiangjiu gongcheng gongzuo weiyuan hui 2007b, 266. While the reading edition would appear to be aimed at a gen-eral audience, the documentary edition would presumably target a scholarly audience. Such an edition, to the best of my knowledge, has not been published so far. In the case of *The Legend of Darkness*, we have one edition that prints the available traditional manuscripts (Zhongguo minjian wennxue yanjiuhui Hu-beii fenhui 1986) and one edition that prints the available traditional manu-scripts, three modern reconstructions, and a selection of articles (Shennongjia linqu feiwuzhi wenhua baohu zhonngxin 2014).

24. In the 2009 edition, the good-hearted Guo Dingxiang provides Zhang Wanliang with the money he will need for his expenses at the academy.

25. In his record of his first meeting with the carpenter Qian, Cao Jiazhen (2017, 291) mentions the episode "The Third Beating and the Third Divorce," which would imply that Qian's version at one time included the episodes of the comparison of riches ("The First Beating and the First Divorce") and Wang's visit to Miaoxiang and its aftermath ("The Second Beating and the Second Divorce").

26. Gao Tianxing 2009, 10.

27. Henansheng Gushixian wenhuaju 2009b, 275.

28. Gao Tianxing 2009, 10.

29. The 2007 edition counts thirty-one chapters but the 2009 only thirty. While the latter edition includes two chapters that are absent from the 2007 edition, it combines three chapters from the 2007 edition—"Jumping into the Stove" (Touzao 投灶), "Visiting the Underworld" (Youyin 游阴), and "Gaz-ing Home" (Wangxiang 望乡)—into a single chapter called "Jumping into the Stove," and it combines two chapters, "A Meeting of Souls" (Hunhui 魂会) and "Appointment as the Stove God" (Fengzao 封灶), into a single chapter, "Ap-pointment as the Stove God."

30. Henansheng Gushixian wenhuaju 2009a, 227–35.

31. This modern hesitation to remarry on the part of Guo Dingxiiang, based on traditional values, sharply contrasts of course with the traditional account of the second marriage as recorded by Yang Xianru and in older versions in which Guo Dingxiang remarried immediately, without any qualms.

32. Henansheng Gushixian wenhuaju 2009a, 31–33. This passage is very clearly written in the first person and so appears to derive from a play.

33. Henansheng Gushixian wenhuaju 2009a, 59–63.

34. Henansheng Gushixian wenhuaju 2009a, 71–85.

35. In her articles on the literary qualities of *Guo Dingxiang*, Cai Yaling (2012, 2013, 2014) refers both to the 2007 edition and to the 2009 edition.

36. Henansheng gushixian wenhuaju 2009a, 1. These poems are also included in the 2017 reprint. The format of five seven-syllable lines is common for *shange* 山歌 (mountain songs) in this part of Henan. See Wang Daoyun 1991.

37. Honko (2000) combines contemporary research studies with discussions of ancient works believed to have originated in oral epics.

38. Bender (2019) surveys the issues involved in the editions of long songs/ epics from China's minorities; McLaren and Zhang (2017) discuss the issues involved in the textualization of the long "Wu Songs."

39. Ready (2019, 101–58) summarizes the many forms of accidental and deliberate changes to the oral texts in the process of recording and editing oral epics in the nineteenth and twentieth centuries worldwide.

40. In the case of all three published editions of *Guo Dingxiang*, the editors report that they had collected considerably more lines than they included in their edition. Most likely, most omitted lines would have been repetitive; they may also have been made up of moral digressions without much relevance to the story at hand.

41. On composite texts, also from China, see Ready 2019, 155–56.

42. See the following description of the long Wu-dialect songs: "Most singer-farmers interviewed in the 1980s and 1990s could only sing short episodes rather than the 'full' story. In other words, one episode in song could be considered a separate song but was also understood to belong to a cycle of songs narrating a sequence of events in line within a familiar structure" (McLaren 2022, xxiv). Some episodes may be much more popular than other episodes from the same song cycle and be known to a considerable number of singers, while other episodes may seem to be taboo because of their "unlucky" contents. This mode of existence also means that folk epics in their natural habitat have no fixed length.

43. Cao Jiazhen 2017, 293.

44. Zhang Wanliang's visits to Wang Manxiang and to Wang Miaoxiang could easily have provided an opportunity for extended descriptions of their lovemaking. One also wonders whether the scene of the servant girl Meixiang's meeting with the student Li Erlang when she has to deliver a letter to the Southern Academy would have originally included some flirtation and perhaps even more. For an illuminating study of the implications of obscenity in the editing of oral texts, see the discussion of the various versions of "Wuniang" 五娘 in McLaren and Zhang 2017.

45. Liu Wenwen 2018, 41.

46. Xinyangshi minjian wenhua yichan qiangjiu gongcheng gongzuo wei- yuan hui and Gushixian minjian wenhua qiangjiu gongcheng gongzuo weiyuan hui 2007b, 266. Bai Gengsheng has published extensively on the religious culture of the Naxi ethnic group; he is not only a well-known academic authority in folklore studies but also a high-ranking Chinese Communist Party member.

47. Saussy 2017. See also Saussy 2022, 78–84.

48. No wonder, therefore, that several emergent nations constructed their own epics on the basis of living folk traditions (for instance, the Finnish *Kalevala*, which grew in every new edition) or claimed to rediscover an ancient epic tradition.

49. For a clear survey of these discussions, see Lin Gang 2007a. The Chinese original of this article was published as Lin Gang 2007b. For the "Weniad," see Wang 1975. Also see Chan 1974; Yu 1972.

50. Qi Lianxiu, Cheng Qiang, and Lü Wei 2008, 111–12 treat the epic as the product of a tribal society and the long narrative poem as the product of a class society (445–49).

51. Duan Baolin 2010; Chen Jianxian and Lin Jifu 2005. This dominant Chinese attitude toward the epic is reflected in the organization of materials in Mair and Bender 2011, even though the introduction to the section titled "The Epic Traditions" (213–15) points out that narrative songs of epic length and substance are also encountered among the Han.

52. For surveys of studies on the epic in China, see Feng Wenkai and Bai Cunliang 2014; Feng Wenkai 2019; Yin Hubin 2013.

53. Børdahl 2002, 316. For a preliminary survey of part of this immense body of literature, see Idema 2010b. Chinese scholars tend to associate many of the genres that make up this body of literature with professional entertainers in urban areas and do not classify them as oral literature.

54. Chinese scholars have not picked up the category of "folk epics" as it is used in South Asian studies.

55. Duan Baolin 2010, 166–75. Chen Jianxian and Lin Jifu 2005 include *Hei'an zhuan* 黑暗传 (Tale of darkness) from western Hubei as an example of a Chinese-language creation epic.

### Appendix II: *Selections from* Guo Dingxiang (the complete edition, 2009)

1. The character for "one" (*yi* 一) is written with one horizontal stroke.

2. A green hat is the prescribed headgear of pimps, so a green hat makes its wearer a cuckold.

3. The old man in the moon ties prospective marriage partners together with a red string.

4. The ruling families of the ancient states of Qin (modern Shaanxi) and Jin (modern Shanxi) often intermarried.

5. The Odes and Rites are two of the Five Classics.

6. The phoenix here refers to chicken, dragon to fish.

7. Guangzhou 光州 is an old designation for the area of southeastern Henan.

8. In a famous story from the Tang dynasty, a man falls asleep below an acacia tree and experiences a glorious career as the prefect of Southern Bough. When he wakes up, he notices an anthill below the tree's southern branch and realizes that it was only a dream.

9. "Hanging heart" refers to a doubting mind.

# References

Anhuisheng wenhuaju 安徽省文化局, comp. 1959. *Zhongguo difang xiqu jicheng: Anhui juan* 中国地方戏曲集成安徽卷 [Complete collection of Chinese regional operas: Anhui]. Beijing: Zhongguo Xiju Chubanshe.

Bai Gengsheng 白庚胜. 2007. "Zhongyuan shishi, wenyuan juexiang" 中原史诗文苑绝响 [An epic of the central plains, an inimitable work from the garden of letters]. In *Guo Dingxiang: Zhongguo Hanzu minjian shenghuo shishi* 郭丁香中国汉族民间生活史诗 [Guo Dingxiang: An epic on folk life of the Han nationality of China], compiled by Xinyangshi minjian wenhua yichan qiangjiu gongcheng gongguo weiyuan hui 信阳市民间文化遗产抢救工程工作委员会 and Gushixian minjian wenhua qiangjiu gongcheng gongzuo weiyuan hui 固始县民间文化遗产抢救工程工作委员会, 1–6. Zhengzhou: Henan Renmin Chubanshe.

Bender, Mark. 2019. "Co-creations, Master Texts, and Monuments: Long Narrative Poems of Ethnic Minority Groups in China." *Chinoperl: Journal of Chinese Oral and Performative Literature* 38 (2): 65–90.

Bo Songnian. 2021. *Zhongguo zaojun shenma* 中国灶君神祃 [China's Stove Lord prints]. Beijing: Renmin Meishu Chubanshe.

Børdhal, Vibeke. 2002. "Epic and Asian Folklore." *Asian Folklore Studies* 61:311–20.

Cai Yaling 蔡亚玲. 2012. "Lun zaoshu *Guo Dingxiang* de yishu tese" 论灶书郭丁香的艺术特色 [On the artistic characteristics of the stove tale *Guo Dingxiang*]. *Xinyang shifan daxue xuebao* 32, no, 3: 79–82.

Cai Yaling. 2013. "Zhen shan mei yu jia chou e de jiaoliang—zaoshu *Guo Dingxiang* nüxing xingxiang leixing tanxi" 真善美与假丑恶的较量—灶书郭丁香女性形象类型探析 [A comparison of the true, good and beautiful with the false, ugly and bad—an inquiry into the types of images of female characters in the stove book *Guo Dingxiang*]. *Yuwen zhishi*, no. 2: 10–12.

Cai Yaling. 2014. "Zaozhu *Guo Dingxiang* xushi yishu lunxi" 灶书郭丁香叙事艺术论析 [An analysis of the narrative artistry of the stove tale *Guo Dingxiang*]. *Pinxiang gaodeng zhuanke xuexiao xuebao* 31 (4): 63–66.

Cai Yaling. 2016. "Qingdai Yunan hunsu wenhua tanjiu" 清代豫南婚俗文化探究 [An inquiry into the culture of wedding customs in Southern Henan during the Qing dynasty]. *Lantai shijie* 1:145–46.

Cai Yuyan 蔡雨燕 and Gong Chuhan 宫楚涵, comps. 2015. *Zhongguo difang xiqu jumu huikao* 中国地方戏曲剧目汇考 [An inventory of the items in Chinese regional opera]. 2 vols. Beijing: Xueyuan Chubanshe.

Cao Jiazhen 曹家振. 2017. "Houji" 后记 [Epilogue] to *Xinyang lishi wenhua congshu: Guo Dingxiang* 信阳历史文化丛书郭丁香 [Series on Xinyang's historical culture: Guo Dingxiang], edited by Dong An 董安, 291–94. Zhengzhou: Zhongzhou Guji Chubanshe.

Cao Jiazhen 曹家振, Peng Huahou 彭华后, and Li Haihua 李海华, comps. 1981. "Guo Dingxiang" 郭丁香. *Minjian wenxue*, October 1981, 29–49.

Cao Jiazhen 曹家振, Peng Huahou 彭华后, and Li Haihua 李海华, comps. 1987. "Guo Dingxiang" 郭丁香. In *Zhongguo xin wenyi daxi (1976–1982): Minjian wenxue ji* 中国新文艺大系（1976–1982）民间文学集 [A great survey of China's new literary arts (1976–1982): A collection of folk literature], 485–504. Beijing: Zhongguo Wenlian Chubanshe.

Cao Jiazhen 曹家振, Peng Huahou 彭华后, and Li Haihua 李海华, comps. 2003. "Guo Dingxiang" 郭丁香. In *Zhongguo geyao jicheng: Henan juan* 中国歌谣集成河南卷 [A complete collection of Chinese folk song: Henan Province], 559–79. Beijing: Zhongguo ISBN Zhongxin.

Chan, Marie. 1974. "Chinese Heroic Poems and European Epic." *Comparative Literature* 26 (2): 142–68.

Chard, Robert L. 1990. "Folktales on the God of the Stove." *Chinese Studies* 8 (1): 149–82.

Chard, Robert L. 1994. "The Stove God and the Overseer of Fate." In *Minjian Xinyang yu Zhongguo wenhua guoji yantaohui lunwenji* 民間信仰與中國文化國際研討會論文集 [Papers of the international conference on popular beliefs and Chinese culture], 2:655–82. Taipei: Hanxue Yanjiu Zhongxin.

Chard, Robert L. 1995. "Rituals and Scriptures of the Stove Cult." In *Ritual and Scripture in Chinese Popular Religion: Five Studies*, edited by David Johnson, 3–54. Berkeley, CA: Chinese Popular Culture Project.

Chard, Robert L, trans. 2000. "The Precious Scroll [Baojuan] on the Lord of the Stove." In *Sources of Chinese Tradition*, 2nd ed.. vol. 2, edited by Wm. Theodore de Bary and Richard Lufrano, 126–33. New York: Columbia University Press.

Chen Jianxian 陈建宪 and Lin Jifu 林继富. 2005. *Minjian wenxue zhi xia* 民间文学志下 [Gazetteer of folk literature, part 2]. Vol. 21 of *Zhongguo minsu tongzhi* 中国民俗通志 [Comprehensive gazetteer of Chinese customs], compiled by Qi Tao 齐涛. Jinan: Shandong Jiaoyu Chubanshe.

Chen Yongsheng 陈永省, comp. 1992. *Henan minjian wenxue jicheng: Xinyang diqu gushi* 河南民间文学集成信阳地区故事 [Complete collection of Henanese folk literature: Stories from the Xinyang region]. Zhengzhou: Henan Nongmin Chubanshe.

Confucius. 1979. *The Analects*. Translated by D. C. Lau. Harmondsworth: Penguin Books.

Dong An 董安, ed. 2017. *Xinyang lishi wenhua congshu: Guo Dingxiang* 信阳历史文化丛书郭丁香 [Series on Xinyang's historical culture: Guo Dingxiang]. Zhengzhou: Zhongzhou Guji Chubanshe.

Duan Baolin 段宝林. 2010. *Zhongguo shishi bolan* 中国史诗博览 [A comprehensive survey of China's epics]. Vol. 2 of *Shenhua yu shishi* 神话与史诗 [Myth and epic]. Beijing: Minzu Chubanshe.

Duan Jinlong 段金龙 and Zhang Rui 张瑞. 2020. "Gushi shexi yanjiu de xianzhuang, wenti ji tupo lujing" 固始社戏研究现状问题及突破路径

[Problems in the current situation of the study of Gushi's village plays and the road forward]. *Xinyang nonglin xueyuan xuebao* 30 (4): 92–95.

Fang Bo 方波. 2009. "Xuyan" 序言 [preface] to *Guo Dingxiang (quanben)* 郭丁香全本 [Guo Dingxiang: Complete edition], compiled by Henansheng Gushixian wenhuaju 河南省固始县文化局, 1–2. Zhengzhou: Henan Renmin Chubanshe.

Feng Wenkai. 2019. "Shishi yanjiu qishiniande huigu yu fansi (1949–2019)" 史诗研究七十年的回顾与反思 [A review of and a reflection on seventy years of research on epics]. *Minjian wenhua luntan*, no. 3: 18–29.

Feng Wenkai 冯文开 and Bai Cunliang 白村良. 2014. "Shijiu shiji houqi zhi ershiyishiji chu Zhongguo shishixue yu yanjiuzhe de zhishi jiegou de guanxi" 19 世纪后期至21世纪初中国史诗学与研究者的知识构成之关系 [Chinese studies on epics from the late 19th century to the beginning of the 21st century and their relation to the knowledge formation of the scholars concerned]. *Minsu yanjiu* 118 (6): 20–24.

Gao Tianxing 高天星. 2009. "Zhongguo Hanzu shehui minsu xushi changshi *Guo Dingxiang—Guo dingxiang* de faxian, zhengli yu yanjiu ganyan" 中国汉族社会民俗叙事长诗郭丁香—郭丁香的发现整理与研究感言 [The long narrative poem on folk customs in the society of the China's Han nationality *Guo Dingxiang*—thoughts on the discovery, editing and study of *Guo Dingxiang*]. In *Guo Dingxiang (quanben)* 郭丁香全本 [Guo Dingxiang: complete edition], compiled by Henansheng Gushixian wenhuaju 河南省固始县文化局, 3–16. Zhengzhou: Henan Renmin Chubanshe.

Gao Tianxing 高天星. 2017. "Xu" 序 [preface] to *Xinyang lishi wenhua congshu: Guo Dingxiang* 信阳历史文化丛书郭丁香 [Series on Xinyang's historical culture: Guo Dingxiang], edited by Dong An 董安, 1–10. Zhengzhou: Zhongzhou Guji Chubanshe.

Gaomu Lizi (Takaki Tatsuko) 高木立子. 1999a. "Zhongguo 'fenshoude fuqi zaifeng' leixing gushi yanjiu (1)" 中国分手的夫妻再逢类型故事研究 (1) [A study of Chinese stories of the type "the reunion of separated couples," part 1]. *Chizhou shizhuan xuebao*, no. 1: 14–20.

Gaomu Lizi (Takaki Tatsuko) 高木立子. 1999b. "Zhongguo 'fenshoude fuqi zaifeng' leixing gushi yanjiu (2)" 中国分手的夫妻再逢类型故事研究 (2) [A study of Chinese stories of the type "the reunion of separated couples," part 2]. *Chizhou shizhuan xuebao*, no. 2: 15–20, 24.

Gaomu Lizi (Takaki Tatsuko) 高木立子. 2000. "Zhongguo 'fenshoude fuqi zaifeng' leixing gushi yanjiu (3)" 中国分手的夫妻再逢类型故事研究 (3) [A study of Chinese stories of the type "the reunion of separated couples," part 3]. *Chizhou shizhuan xuebao* 14 (1): 33–38.

Graham, D. C. 1930. "The Original Vow of the Stove God." *Chinese Recorder* 61:781–88, 62:41–50, 110–16.

*Gushixian quyizhi* 固始县曲艺志 [Gazetteer of the minor performance arts of Gushi District]. 1989. Gushixian: Gushixian Cultural Bureau.

Henansheng Gushixian wenhuaju 河南省固始县文化局, comp. 2009a. *Guo Dingxiang (quanben)* 郭丁香全本 [Guo Dingxiang: Complete edition]. Zhengzhou: Henan Renmin Chubanshe.

Henansheng Gushixian wenhuaju 河南省固始县文化局. 2009b. "Houji" 后记 [epilogue] to *Guo Dingxiang (quanben)* 郭丁香全本 [Guo Dingxiang: Complete edition], compiled by Henansheng Gushixian wenhuaju, 273–77. Zhengzhou: Henan Renmin Chubanshe.

Holm, David. 1991. *Art and Ideology in Revolutionary China*. Oxford: Oxford University Press.

Honko, Lauri, ed. 2000. *Textualizations of Oral Epics*. Berlin: De Gruyter.

Hu Chongjun 胡崇峻, ed. 2021. *Hei'an zhuan* 黑暗传 [The legend of darkness]. Wuhan: Wuhan Daxue Chubanshe.

Hu Yongliang 胡永良, ed. 2013. *Haiyan saozi: Wenshu xuanji* 海盐骚子文书选集 [A selection of *saozi* texts from Haiyan]. Hangzhou: Xiling Yinshe Chubanshe.

Idema, Wilt L. 2008. *Meng Jiangnü Brings Down the Great Wall: Ten Versions of a Chinese Legend*. Seattle: University of Washington Press.

Idema, Wilt L. 2009. *Filial Piety and Its Divine Rewards: The Legend of Dong Yong and Weaving Maiden, with Related Texts*. Indianapolis: Hacket.

Idema, Wilt L. 2010a. *The Butterfly Lovers: The Legend of Liang Shanbo and Zhu Yingtai—Four Versions, with Related Texts*. Indianapolis: Hacket.

Idema, Wilt L. 2010b. "Prosimetric and Verse Narrative." In *The Cambridge History of Chinese Literature*, edited by Kang-I Sun Chang and Stephen Owen, 2:343–412. Cambridge: Cambridge University Press.

Idema, Wilt L. 2015. *The Metamorphosis of "Tianxianpei": Local Opera under the Revolution (1949–1956)*. Hong Kong: Chinese University Press.

Idema, Wilt L. 2022. "The Textualization of *Guo Dingxiang*." *Chinoperl: Journal of Chinese Oral and Performing Literature* 41 (1): 7–36.

Jiang Fan 江帆. 2001. 'Nüxing mingyun de bieyizhong quanshi: Duo minzu chuanchengde gushi "Zhang lang xiuqi" jiexi" 女性命运的 别一种诠释—多民族传承的故事张郎休妻解析 [A different explanation of women's fate: An analysis of 'Mr. Zhang divorces his wife,' a story transmitted by many nationalities]. *Minzu wenxue yanjiu*, no. 4: 25–28.

Jiang Yan 姜燕. 2007. *Xianghuoxi kao* 香火戏考 [An inventory of ritual plays]. Yangzhou: Guangling Shushe.

Ko, Dorothy. 2001. *Every Step a Lotus: Shoes for Bound Feet*. Berkeley: University of California Press.

Landsberger, Stefan. 1996–97. "Mao as the Kitchen God: Religious Aspects of the Mao Cult during the Cultural Revolution." *China Information* 11 (2–3): 196–214.

Li Chen, Fan Pen. 2004. *Visions for the Masses: Chinese Shadow Plays from Shaanxi and Shanxi*. Ithaca, NY: Cornell East Asia Series, Cornell University Press.

Li Chen, Fan Pen, trans. 2009. "All Three Fear Their Wives (Sanpaqi): A Post-midnight Shadow Play." *Asian Theatre Journal* 26 (2): 197–214.

Li Chen, Fan Pen, trans. 2010. "'Baldy's Wedding Night': A Post-midnight Marionette Play from Shaanxi." *CHINOPERL Papers* 29:133–41.

Lin Gang 林岗. 2007a. "'Epic in Chinese': A Tentative Insight into the Problem under Discussion in the 20th Century." *Social Sciences in China*, Summer 2007, 69–78.

Lin Gang. 2007b. "Ershishiji Hanyu 'shishiwenti' tanlun" 二十世纪汉语史诗问题探论 [An exploratory discussion of the problem of the Chinese epic in the twentieth century]. *Zhongguo shehui kexue* 2007 (1): 131–42.

Liu Shouhua 留守華, ed. 2015. *"Hei'anzhuan" zhuizong* 黑暗傳追蹤 [Tracing *The Legend of Darkness*]. Taipei: Xiuwei Zixun Keji Gufen Youxian Gongsi.

Liu Wenwen 刘文文. 2018. "Shenghuo wenhua shijiaoxia de Yunan diqu zaoxi yanjiu" 生活文化视角下的豫南地区灶戏研究 [A study of the stove plays of southern Henan from the perspective of life culture]. MA thesis, Heilongjiang University.

Mair, Victor H., and Mark Bender, eds. 2011. *The Columbia Anthology of Chinese Folk and Popular Literature*. New York: Columbia University Press.

McLaren, Anne E. 2022. *Memory Making in Folk Epics of China: The Intimate and the Local in Chinese Regional Culture*. Amherst, NY: Cambria.

McLaren, Anne E., and Zhang, Emily Yu. 2017. "Recreating 'Traditional' Folk Epics in Contemporary China." *Asian Ethnology* 76 (1): 19–41.

"Pan Jing'e: Changpian zaoshu *Guo Dingxiang* jiechu chuanchengren" 潘景娥—长篇灶书郭丁香杰出传承人 [Pan Jing'e: An excellent transmitter of the stove tale *Guo Dingxiang*]. 2011. *Zhongguo shehui kexuebao*, January 20, 2011.

Po Sung-nien and David Johnson. 1992. *Domesticated Deities and Auspicious Emblems: The Iconography of Everyday Life in Village China*. Berkeley: Publications of the Chinese Popular Culture Project.

Qi Lianxiu 祁连休, Cheng Qiang 程蔷, and Lü Wei 吕微, eds. 2008. *Zhongguo minjian wenxueshi* 中国民间文学史 [A history of Chinese folk literature]. Shijiazhuang: Hebei Jiaoyu Chubanshe.

Ready, Jonathan L. 2019. *Orality, Textuality, and the Homeric Epics: An Interdisciplinary Study of Oral Texts, Dictated Texts, and Wild Texts*. Oxford: Oxford University Press.

Ruitenbeek, Klaas. 1993. *Carpentry and Building in Late Imperial China: A Study of the Fifteenth-Century Carpenter's Manual "Lu Ban Jing."* Leiden: E. J. Brill.

Saussy, Haun. 2017. "The Absent Epic: China and the Politics of Narrative." Lecture at the American Academy in Berlin, last accessed October 22, 2021. https://www.americanacademy.de/the-absent-epic/.

Saussy, Haun. 2022. *The Making of Barbarians: Chinese Literature and Multilingual Asia*. New Haven, CT: Yale University Press.

Shandongsheng xiqu yanjiushi 山东省戏曲研究室. N.d. [1986?]. *Shandong difang xiqu chuantong jumu huibian Liuqinxi disanji* 山东地方戏曲传统剧目汇编柳琴戏第三集 [A complete compilation of traditional items in Shandong regional opera. Liuqinxi. Third collection]. N.p. [Jinan?].

Shennongjia linqu feiwuzhi wenhua yichan baohu zhongxin 神农架林区非物质文化遗产保护中心, ed. 2014. *Hei'an zhuan*. 黑暗传 [The legend of darkness]. Wuhan: Hubei Renmin Chubanshe.

Si Zhulin 斯竹林. 2023. "Zaoshen xingxiang de renzhi yu chuanshuo muti de shengcheng—yi Zhanglang xiuqi xing zaoshen youlai chuanshuo wei li" 灶神形象的认知与传说母题的生成—以张郎休妻型灶神由来传说为例 [An understanding of the image of the stove god and the development of the motifs of the legend—based on the legends of the origin of the stove god of the type "young man Zhang divorces his wife"]. *Minjian wenhua luntan* 2023 (1): 66–74.

Stein, Rolf A. 1970. "La légende du foyer dans le monde chinois" [The legend of the hearth in the Chinese world]. In *Échanges et communications: Mélanges offerts a Claude Lévi Strauss à l'occasion de son 60ême anniversaire* [Exchanges and communications: Papers presented to Claude Lévi Strauss on the occasion of his sixtieth birthday], compiled by Jean Pouillon and Pierre Maranda, 2:1280–305. The Hague: Mouton.

Wang, C. H. 1975. "Towards Defining a Chinese Heroism." *Journal of the American Oriental Society* 95 (1): 25–35.

Wang Daoyun 王道云, comp. 1991. *Xinyang diqu geyao juan* 信阳地区歌谣卷 [Folk songs from the Xinyang region]. Zhengzhou: Zhongyuan Nongmin Chubanshe.

Wang Huili 王会丽. 2019. "Zaoshu *Guo Dingxiang* toukou chengshi fenxi" 灶书郭丁香头口程式分析 [An analysis of the oral formulas in the stove tale *Guo Dingxiang*]. *Kaifeng jiaoyu xueyuan xuebao* 39 (4): 50–52.

Wang Jiaju 王稼句, comp. 2006. *Wan Qing minfeng baisu* 晚清民风百俗 [Popular customs of the late Qing]. Nanjing: Jiangsu Renmin Chubanshe.

Wang, Xing. 2020. *Physiognomy in Ming China: Fortune and the Body*. Leiden: Brill.

Wei Xiuping 位秀平. 2006. "Yunan Gushixian zaoshu *Guo Dingxiang* yanjiu" 豫南固始县灶书郭丁香研究 [A study of the stove tale *Guo Dingxiang* from Gushi District in southern Henan]. MA thesis, Henan University.

Xia Wanqun 夏挽群. 2007. "Dingxiang changge gujin" 丁香长歌古今 [The long song of Dingxiang in past and present]. In *Guo Dingxiang: Zhongguo Hanzu minjian shenghuo shishi* 郭丁香中国汉族民间生活史诗 [Guo Dingxiang: An epic on folk life of the Han nationality of China], compiled by Xinyangshi minjian wenhua yichan qiangjiu gongcheng gongguo weiyuan hui 信阳市民间文化遗产抢救工程工作委员会 and Gushixian minjian wenhua qiangjiu gongcheng gongzuo weiyuan hui 固始县民间文化遗产抢救工程工作委员会, 1–4. Zhengzhou: Henan Renmin Chubanshe.

Xinyangshi minjian wenhua yichan qiangjiu gongcheng gongguo weiyuan hui 信阳市民间文化遗产抢救工程工作委员会 and Gushixian minjian wenhua qiangjiu gongcheng gongzuo weiyuan hui 固始县民间文化遗产抢救工程工作委员会, comps. 2007a. *Guo Dingxiang: Zhongguo Hanzu minjian shenghuo shishi* 郭丁香中国汉族民间生活史诗 [Guo Dingxiang: An epic on folk life of the Han nationality of China]. Zhengzhou: Henan Renmin Chubanshe.

Xinyangshi minjian wenhua yichan qiangjiu gongcheng gongguo weiyuanhui 信阳市民间文化遗产抢救工程工作委员会 and Gushixian minjian wenhua qiangjiu gongcheng gongzuo weiyuan hui 固始县民间文化遗产抢救工程工作委员会. 2007b. "Houji" 后记 [epilogue] to *Guo Dingxiang: Zhongguo Hanzu minjian shenghuo shishi* 郭丁香中国汉族民间生活史诗 [Guo Dingxiang: An epic on folk life of the Han nationality of China], compiled by Xinyangshi minjian wenhua yichan qiangjiu gongcheng gongguo weiyuan hui 信阳市民间文化遗产抢救工程工作委员会 and Gushixian minjian wenhua qiangjiu gongcheng gongzuo weiyuan hui

固始县民间文化遗产抢救工程工作委员会, 261-67. Zhengzhou: Henan Renmin Chubanshe.

Yang Fuquan 杨福泉. 1994. *Zao yu zaoshen* 灶与灶神 [Stove and stove god]. Beijing: Xueyuan Chubanshe.

Yang Xianru 杨纤如. 1981. "Jieshao changzao" 介绍唱灶 [An introduction to stove singing]. *Quyi yishu luncong* 1981 (2): 60–64.

Yen, Chun-chiang. 1967. "Folklore Research in Communist China." *Asian Folklore Studies* 26 (2): 1–62.

Yin Hubin. 2013. "The Paradigm Shift of Epic Studies in China." In *Folk Traditions in Modern Society*, edited by Pekka Hakamies, Sun Jian, and Vibeke Børdahl, 126–39. Shanghai: Fudan University Press.

Yu, Anthony. 1972. "Heroic Verse and Heroic Mission: Dimensions of the Epic in the *Hsi-yu chi*." *Journal of Asian Studies* 31 (4): 879–97.

*Zhang lang xiuqi—Ge Dingxiang jiezhi ji* 張郎休妻葛丁香戒指記 [Young Zhang divorces his wife—Ge Dingxiang: The tale of the ring]. n.d. Shanghai: Chunyin shuzhuang. Reprinted in *Suwenxue congkan* 俗文學叢刊 [Folk Literature], 573:323–36. Taipei: Xinwenfeng, 2001–16.

Zhang Lingyi 张凌怡, Liu Jingliang 刘景亮, and Li Guangyu 李广宇. 2007. *Henan quyi shi* 河南曲艺史 [A history of Henan's minor performative arts]. Zhengzhou: Henan Renmin Chubanshe.

Zhao Xiangxin 赵向欣. 2007. "Zaoxi de wenhua moshi: Yi *Guo Dingxiang* weili" 灶戏的文化模式—以郭丁香为例 [The cultural model of stove plays, taking *Guo Dingxiang* as model]. *Xinyang shifan xueyuan xuebao* 27 (4): 99–102.

Zhongguo minjian wenyi yanjiuhui Hubei fenhui, ed. 1986. *Hanzu changbian chuangshiji shishi: Shennongjia "Hei'an zhuan" duozhong banben huibian* [A long creation epic of the Han ethnicity: A collective edition of the various editions of Shennongjia's "The legend of darkness"]. [Wuhan:] Zhongguo Minjian Wenyi Yanjiuhui Hubei Fenhui.

*Zhongguo quyi zhi: Henan juan* 中国曲艺志河南卷 [The gazetteer of China's minor performative arts: Henan]. 1995. Beijing: Zhongguo ISBN Zhongxin.

Zhou Ruchang 周汝昌, ann. 1974. *Fan Chengda shixuan* 范成大詩選. Hong Kong: Zhongliu Chubanshe.

Zhu Hengfu 朱恒夫 and Huang Wenhu 黄文虎, comps. 2011. *Jiang Huai shenshu* 江淮神书 [Divine books from the Jiang-Huai region]. 2 vols. Shanghai: Shanghai Guji Chubanshe.

Zou Zhenqi 邹振起 and Pei Shihu 裴世虎, comps. [1989?]. *Gushixian xiquzhi* 固始县戏曲志 [Gazetteer on traditional theater in Gushi District]. Gushi: Gushixian Wenhuaju.